W9-AQK-200

"A smoothly handled, intriguing, sometimes unsettling drama."

—*Kirkus Reviews*

"A disturbingly haunting tale of humanity's next evolutionary step. Thoughtfully written."

—*Library Journal*

"A fascinating, occasionally bold, work."

—*Publishers Weekly*

"Stephanie A. Smith's first foray into SF is a remarkably humane exercise in the psychology of collapse and survival."

—Thomas Easton, *Analog*

other nature

Stephanie A. Smith

 TOR®   A Tom Doherty Associates Book / New York

This is a work of fiction. All the characters and events portrayed in this novel are either fictitious or are used fictitiously.

OTHER NATURE

Copyright © 1995 by Stephanie A. Smith

All rights reserved, including the right to reproduce this book, or portions thereof, in any form.

This book is printed on acid-free paper.

Edited by David G. Hartwell

A Tor Book
Published by Tom Doherty Associates, Inc.
175 Fifth Avenue
New York, N.Y. 10010

Tor Books on the World Wide Web:
http://www.tor.com

Tor® is a registered trademark of Tom Doherty Associates, Inc.

Design by Lynn Newmark

Library of Congress Cataloging-in-Publication Data

Smith, Stephanie A.
    Other nature / Stephanie A. Smith.
        p.   cm.
    "A Tom Doherty Associates book."
    ISBN 0-312-86352-7 (pb)
    I. Title.
PS3569.M5379768087   1995
813'.54—dc20   95-30307
                                                                      CIP

First hardcover edition: October 1995
First trade paperback edition: June 1997

Printed in the United States of America

0 9 8 7 6 5 4 3 2 1

For Jennifer and William, Alex and Jules.
But finally, and most importantly, to John,
for putting up with me with
more patience than most.

Contents

A love of other nature in my brest
with violence came.

—Ovid, *The Metamorphoses*
(trans. Arthur Golding 1567)

BOOK ONE

spring

1

Leave-taking

(4:30 a.m.)

Emily Zafieras woke, knowing she'd missed the alarm, knowing it was almost too late. Sean was in the next room, dressing, humming to himself. She groaned and glanced across the tumbled expanse of blue blanket at the alarm clock, but could not see the time. Groggy, she turned on her back, wishing for a few more minutes and knowing that Edward Jackson, always punctual, would be at the door soon. Sean and Ed needed to be on the road before daybreak, if they were to reach Sheila's by nightfall.

Sean's all-too-familiar humming stopped. Emily sat up and wondered: what the devil was making—could make?—that heartrending, not-quite-music that woke her in the middle of the night, night after night? It was not Sean—or any of her neighbors, she was sure. It was not even music. Yet it held her as if it were, vibrantly low, inexplicable.

You, not me, she thought at the half-closed double doors to the next room, *you, Sean Rider, are supposed to be the light sleeper!* Last night was the sixth night in a row that she'd been the one who'd lain sharply sleepless, when she ought to have slept, when she needed sleep—while he had slept. And he'd told her, too, that she must be hearing things. She'd almost willed herself to believe him. Except. Last night she'd heard it again and had hoped that this time he might listen, or that this time the mellifluous but unmelodic sound would coalesce into definition—into the waters, or the wind, or the muffled retreat of a dream, so that she could have been hearing things. But no—it had drifted maddeningly into a waking silence. And Sean had slept on.

Emily stirred, feeling ill enough to lie down again. But she'd promised Sean breakfast—and she couldn't bear the thought of breaking that promise, not on this, their last morning together. Maybe their last ever. She put that thought aside in painful haste, dressed, and went down to the kitchen. The old house was strangely cold. Once the oil lamps were up, and the woodstove's potbelly glowed red-black, she went out the back door for the rainwater that had collected overnight.

She eyed the pail; even in the semidark, she could see the water was brackish. It had a metallic, bitter odor. She lifted the pail. Turning toward her low-roofed home, perched solitaire upon a small rise, she saw the kitchen steaming from the stove's heat. She smiled, forgetting the relentlessly bad water for a moment. Her home looked brave, the yellow light wavering through open windows. There was something satisfying, she felt, about getting up before sunrise. The dark had a different quality from the nappy, worn-down velvet of late evening. It felt new-spun, shot with a promising soft gray. In the uncertain light, her kitchen seemed comfortable, rather than shabby. Things that were normally dull gleamed. She wanted to be inside there; she wanted to gleam. Even weak tea would taste good to her in that beckoning warmth.

As she headed toward the house with her pail, she paused to gaze down along the wide coastal path that lead into the town of Monkar. Below the ragged path and parallel to it was a small cove, very sheltered; a neat half-moon of shore bounded on either side by high, craggy basalt. To her right, the black rocks were met by a rolling hill. Atop the hill sat a boulder, perched awkwardly but soundly near the ruins of what had once been—or so most people thought—a lighthouse. To her left, the basalt became a series of caves that sloped back into a sandy coast.

Later that day she'd promised herself that she would visit Maria Monkar, who lived just beyond town center, near these sea caves. The two women hadn't had the chance—they hadn't really made the time—to be together. She missed Maria, missed her in a way that made for an irritated and irritable restlessness. This restlessness translated itself suddenly, on the spot, into a reluctance to go back inside the house.

So Emily lingered as what was left of the moon's light leached the cove, making the sea look black and the sand gray. Here and there a fleck of white showed; sea foam or the overturned hull of a dinghy. The sea had merged with the night sky, except that she fancied the water darker than the air, for it only reflected light, while the sky held bursts and trails of stars. It all seemed so spare, yet it inspired extravagance. She had a sudden desire to run naked over the sand; dash to the water and take a neat dive, letting the shock of the cold make her muscles clench, her ears ring.

She stared down at the waves and sand, musing at nothing. Then she started. The waves seemed to be growing. Just offshore, there was some sort of disturbance—a roiling, irregular whirlpool. Fish? Not likely. Could it be a swimmer—or? What? Her heart beat faster. She squinted into the dark. Might something of this strange disturbance be connected to her night music? She strained, tensing with hope, listening. But there was not a sound save the sea itself. Then she remembered that one of Monkar's few children, Tomas Nitehammer, often swam there at dusk, despite the sheer danger of night swimming. His father, Nathaniel, usually joined him. And, too, just lately, Nathaniel had claimed that he'd seen seals out there.

Seals! Emily smiled to herself, as she scanned the foamy

dance of the waves. No one believed in Nathaniel's seals—how could they? It was a too, too hopeful thing. Anxiously, she watched the rippling waters, half hoping. But as she watched, the sudden roil smoothed. The sea held calmness.

Shrugging, she swung the pail before her into the kitchen. Her numbed fingers and cold nose tingled with the heat. She whistled to keep out the uneasiness, until she caught sight of Sean huddled near the stove, his shock of blood-red hair pulled tightly back into a severe tail. His traveling gear was packed and set in another huddle by his feet, and he stared up at her with an almost angry blue glance. It cut her whistle short.

"You sound happy," he said.

"Happy?" She shook her head. "Not really." She hesitated, then added, "I thought I saw something out there in the sea."

He laughed and shrugged. "You've been listening to Nathaniel?" His long-lashed eyes, his childishly round face, and still sleep-placid lips wore no hint, now, of any anger. "Try to take care while I'm gone," he said.

"I'll try." She looked at him, seeing, with a pang, how haggard he seemed. Not long ago, she'd heard him say, "Gravity's bound to catch up with the flesh." He'd laughed then, and had cut her a glance so sharp she'd thought the comment a reproach to her low-lying breasts. But a few days later, when this same comment came flying at her through the bedroom doors, she'd discovered that he'd not been talking to her at all. He'd been staring in the mirror, talking to himself.

She stared at him now, hoping to put her concern into the silence of a glance. Then she turned and plugged the sink, broke the paper-thin sheeting of ice, and emptied the bucket.

"Em," he said. "I have to go. And besides. We both wanted it this way. We both needed it this way."

"I know," she said quietly, keeping her back to him.

*   *   *

Sean watched Emily's shoulders as she scrubbed dishes. He didn't know what more to say and so tried to get rid of the tension he felt by giving himself a stretch and a shake. He'd been ready to get on with the morning, to pick up his gear, start off—and yet, and yet, seeing Emily just then, with her pale face all reddened by the cold, her lips giving out that jaunty whistle, he felt a late-rising reluctance to leave. His mood of adventure and expectation had shifted when he'd heard her whistling. And he'd thought: *Hell—she isn't going to miss me!*

He added wood to the fire and banged the stove door shut. What was the matter with him? Hadn't he begged and cajoled Ed into this journey? Hadn't he talked it all out with Em? Hadn't they both agreed that she should stay and he should go? He sliced off a wedge of corn bread from the tinned loaf. He'd had a time of it persuading town council that there was more to this trip south than his own loss or his own gain; that if he and Ed could just find Linda, even just talk to her (though the idea that she wouldn't want to come back with him seemed as impossible as thinking about her possible return), she might be able to help Monkar change or grow in ways they couldn't foresee.

Emily set the kettle on the stove top to boil and asked, "Have you packed everything?"

"As far as I know."

She nodded. "Tea?"

"Please."

She pulled a glass beaker marked UBAS off the windowsill, uncorked it, and scattered a handful of leaves into the bottom of the blue pot. Setting the pot in front of him, she said, "Eggs?"

"Jesus, Em, what do you think?"

"All right," she said, clearly surprised.

Angry at himself now, he said, "I'm sorry. I'm edgy."

"I guess." She glanced at the back door. "Ed's supposed to arrive—?"

"Soon."

"Eggs," she said, but made no move to start cooking. Her dark gray eyes seemed to grow darker, less soft. Sean cocked his head so that he wouldn't have to look directly at them, so that when he said, "Yes?" he would see only her mouth, and not those gray eyes that always spoke more—but what?— than her lips did. But she said nothing. She turned to the dishes in the sink. With her back to him again, he felt the clutch of uneasiness in his chest loosen up a bit. As the quiet between them grew, he felt calmer—up to a certain point, up to that point when the silence, too, became irritating. He really hadn't meant to be so prickly. He sat down to slice off another piece of bread and then said, "It'll be all right, Em. I have everything I need. Forget the eggs."

Her shoulders drew down a little as he spoke and she leaned against the sink, bending her head toward the suds.

He thought she might say something more, but no. As she noisily scrubbed, he watched her impale herself upon his silence.

It had been happening like this between them for a long time; almost eight years, ever since it became clear to them that Linda was truly gone. Though now—well, according to Edward, Linda was not dead, as most everyone in Monkar had come to believe. Even her twin sister, Christine, had given up. Eight years since Linda had disappeared from Monkar and, somehow, her loss had shut the doors to Sean and Emily's hearts; there were no words either one of them had found that would jar those doors open. They went on living together, but why was hard to say. They cared deeply for one another—but they had both been in love with Linda.

Sean often felt angry at this in sudden little moments of frustration, yet no anger ever seemed to come from Emily— although sometimes, Sean reminded himself, she would rap out sarcasm. But nothing hot and loud. Not like his mother had done, when she was alive. Her anger had been steady and scorching. And not like Linda, whose anger had always been close to the surface, quicklime corrosive.

Tying up the strings of his pack, he turned his gaze from Emily's back and leaned closer to the woodstove. At that moment, he preferred the laden silence to pointless talk. His mood lightened a little in the silence, but he still said nothing, afraid if he did, she would cry. He folded his hands and then cracked his knuckles. He picked up his jacket.

Emily, pouring out their tea, tried not to watch Sean as he slid on his jacket and checked over his gear again. She tried not to see how eagerly he buttoned himself into that jacket because she was trying not to remember how long it had taken her to quilt it, how carefully she had stitched up the front and made those buttonholes neater. Not-watching him, not-hearing him lace his boots and drink his tea down slow made her feel suffocated. She touched her throat, trying to swallow away the pain.

As they finished breakfast, she kept her own counsel; he did not say more than to ask after a household trifle and to give her instructions about his clocks. Their house had ten of them, all of which had to be wound daily. He had collected them by trading between the outlying enclaves of Monkar on the coast. Once or twice, roving far afield, he had simply found one.

Sean Rider was, in fact, famous in Monkar for two things: his fascination with clocks and his ability to get the best out of a trade. He often returned from a trip with a load of seemingly useless odds and ends that somehow became, in his capable hands, useful. He had an amazing facility for repair—from pots to peelers, from knives to a kevel. Blankets, sweaters, and, mostly for himself, clocks. The first three timepieces he'd restored had been ancient but serviceable mantel clocks, squat and cheery. They'd been followed by many more, from blank digitals to battery divers, neither of which he could yet repair, although he hoped to find out how, down south; pendulums to pocket watches, some whose mechanical movements could be coaxed back to life; chimers to electronic buzzers. But without electricity, the alarms sat rusting on the back porch among the hothouse plants.

Eyeing the heavy tangle of clock keys, she remembered that Sean wasn't the only person to fancy clocks so—Tomas Nitehammer seemed to find them fascinating, too. She frowned. One day last summer, she'd come back from a walk on the beach to find the child in the living room, with several of Sean's clocks in a circle around him. There on the worn rug he sat, smiling, spinning the hands of one clock round and round, making a curious click-click sound of his own. She'd rushed in and scolded him, forgetting about his small, misshapen ears, forgetting that he was deaf. He hadn't cried. He'd just stared at her, then he'd shoved past her and on out the back door.

Remembering this, she forgot the bunch of clock keys, until Sean said, "Will you keep time for me or no?"

She nodded, closing her fingers around the cold metal.

Sean hoisted his gear to his shoulders and patted his pockets. He said, "Ed out there yet?"

She went to the kitchen's back door and peered through the rusting, unraveling screen. "No," she said.

"I'll just double-check upstairs," he said.

"Right." Emily looked out across the yard, as Sean left the kitchen. A late frost had stiffened the grass near the stoop, where the back-porch tallow lamp flickered. The sun had still not yet risen, but some of the stars, so brilliant against the night sky, had waned. She stood at the door, thinking again of the sounds that had wakened her, thinking back on her restless night.

The moonlight had made the blanket's folds seem deeper, more secretive than the moon's own calm face. Terribly awake, she'd let the edge of the quilt slip off her shoulders and sat up on top of the pillow, her knees pulled against her breasts. Her skin had tightened and pimpled in the chilly air. And she'd thought: *These sounds, maybe they are the waves or the stars, singing?* She'd smiled at this fancy. A good idea, watery music or singing stars. Her great-grandmother would have appreciated it; to Aretina Zafieras, everything had had a voice.

"Why, fishmen's nets can lull the fish with their music!" she'd often said with a knowing chuckle. Emily supposed that whatever her great-grandmother had truly remembered of her childhood was, at best, fragmentary. Still, before she died, she bequeathed those fragments to Emily, who cherished the stories and tended them with as much care as Sean tended his clocks.

When she'd finally crept back into bed, slipping beneath the blue expanse as if under a winter sky, both comforter and sheets had lost their warmth. She eased down until the blue cotton edged over her chin. And as she turned her back on Sean, he sighed in his sleep and turned toward her.

She sighed now and was about to call out to Sean, when Edward Jackson appeared on the back stoop below her, breaking up her reverie. A big man, he stepped up onto the porch gingerly. She went out to meet him, trying to keep her anxiety at bay. Although Ed was a veteran rover, he hated cities, as did everyone in Monkar—hated deecees on principle, was terrified, as were they all, of trolling—and then there was the mysterious "ubes," a name most southerners used as a curse, but for what? Some in Monkar thought it was a forgotten acronym for a disease, others shrugged it off as simple urban hate-mongering—but again of what? Still others thought it might be some urban primitivism, a tribal affiliation or maybe a gang. Indeed, none from Monkar had gone into a city and none of them had sought contact outside their own several enclaves since Emily could remember. They heard rumors of other places now and again. Tales traveled, but, really, anything could be true.

So it was a risky thing Sean had asked Edward to do. She smiled at him, shrugging her shoulders against the cold, and gave him her hand, then a kiss. His dark cheek was chilly and he smiled curtly, as was customary for him. He glanced over her head to the doorway. Sean stepped out behind her and let the screen slam. When he put both hands on her shoulders, she shivered.

Edward gave them another one of his quick excuses for a smile and said, "Ready?"

Emily slipped out from under Sean's hands. " 'Ware the trolls now," she said.

Sean laughed. "We'll be back before the winter."

She nodded. She did not believe they'd be back until the following spring was well-nigh over—if they came back at all. Sean would not admit to her fears; Emily would not speak about them, either, because she could just hear Sean: "Sure it's dangerous. Do I need a reminder?" But it would be a rough journey, rougher than Edward's last scavenging trip south, a year ago, when he had neatly avoided trolls and then had nearly been killed by sheer accident. It was on this trip that he'd spotted Linda Nottage. Had seen her, he claimed, in what had looked to be a deecee crew repairing a roadbed skirting the bay. He didn't dare stop then, or try to talk to her, but he swore it was Linda. When he'd gotten home, he'd told the Nottages. And of course he'd told Sean and Emily.

Emily would never—*never*—forget the look on her lover's face when Edward had spoken Linda's name. Nor would she forget the thrilling rebound of her own feelings. Linda! Linda . . . alive?

She kept her expression calm and her fears shut within, as Sean hugged her and smoothed her hair back from her face. She pressed her lips together anxiously. Going to the Area from a dead-town was always risky. Although no one in Monkar was exactly sure how the deecees managed to govern anymore, let alone what they might or could do, everyone was sure of two things: dead-townies were feared and treated as targets by most anyone but another townie.

Leaning over, Sean whispered suddenly, "Try to miss me."

Tears sprang to her eyes. "Damn you," she said softly.

For an answer, he kissed her, as gentle and as convinced as the day they'd first kissed. She didn't push away, as she had done that first time, no, she kissed him back and so intently that she scared herself. Stepping away from him, she slapped Edward affectionately on the back. Then she folded her arms and watched Sean leave home.

As his home dropped from sight, Sean kicked a stone down the path and resisted the urge to turn around. He kicked the stone again, sending it on a skittering journey. The confidence he had felt early that morning went down after it. Squaring his shoulders, he followed Edward and tried not to think about Emily.

The sky had lost all the stars, although the bright moon still held sway, as if loath to give over to the sun. He felt Emily's gaze following him even if she could no longer see him. She always wanted that last caress, that one extra hug by which she would prove to herself that he loved her more than anyone and anything. He would not do it; he was tired of proving his love to her. She needed too much, always. He kicked the stone again.

Edward said, "Jay asked me to call it off."

"JP? He's crazy. How could he even think you'd call it off at this point?"

"Hope. Hoped I'd stay. You, too."

"And what'd you tell him?"

"Told him no, of course. Told him—" Edward stopped.

"Well?" prompted Sean.

"I—he's—I—"

Sean glanced at his friend. "What's wrong?"

"Emily's looking poorly to me."

"*What?*"

"Poorly. As in not well."

"Probably just tired."

"Looked more than tired—"

"Come on, Ed."

"I'm telling you what I see."

"She's fine," said Sean.

"*You* sleep?"

"Yeah."

Sean kicked his stone up past the rise in the road. As the two of them climbed after it, they found Nathaniel Nitehammer waiting for them on the other side. Smiling, easy, he stood, his long legs apart, rolling the stone around in the palm of his hand. The light wind blew his uncombed hair about his thin face.

"Lose something?" he asked, tossing the stone lightly overhead and catching it.

All three men laughed. Nathaniel put the stone in his pocket and blew on his bare hands. He said, "I thought I might run into you this morning."

Sean poked Nathaniel gently in the ribs. "Is that so? Have you suddenly decided to join us?"

Edward coughed nervously, but Nathaniel chuckled and said, "Oh, no. I leave such feats of daring to the young. Just wanted to say good luck."

"You're ancient, really ancient," said Sean dryly. "We'll have to visit you in your rocking chair, any day now."

Nathaniel chuckled and gestured toward the sea. "I thought I'd take a look around the caves."

"For your seals?" said Sean.

"Maybe."

Sean eyed him. "Emily was muttering about having seen something odd this morning."

Nathaniel glanced up toward the cove sharply. "Really?"

"Yeah. But she didn't think it was a seal."

"No," said Nathaniel, nodding. "No one does."

No, thought Sean in silent agreement. But then again, no

one would believe that *he'd* once seen live seahorses—not pictures, not photographs, but tiny, living beings. Yet he had. He remembered them vividly, even though he'd been very, very young; they'd startled him with their vibrant movement and colors—purple, orange, and yellow. They'd spun and floated in the aquarium, the same size, the same bony elegance, yet each a different hue. Most people told him that a childish imagination had enlivened old photographs and had given him seahorse fancies. Such delicate creatures belonged to the far distant past.

"Look, Nate," said Ed, "I doubt there are any seals left."

"But you will ask Sheila—?"

"Sure," said Ed, smiling quickly. "God, you're as stubborn as Jay! Got an idea, can't let it go."

"I'm positive," said Nathaniel, "that seals used to haul out here. They might've come home."

Ed shrugged. "Maybe."

"We're going to be late starting," said Sean. "Nathaniel—I was joking, but you didn't want to come with us, did you?"

"No. I've got Tomas. He—he might need me. You understand."

"Yeah," said Sean. "Yeah, right."

Nathaniel held out the stone he had picked up. "Want it?"

Sean laughed. "Good God, no! Got enough to carry. Keep it."

Nathaniel waved and pocketed the stone again. Then he turned around, heading toward the cove. He was used to being either teased or ignored. He had caught only one quick glimpse of something in the sea caves at the end of the cove, but he thought it had been a seal. And, after having patiently searched through the paper trash he'd saved from what had been left in the lighthouse on the hillside above Monkar, he was convinced that the cove might have been a pupping ground. If so, the chances were more than just good that a small herd had returned.

What luck if they had! He'd read once that seal meat was fatty, that seal oil burned well and sealskin was waterproof—it could mean a much better winter, next winter, if he could catch one and prove he wasn't dotty. Of course he had no real idea how to slaughter such an animal—not as he'd been told his ancestors could. They'd lived upon the seal, supposedly, in ancient times. He'd never touched one, let alone killed one. But he'd get to that problem later.

He climbed up over the first rise and headed toward the road near the water that led to the dock. A storm had flattened part of it, on the day that Barbara Monkar had died. No one had bothered to shore up the pier. Lately they'd had enough trouble finding material to fix the buildings in town with, let alone trying to reconstruct a port, for which they had no use— although Nathaniel had been urging council to begin repairs on one of the boats left in dry dock.

He stopped for a moment to scan the beach. His son usually accompanied him to the sea caves. But this morning Tomas had not been home when Nathaniel had started out for the beach. He'd hoped the boy would be waiting for him near the dock. But it was deserted. Nathaniel waited for a few minutes, in case the boy should show up. He wasn't worried. Despite his deafness, Tomas had learned how to take care of himself pretty well in most ways.

Even so, thought Nathaniel, *it's better that I stay. Just in case. He might need me.* He took off his shoes and shook the sand out of them. He looked around—still no Tomas. He tucked his shoes under his arm and ran toward the sea caves. His stride was clean and even, his long toes dug into the firm, wet sand. He liked the feel of the brisk wind in his hair, slapping his face. His skin grew damp from the sea's mist; he ran to the rock outcropping and nestled his shoes in a high crevice, out of the sea's reach; then, he climbed.

Atop the bluff, he glanced up and down the two beaches and the scattered expanse of Monkar, looking once more for Tomas. The boy was nowhere to be seen, but there were signs of other people astir; a few lights twinkled out from among the huddled darkness of town center; the Nottage-Patterson house, of course, sprawled across several lots, growing as it did piecemeal and smack in the middle of things; next door and facing the open square, in the center of which stood a crumbling clock tower, the long, squat, flat-roofed council house, which was dark; the semicircle of swapping lean-tos, tented until the next gathering; the several repaired rows of neat, ugly one-floor box dwellings where he lived, only one of which—Alice Rey's—was lighted; beyond that, he couldn't make out any of the others, except Maria Monkar's sagging excuse for a cottage at the very edge of town. Smoke curled from the broken chimney, and as he watched, her lights went out.

Nathaniel pictured Maria as he knew she would be, rumpled, her hair a nest, her eyes half-lidded as she padded around her tiny house, as quiet on her feet as her cats were. He folded his arms against his chest and looked away. Closer to the basalt rocks, down toward the water on the sand, he saw three people gathering driftwood. They were building a bonfire—a small pit and a ring of gray stones, kindling. He squinted, cupping his hand over his eyes—Tomas? No—it was JP Nottage and his sister, Christine. And who . . . Maria? Surprised, he stepped hastily aside and crouched down. Yes, it was Maria. He shifted his weight—the rocks were a bit loose—anxious to keep hidden. Maria didn't like him to poke around the sea caves.

Suddenly the earth gave way under his heel and, without time for a cry, he fell.

Down on the beach, the bonfire for the departing expedition leapt into life as Maria Monkar touched off the dry bunchgrass that she, Christine, and John-Peter (Jay or JP) Nottage had collected. Christine added a few more bundles of the stuff to the flame, while JP handed hot tea around to all. They were waiting for Ed Jackson and Sean Rider, as well as for the mapmakers, Ty and Marah Logan. After a few minutes, several others appeared, to stand near the growing fire—Malini and Seth Leeman; Ki and Jiro Rey; Denuda, her brother, George Patterson, and his first living child, Lindi; Alana Madraguda, Yvon Jones, Ceyda Stein, Guilia Dais, Jia Zheng, Pat Jiminez . . . Maria smiled at them all, spoke to a few. It was a good turnout, for so early an hour. Bitterly cold, she held onto her mug of tea with both hands and sipped it.

She knew she had startled Christine by showing up to help with the bonfire, because she'd been making it clear that she didn't approve of this crazy expedition.

And now? Now that Chris had decided to go along? It was worse. Maria frowned thinly to herself, knowing Sean's reaction, and knowing, too, that she would be the one who would startle both Chris and Sean before the morning was over. She fingered the thin folio in her pocket and wondered what Sean would say when she gave it to him—if she was able to get him to accept it at all! He'd often argued in council that her book-making was a waste—of time, of resources. Then, when Emily began to help her, Sean had ceased speaking to her altogether, save for necessity's sake. She sipped her tea. She didn't really loathe him anymore, though; she'd grown neutral.

"Will you miss me?" said Christine. She'd stepped nearer to Maria, cradling a cup of tea in her hands.

"That," said Maria, smiling, "is a silly question."

"Good, because I'll miss you—and your tea—dreadfully."

The two women laughed. Maria said, "Be careful. Come home safe. That's a piece of advice I'd like to tattoo on your eardrums, so that you will hear it every day."

"I'm careful."

"Still, being on the road . . ."

"Old habits die hard and I remember. I remember getting to Monkar. And I remember the Area."

Maria sighed. "Perhaps. But I didn't think you'd care to try going down there again."

"Care to? No," said Christine, shrugging. "But this isn't about staying. It's for Linda."

"Of course."

"Well, I can't just wait here, can I?"

"No," said Maria slowly, evenly. "No."

"And we're not fleeing. We're not homeless. . . ."

Uneasily, Maria said, "Of course not."

"I thank God for that. When I think of how Sandra's kids—" Christine dropped her gaze. "I'm sorry," she said.

Maria threw out the dregs of her tea. "For going?"

"No. For speaking about the kids. It was thoughtless."

"Why?"

"Because I should have been . . . because of Carlo."

"Here, don't be sorry." Maria touched her cheek to Christine's and then ran her fingertips over the younger woman's thick, short-cropped hair. "He's gone," she said. "Like so many. Speaking or not won't change it."

"Maria—"

"Please—you ought to start this journey without sadness! You've got a sister waiting for you on the other end."

Christine laughed gently. "Only the rumor of her."

"Don't you trust Edward?"

"He could have been mistaken."

"Still—"

"Oh, Ed's reliable. But I'm worried, too."

"As you should be." Maria glanced over her shoulder. "Sean doesn't know yet that you're going?"

"Ed was supposed to have told him." Christine sipped at her tea and pulled up her collar, facing herself toward the fire. "I don't know how I could have let Sean talk me out of going in the first place. Linda's not just my sister. I'm her. She's me."

Maria nodded. By the uneven light of the bonfire, Chris's saddened brown face seemed both darker and younger than it was—which, to Maria, heightened the facticity of Chris's statement, though it hardly needed heightening. Chris and

Linda had been—were?—identical twins. For several years after Linda's disappearance, indeed, Sandra, the twins's older sister, hadn't been sure that Chris would survive the loss.

Maria said, "How's Sandra taking it now?"

Chris sighed. "Not good. She doesn't believe that Linda might be alive." She shrugged. "Do you?"

"It's possible."

"But you still disapprove?"

"Yes." Maria listened to the lapping of the water; it was just light enough to see the ruffled waves rise up on the flat sand and then slide back out again, leaving a wet and uneven trail. The tide was coming in. She said, "It isn't up to me, is it? Just you take care."

"I will. Oh—there's Ed and Sean." Chris darted off.

Maria hung back, watching.

Edward Jackson, Sean Rider—and even the Nottages—were all, so far as Maria was concerned, still newcomers to Monkar. She measured her responses to them; even after so many years, she was still cautious with them. She watched.

Sean Rider was big, broader than most, certainly taller; he wore his long, red hair brushed back off his face in a tail. But though he was large, he had often reminded Maria of a goat. On the other hand, Edward Jackson, who was the shorter of the two, had always seemed the larger. He spoke little, unless badgered, but Maria found if she badgered him enough, he would get started on something and pull her ear with it for hours. He reminded her of a bear and with good reason: dark and heavy-set, he likened himself to one often and with pride, although he had to admit he'd never seen a live bear of any kind.

She stood still, considering the two men, until she saw Sean move off alone to one side of the bonfire. Ed was talking with George Patterson and Ki Rey. Christine was checking over her gear. John-Peter made second rounds with the tea, while those children who could run, ran about the gathering. Maria edged over to Sean and tapped him on the shoulder.

He jumped a little at her touch and scowled.

"Sorry," she said.

"Maria." His frown deepened. "What are you doing here?"

"Came to see you off."

His expression softened. "Good."

She chuckled. "I wouldn't come along, Sean. Never in a million years. Is that what you were thinking?"

"I've a right. JP and Christine—"

"So?"

"So? I planned it for Ed and me alone."

"Won't eight hands be better than four?" She shot him a narrow glance. "Listen, you take care of Chris—"

He laughed. "And that had better be a joke, Maria. Both Linda and Christine have always taken care of themselves."

"All right then, just don't make it harder for her. Anyhow," she continued, rushing herself before she got too annoyed with him, "I wanted to give you this." She handed him the small book, along with an old-fashioned, manufactured pencil. "For the trip. We need to know as much as we can about what's going on out there. Keep a journal."

He held the two objects away from him, as if he would give them back to her instantly. But before he could either speak or do anything, she moved aside and said, "Keep it. Use it. Tell us what you see." And then she left him.

Sean watched Maria in surprise. She headed away from him and toward her home at a clip he would've thought too swift for her—she wasn't a young woman, and he never considered her agile. But before she disappeared, Christine ran up and caught her. The two women spoke. Maria shook her head. Then they embraced.

Sean turned away and stepped closer to the fire. Watching them make their farewells irritated him. Christine was coming along! He pocketed Maria's gifts absently and stood staring into the blaze with his hands on his hips, his shoulders hunched. How many times had he discussed the trip with Christine? And how many times had he persuaded her to stay home? Half a dozen, at least. He shut his eyes. Everybody seemed to be crowding him! Ed, with his remarks about Emily "looking poorly"; Emily's pathos; Maria's book; Nathaniel's genial and more or less unspoken reminder that he had to take care of Tomas because no one else would. And now, Chris's impudent, perverse decision to just come along.

He glanced up. Christine had returned and stood with her brother on the other side of the fire. Everybody was just standing around, waiting for the mapmakers' arrival. Ed had given elaborate instructions for the map alterations, so that it would include which sections of road had troll-mark; he'd been hovering over the mapmakers like a cook over a pair of unreliable pots.

Sean watched Ed waiting. Although he felt accuracy was always a good idea, he feared more troll-mark than Ed had either remembered or had even chanced to see. *Still,* he thought, *a new map can't hurt.* He eyed the waning moon and then rummaged inside his shirt for the pocket watch he wore on a string around his neck. It was getting late.

Sean stamped his feet to warm up his toes and slid his hands into his pockets. He felt his chest clutching up again as he gazed at Chris. Why, after all their arguments, had she decided to be an idiot? He watched her, covertly, he hoped, and waited for JP to move away from her side. If he could get Chris to give it up, JP would quit, too.

But he did not need to wait. Christine herself walked over to Sean. "Surprised?" she said lightly.

"Appalled," he answered, smiling.

"I couldn't just sit home."

"The last time we talked, you said different—a small group travels faster than a large one."

"Four people isn't a large group. Besides—it's Linda."

"Yeah?" He cracked his knuckles. "Since when," he said

slowly, knowing the deep bite his words would have, "did she really matter all that much to you?"

Christine stared at him, flushing. She folded her arms. "My, my," she said harshly, "aren't we cruel this morning."

"Cruel? I'd say truthful. Why don't we ask Sandra?"

"Sandra's no friend to you."

"All right—how about Linda then?"

She glared at him. "*You* should talk about Linda!"

"I remember well enough what she used to say about you."

Christine laughed. "You don't know anything about anybody, do you? You never have and you never will."

"Stop it," said Edward. He stepped between the two. "We're going to have trouble enough on the road, without bickering like spoiled kids. I want peace. Understand?" He looked to Christine, then to Sean, who, cooling his temper down, said, "Look, Ed, she'd agreed to stay. And we don't even know if Linda's really down there, anyhow."

"If that's your reasoning," said Chris, "no one should go."

"Now wait—"

"Linda's my twin!"

"She's my wife!" he cried.

Both Ed and Christine looked at him. Neither spoke.

He laughed uneasily. "Well? She *was* mine. We'd made vows. Does that suit the two of you better? Good God, we don't even know whether she's alive and already we're arguing about her!"

"Why don't you stay here, Sean?" said Chris flatly. "JP, Ed, and I will go. Stay here. With Emily."

He glared. "Watch yourself, Chris. My temper isn't as generous as it used to be."

"When was it ever?" She turned her back on him.

"Sean—" said Edward.

"What?"

"Have you considered it?"

"What—strangling Chris?" he said to her back. She stiffened, so he added, "Plenty of times."

"No," said Ed, "I meant staying here."

"Don't you think I've reconsidered?" Sean sighed and dug one heel into the sand. "Emily knows why I'm doing this. Better than anyone. Emily knows. So drop it, all right?"

Sean walked off, leaving Ed and Chris to ponder, he hoped, just what it was that Emily "knew." As he sat down in the sand next to his pack and stretched his feet out toward the dwindling fire, he wondered, was Emily really not looking well? He frowned, picturing her face as he had seen it that morning, when the alarm rang. He'd woken instantly, as usual, and, as usual, she'd turned over, her eyelids trembling but not opening. Her skin was very white, whiter than his own, yet more olive than the white of the pillowcases. There were dark patches under her eyes. But they had always been there, her skin was simply darker there. Asleep, she'd looked contented—

"She's fine," he whispered. "She's fine." He swallowed back nerves and looked off toward his home. He could barely see it now in the distance, the kitchen light pinprick-size. He'd not been able to bring himself to say to Emily, out loud, that Linda was the biggest mistake he'd ever made. This trip was the sort of chance people seldom, if ever, got: the chance to rectify an error that had marred everything he'd felt since. But he knew that Emily knew. He gritted his teeth and wondered what she was doing.

And Emily, in the bedroom, wondered if Sean had left yet. Pulling on a sweater, she wondered where Sean would be by noon. Then she put the thought away from her. All she had to worry about was where she would be and what she would be doing.

Still, it was a hard habit to break, this worrying about Sean. As she made a second cup of tea, she found herself staring out the back door and wondering again about him. She shook her head, set the mug down, and left. She wanted to watch the sun rise on the beach. She wanted to be away from their house, the home they'd made together in those days past when she had thought she knew how to talk to him. Yet she had decided she wanted him to go. If he could find out what had happened to Linda, maybe his nightmares would cease. Meanwhile, in his absence, maybe she could decide what to do about the two of them. Or rather the three of them—she, he, and Linda—since, no matter what passed between herself and Sean, Linda was with them, always.

And Sean did want to go, almost desperately—he wanted the cold nights, the surreptitious campfires, the known and unknown threats. In the last few days, she'd often wondered: Was his desire part of his unprofessed guilt about Linda's fate, which she thought hunted him down in his happiest moments? Could be. But Emily suspected it also had something to do with that creeping sense of aimlessness he spoke of from time to time. She knew that aimlessness. She'd felt it, too, especially and acutely after her second stillbirth.

The gravel of the road to the cove was lightly frosted. Emily's boots melted footprints in it as she jogged halfheartedly down the incline. At the water's edge, she stopped to listen; she closed her eyes and folded her arms across her chest and listened. She could almost hear the strange night music, a not-song lingering at the edge of the mind, playing for the inner ear. Yet on several occasions, it had been more a wail than music; high-pitched, birdlike, one night almost a scream, a human shriek that had quite unnerved her, because it had resurrected old memories of the place where she'd been born.

It had never been silent in Vanseaport; the city had always been on alert. She didn't remember much of that time. Snatches of dark hallways, a malodorous room, a soft, pale face she knew to be her mother's, but little else—moments like nightmare and often as vivid, but never continuous nor attached to blame or sorrow the way Sean's dreams were. But then Sean had been with his family in the Area until he'd been a teenager, while she'd been taken away from Vanseaport by her great-grandmother when she'd been four. Aretina had been a small, angry person, too full of memories. She'd had a smooth face, startlingly unwrinkled and unlined, framed by starkly white hair braided as Emily now braided her own. Toward the end of her life, she'd lost track of the present, but even senile, she had never feared either her own judgments or their consequences. Aretina, with an astonishingly youthful vigor born, Emily believed, of sheer desperation, had fled Vanseaport and had found her grandson, Emily's father, in Monkar. Whatever had become of the soft, pale face, Emily did not know.

She smiled because the beach was empty and she felt oddly comforted by the predawn lighting of the sky. She got to her knees in the sand and bowed her head. Though she'd lost the particulars of the faith her great-grandmother had taught her, she'd never lose the habit of prayer. When she opened her eyes, she was shocked to find the Nitehammer child, Tomas, kneeling in an attitude of prayer in front of her. She started to her feet.

He scrambled backward.

He'd always been both alluring and frightening; his eyes— oval, grayish-green, and glassy—were strange, too large. They dominated his snub-nosed face and seemed to hide it, unless they were screened behind his overgrown hair—then, with his thin-lipped mouth unsmiling, he seemed sullen. She thought him both lovely and a little horrifying. Certainly unteachable. And the way he watched people, never speaking, never having learned to speak, in fact, except for an odd noise he made infrequently, a clicking in the back of his throat. She brushed sand off her knees and started to the rocks, hoping the boy would leave.

Instead, he followed her.

She walked faster.

So did he. She stopped and frowned at him. She didn't

want his silent presence, she wanted to be alone. She motioned him away brusquely. She turned to point at the ruins of the dock. She hoped he would go. But when she turned back to him, he was crouching in the sand, staring away from her. Suddenly he ran off, with a spring and fluidity that was so startlingly lovely and unexpected, it took her breath away. He ran toward the rocks and climbed, until he disappeared.

She waited a few minutes, to see if he would return, but when he didn't, she assumed he had climbed onward, to the sea caves. She continued her walk. She had a spot among the rocks high above the beaches, a natural windbreak from which she could meditate, watch the sea. Settling herself on the grassy perch, she glanced around for Tomas, but saw nothing save two abandoned shoes tucked into a crevice below her. She shrugged to herself and leaned back out of the wind.

2

Accidents

THE TIDE WAS coming in. On the beach, a few yards from the back of her house, Maria bent down and picked a tiny shell out of the sand. She had almost stepped on it and she would have hated to break it, there being so few to be found. She put it in her pocket and stretched. Her joints ached. At the water's edge, she stepped into the surf. Her bare feet were numbed from the cold. She liked the numbness; it braced her, wakened her from nighttime fogs and all-too-frequent choking dreams.

It was her custom to walk the shoreline before sunrise. Some days, she stayed at the ocean's edge until well after the sun rose. Not today, though. She'd hiked over to the leave-taking, given Christine her love, delivered her book to Sean, and now—now, she would speak to Emily.

Leaving the shore, she began to climb the bluff. At the first switchback, she suddenly stopped. The sun slipped up over her shoulder and ran beams aslant across the rocks and blond scrub. There, a few steps beyond the switchback, the narrow track split. The wider trail led upward toward Gideon's Point and, past there, to Emily; the thready one led down, to the sea caves.

She stood gazing at the lower path. She hadn't taken it for—well, since Carlo had died. It was overgrown, almost too weedy to follow. Uncertainly, she stepped onto that winding thread of dirt, away from Emily, through basalt and grass, down toward the sea caves. Briefly glancing around, she wondered if Nate was out after his imaginary seals. She hoped not. She just didn't want to run into him. She reopened the choked way, imagining as she went that her energy and noise would prove she had spirit enough to entertain any morbid little child-ghost lingering there.

She knew that it was last night's dream that had pushed her onto this path and drew her to the caves. So be it. She knew also that she wouldn't be able to walk out upon the sand or even to get close to one of the caves—not at high tide. So be it. She just wanted to go, to go and be with Carlo.

She sighed; she had not been plagued with his memory so much in a while. Yet today her lost son's ungainly body came into her view at every turn—his hunched shoulders and narrow oval head, his pointed, snub nose and oddly lipless mouth, his thick-lidded eyes and hands so fleshy as to be nearly fingerless, his misshapen penis and curled-in toes, those hampering accidents of birth that had become more pronounced as he grew. He'd appeared first in her dream; then, in Christine's departing conversation, both of which had called him too vividly forth, reminding her that she, too, had once traveled, albeit on a much, much shorter trip, in search of someone already lost.

She knocked aside a thistle and stepped down to a ledge in the path. A crow flapped clumsily past her and settled on a nearby rock. When it moved off, she saw that it flew without grace, burdened by a flabby, white tumor. She gritted her teeth and dropped farther down to a small plateau that inclined to, then disappeared at, a scoop of beach, a mere slice of sand. The sea caves were visible only if one knew how and where to look, because the tide was nearly high.

The wind blew whitecap froth on the wave tops; she wrapped her jacket close about herself and sat down on the flat, mossy stone. She would allow herself to think of Carlo now. She would let open the way to that heart chamber where he was hidden. In doing so, she let a shy child sneak out of her memory to dance, as he could never have done in life, on the plateau beside her. She sat, watching her memory's image of Carlo, until the rising tide beat against the bluff, railing and foaming, filling the sea caves and bubbling white where the entrances were, giving life to the anenomes and spraying the barnacles that grew on those rocks. Watching her child's ghost dance in the grass above that spit of land on which she had buried him, she forgot time and somehow, the loss of him seemed less sharp.

At last, she made Carlo vanish back into the dew and mist out of which his dream-flesh had taken substance. The air was warm, even though the wind was chilly; there, on the mossy stone, it was almost hot. She lay back and put her hands behind her head. The light gauzy fog had burned off, except at the very tops of the hills far beyond Monkar, where it caught and hovered at the evergreen spires, long, still pennants of fading fleece.

She had just closed her eyes when a shrill wail brought her instantly to her feet. The cry died on the wind, but her heart held it. She scanned as far as her sight could reach but nothing that could have made so thin and desperate a cry came to view. She sat down slowly.

Carlo—Carlo again, back again unbidden, haunting her with this agony of sound. Hadn't she heard that cry before, right here, in nearly this same spot? Hadn't he screamed like that, just once and piercingly, when death had grasped him unawares?

She had been down by the sea caves. Curiosity had brought her often to them at low tide. She had been sure that she would find something inside one of them, someday—

perhaps an ancient glass float, or a more recent relic, say, a shoe, from those times when there were many, many people here, people who lived freely all along the coast.

On the day he died, Carlo had been asleep on the blanket she had spread for him. She had glanced at the boy from time to time as she poked in and around the rocks and caves, waiting for him to wake so that she could show him a tide pool in which she had found a large, violet starfish. She had seen him sit up. She had waved to him.

He stood, to wave back.

Then, for no reason she ever did find out, he had screamed. Once. The sound of it had bounced off the craggy hills.

He fell forward.

She ran to him; she'd run so quickly that later, she neither remembered running, nor had she felt it when a barnacled rock tore her heel—a gash that had trailed blood in the sand behind her. Despite her speed, he was gone before she could touch him. Later on, Alice Rey had said to her over and over again that the child had probably had, for some reason they'd never know, a massive stroke or heart attack; he had not suffered. Alice was as good a doctor as her mother, Janice Rey, had been, as good as her daughter Ki promised to be, strong, kind, and careful. Maria trusted her as much as she had trusted Janice.

But Alice had not heard Carlo scream.

Maria found her hands shaking as she looked around again. All was as it should have been. Nobody was about. Nothing was in sight, not even her memory-phantom of Carlo.

Yet she'd heard something. What?

A second, thinner, higher shriek brought her back to her feet. This time, though, the sound was truly strange, almost inhuman. It made her heart freeze.

The shriek was repeated, staccato, then piercing but at the same time like music; wild, somehow gorgeously frightening—

What the hell? She frowned. The only thing that came to mind—but how could it be? Could there actually be . . . seals?

Nate had been saying for months now that he'd spotted seals up this way. Recently, angered, she'd told him, in front of Sandra Nottage and Alice Rey, two women for whose opinion he cared, that he was nothing but an old fool. Delusional.

Might he have been right? She shaded her eyes. What sort of sound did a seal make? Did it even make a sound? No one knew. A part of her still loved Nate, but since Carlo's death, she'd kept her distance. He reminded her too much of better times, of when her brothers, Jorge and Eduardo, were alive, of herself when she was younger and stronger; he reminded her too much of Carlo, their only child. And there was his own sweet Tomas—so lovely to her eyes, and yet so much like Carlo; he, too, reminded her of all who were gone and especially of his mother, Cait, for whom she had cared. And lately, Nate's imaginary seals had made her even more wary, although not because she really thought him demented. No. Rather, his stories brought to mind how often she dreamt of dead things. Children long dead spoke to her. Animals she had never seen roamed dream-fields. There were days when she woke confused by the nearly birdless skies and taken aback— where had the world gone? Perhaps Nathaniel's seals were imaginary, but far be it for her, so plagued by dreams, to judge their reality. She simply avoided him and had (mostly) kept her opinions to herself.

Yet, at that moment, she grabbed hold of those seals as an explanation for the terrible, gorgeous, daunting sound she'd just heard. She didn't have to believe in them altogether— tomorrow they could become imaginary again. But as she stood alone by the sea in the dawn, she preferred to have an explanation for the wail. The seals were better than nothing. Far better indeed than to believe she'd heard Carlo's ghost.

Unless—was someone in trouble?

At that she stood and headed rapidly back up the path. She would go to town and report what she'd heard, get George Patterson or Ki Rey or Tomas to help her make a quick search; then she could really forget the cry, put it down to imaginary seals or some other benign cause—the dying crow she'd seen? She hurried and ignored the reminiscent pain in her heel. She hurried and did not notice that she was, in fact, running up the hill.

The tide was coming in. Nathaniel watched the whitecaps as they approached the shore. The crescent of sand that usually rimmed the rocks below him had already vanished; the tide pools had been swallowed. The rush of the waters, the unspeaking roar of the sea in its ceaseless fury, contained all sound. It seemed to him more a terrible silence than a terrible noise.

He shifted his position and winced, gasping at the pain that lanced his ankle. He was stuck; he'd fallen only a few feet or so off the Point, but his ankle was wedged awry in a crevice, vised tight. He was pinned to the sea side of the hill.

What a fool, he thought, *hiding from Maria!* He took a deep breath and then called out, but knew his voice was overcome by the sea's basso song. The tide was approaching—fast. He judged by the anenomes sprouting near his shoulder that, if he did not get free, he would drown.

Leaning forward, he tried again to loosen his foot. One side of the crevice had some give to it, but he was pincered at the wrong angle to take advantage of the leeway. He rested his full weight on an elbow. His hands were icy. He shivered in fits.

Shading his eyes from the low-angled sun behind him, he looked over the glittering, warm, and restless waters. The distance between his feet and the sea was rapidly thinning under the pitiless advance of the tide. The sea spray, atomized by the force of the waves, made him so cold in the wind that he thought the chill might carry him off before the tide did. He'd heard that neither drowning nor freezing was painful; he'd heard them called easy ways to die.

A spasm shook him, a streaking pain; each spasm worked a dagger edge of agony a little deeper and a little farther up his calf. He shifted his weight onto the other elbow; as he did, he caught sight of Tomas, scampering like some fantastically large hermit crab, over the rocky face of the hill. Nathaniel's eyes burned—with a grim lunge, he rocked back and forth to loosen the rocks, to make the unyielding earth give way.

The lash of fine-honed pain that raced up his spine told him, when his sight cleared and he could breathe again, that the ankle was more than simply wrenched—it was broken. He felt the bones scrape, he even thought he could hear their edges saw against one another. His stomach turned. Panting, he glanced around for Tomas—why had the boy come now? Why couldn't he have stayed away?

And then came the question that he'd been staving off: Who would watch over his son? Who would see that Tomas ate well and kept warm in winter. Who would teach him? Would Maria? Could she?

"Oh, please—" he murmured at the stubborn rock, "come on—" He gently moved his leg again from side to side; the crevice was crumbling. But at every movement, for every inch, his foot swelled more, to fill the space gained. A trickle of dirt and sand sifted down against his back. He twisted around as best he could. Tomas was climbing toward him. The boy made a tentative, clicking sound as he kneed his way over the bluff, sending down more dirt and sand. Nathaniel shook his head. He mimed, *Go back*. But Tomas persisted until he had crawled to his father's side.

Nathaniel leaned forward, to show how his foot was caught; he pointed to the rising water, then took hold of the boy's shoulders and turned him half around, toward safety.

Tomas shifted away from Nathaniel's grasp. He tried to inch down to where his father was caught, but the hill was too steep. The boy laid his cheek against his father's shoulder, nuzzling as a cat would. Almost instantly he pulled back as if burned.

Startled, Nathaniel touched his own neck and shoulder, running his fingers along the collarbone and up to the edge of his beard. But nothing was broken, he felt neither blood nor pain there. What was the matter with Tomas? He looked questioningly to his son; the boy touched him again with the flat of his warm hand and then hastily crawled away.

Nathaniel tried to twist around and see what the boy was up to. But he could scarcely move. Another sprinkling of pebbles and dirt showered down the hillside and then he felt the pressure of the boy's full weight against his back, as Tomas lowered himself upon his shoulders, wrapped his thin arms around his father's chest, almost cinching him out of breath.

"What the hell?" said Nathaniel. Frightened, he caressed the boy's arms. Swallowing fear, he pulled away from his son and tried to push him toward the top of the bluff. Tomas *must* go, he must leave before the tide came in. He did not hope that his child might help him; the water was moving too quickly. He knew he would be dead long before anyone could interpret Tomas's miming hand motions and odd, strangulated voice.

Again he nudged the boy away and shook him by his thin shoulders. But Tomas scrambled back. Nathaniel glanced at the sea. Water would soon cover his swollen ankle.

"Tomas," he said uselessly, "we will both drown, both of us." He pushed at the boy yet again and roughly now; he tried to wriggle out or wrench from the warm grasp.

"Go!" he shouted. What if he couldn't force the child from him? His weakness and the boy's stubborn refusal were breaking him; he felt an inward cracking. He felt a scream squeezing past his strength . . . a thick panic . . . rich ground for the bloom of his fear, he would just scream, now—

And Tomas let go. He shimmied down next to Nathaniel's side and looked into his father's face. It was a commanding gaze, bespeaking an urgency that strangely quieted Nathaniel's terror—maybe the boy would leave now? But no— Thomas crawled full onto Nathaniel's chest.

"Tomas!" he shouted, resisting. "No!" He would not take his boy with him to death—he struggled . . . and lay motionless. This hug was meant as help. As body heat seeped through Nathaniel's torn shirt down to his cold skin, he knew that Tomas was lending him warmth, to fight off death. Sure enough, as the boon of heat stole into him, he relaxed a little. The spasms stopped. Finally, he took the boy gently by the shoulder. Now Tomas should go, said Nathaniel without speaking. Go for help.

In a few moments, the boy did move off. He nodded at his father and scampered away. The man watched his son, smiling sadly—he had seldom seen Tomas move so gracefully, except for the few times the two of them would race each other across the field near their home. Would he never see that agility again? Angry, he glared at the enemy-sea and at the sunshine sparkling off the blue-green expanse. A new mist drifted around him, moistening everything, the spray-salted rocks, the still, tailed grasses. It wasn't too long before he started to shiver again. His leg muscles cramped. Crazily, he thought he might just gnaw his foot off. Desperate, he wondered: How high would the water rise? Maybe he would be able to keep his head above the waves?

But he knew just how desperate that hope was as he watched the waves grow and dash themselves against the bluff. He started laughing. He wouldn't freeze or drown! How silly of him! Of course not! He would be battered to death first!

Oddly, as he tried again to loosen his foot, he thought about the mythical Andromeda, chained to the sea stack as sacrifice, awaiting the fate the gods had meted out to her. Had she strained against her captivity, as he was doing? Had she felt the cold slap of the sea's wind, had she watched the waters below, hoping for rescue, or hoping to wake and find her fate merely a nightmare? He wondered, too, who would remember poor, lovely Andromeda? What he took for granted was slowly eroding; tales and histories and lives once well known, well remembered, were just forgotten, as his own little life was about to be forgotten, washed over by the sea.

For some time, maybe, Tomas would remember. Yet if Monkar turned the boy out and let him starve? Would he curse a father who had brought him to such abandonment? Nathaniel yanked at his trapped foot and vomited with pain. Trying to recover, he kept still and stared at the sea, thinking, Andromeda had had a stalwart hero on her side, someone to save her. Nathaniel had no one but Tomas and, besides, it was Tomas who needed the savior. Through gritted teeth and muscle contractions, Nathaniel worked on freedom, not for himself but for his child. And as he worked, he found himself mumbling a prayer, a plea, pleasegodpleasegod, the sort of chant he had used when he was a child himself. The sun rose high, to touch his curved back and give him dose of warmth as it chased away the mist. Out of sheer desperation, he screamed.

On another part of the bluff, high above Nathaniel, Emily glanced up—had she heard something? Hastily, she stood.

But it was Tomas's head that appeared among the rocks. Her haste died.

"Go away!" she said, motioning to him. She had hoped he'd gone for good. Why had he come back? Hands on her hips, lips pursed, she waited for him to see her; when he glanced upward, his overlarge eyes bright and his half-hidden face set in a solemn grimace, she motioned him away again. But he ignored this and kept climbing toward her. She motioned more vigorously, until she found herself stamping her foot as if that gesture of impatience would have some effect.

He kept climbing until he reached her perch. He was breathing hard and despite the chill wind, his narrow, oval face was sweat-laced. He straightened up and pointed downward from where he had come. To placate him, Emily peered over the bluff: wet rocks, dressed in varied seaweeds of onyx, maroon, auburn, with a hint of emerald here and there—nothing unusual. She frowned. He gestured, clicking his tongue. It baffled her.

He's harmless, she thought, staring at him. She hadn't really noticed before how spare and almost delicately compact he was, how softly but strongly muscled.

He stared back at her. For a moment, they both seemed to be waiting for something. He opened his mouth, then closed it, then he reached out and tried to drag her bodily to the edge of the bluff. She clawed away from him and jumped back. He grabbed for her, tugging at her sleeve and pointing over the cliff's edge.

This was too much; she was really frightened now. What if he was not harmless? She pushed at the boy—who was not so young, she realized—until he recoiled. Then she began to climb down to the cove. Angry tears threatened to blur her vision as she swiftly abandoned the bluff—her own special place—to the silent, intrusive, downright scary youth. She glared back upward, with half a mind to return and force him to leave her alone there. But as she glanced up, her heart skipped.

Tomas had knelt, his arms reaching out, trembling, toward her. His thick, tawny hair was blown back off his odd face, revealing—or creating?—such a visceral, instantaneous, and complete sorrow that she nearly lost her footing in surprise. She felt smitten with grief, but a grief not her own.

What could it be? How could he bring her to actual tears, tears no longer of anger but of—what? How could he do that to her? Frightened, far too jangled to try to solve the mystery, she climbed down fast, so that her legs shook with the strain of hurry when she touched the sand. As she jogged across the cove and up the rise to the dirt road near her house, she threw a swift glance behind her. Tomas was no longer visible. Relieved that he had not followed her yet again, she slowed her pace.

By the time she reached her kitchen door, she was exhausted and chilled through and through. She stood beside the stove, shivering. What could Tomas want? Why was he so persistent? The only thing that came to mind was the day she'd thrown him out of her house for playing with Sean's clocks. And what of that feeling of grief—absolute sheering grief—that she'd had? It had been like a dose, or a drenching of emotion, so complete and so, well, foreign . . . not hers, yet of her, that she'd felt as if she'd been inhabited by it.

As soon as her fingers were no longer numb, she took off her damp sweater, set it on the back of a chair before the stove, and went upstairs to her bedroom to lie down. She was still shivering. *Damn him!* she thought.

Climbing the stairs, she tried to take in the quiet emptiness of the house, to feel how sweet it was to have the old place to herself. As she smoothed the blue comforter over the bed and ritually shook out the pillows, laying them neatly side by side, she found that two tiny, spindly-legged spiders had been at work since she had risen that morning. They'd spread their fine net right between the ornamental posts of the old headboard. She cleaned away the web. She hated spiders but no matter how many times she cleared them out, they'd always returned, and always in a pair, the same tiny size, the same round bodies, like ghosts of the original two, if there had ever been an originating pair. Sometimes she fancied they'd always been there, a spontaneous creation of the room itself.

Having tidied the bed and cleared it of its infinitesimal intruders, she sat down. She did not yet feel calm. In a moment, she leaned over and opened her sea chest. She rummaged under blankets and sweaters for a heart-shaped bag, got it out from under woolens, and set it on the bed. She touched the sewn flap. She ran an unsteady fingertip along the fine-grained leather.

At last she stood up, left the unopened pouch sitting in the middle of the bed, and paced.

Tomas had upset her, a ragged boy! She shook her head

and stood beside the window. Pulling the curtains back a bit, she scanned the cove for the child. No one. Nothing.

"Damn," she muttered. A few more minutes passed and then, in a rush, she grabbed a sweater from her sea chest and swept out of the room. She would find Maria. Maria would calm her . . . she knew Tomas, she knew Nathaniel well. Maria could go with her. Together they'd talk to the Nitehammers, and tell that boy to leave her alone.

The tide wet his knees with its warm lips. Nathaniel shuddered. His trapped foot had disappeared to sensation at the ankle. He no longer felt toes. He had ceased struggling and watched the sunlight play on the water. He heard the sea's constant boom. He shivered.

Images came to him unbidden. He saw himself as a very small boy, far, far away from any ocean, landlocked, in a crumbling and by then unlicensed deecee clinic, part of a reloc center built in the foothills of the magnificent mountain range near what was left of Salt Lake. The doctor (who had stayed there in the relocation camp stubbornly despite her conscription orders) had tried to save his ailing mother but could do little against the multiple infections, since the deecees had locked down on all medicine distribution. Salt Lake was one of the first places, he'd found out later, that a third-zone designer strep had swept through like a wildfire, taking family after family down—until the deecees had no longer considered the city worth trying to save. A year after his mother died he'd been chased away by rumors that a massive trolling deployment was making its way over the range. He remembered sitting beside his mother in the dirty half-room allotted them, wishing he might go out and play. He wondered at her listlessness and at her fierce, tearful insistence that he stay close at hand. The days had seemed so long to him. He had sat indoors by her, watching the ants on the floor, watching the sun make a slow track across the wide and empty sky. Those few times he'd sneaked away from her, as she dozed, he had felt so crushed by a sense of wrongdoing that he never did have any fun.

How she would've loved Monkar! It was so like the place she'd dreamt of and spoke to him about in her last days that when he'd found it, he thought he'd walked right into her mind.

Another dousing of the sea water drenched his trousers. Spasming, he half rose, but the pain in his ankle drove him back.

He saw his mother's face. The patches of grayish skin under her eyes made her brown cheeks dusty and her restless glance wandered from corner to corner. He wondered if his own face bore her trapped look now—unable, as she had been, to flee, unable to simply drop the yoke of obstinate flesh, he waited to die. Death was so miserable, so unavoidable.

And what would happen to Tomas? Such a gentle baby! He'd never complained. Even his baby cries had never lasted long. He had seldom fussed and so, because he'd been such a good infant, his quietude long went unremarked as a sign of deafness. Nathaniel closed his eyes. Neither he nor Cait had understood what was wrong with Tomas until just before her accident. He could almost hear Cait's voice now, clear and undistorted by the tetanus that had killed her; it whispered to him with the tide's grim music.

He opened his eyes. To his great dismay, Tomas had returned and was crouched beside him on the hillside. Nathaniel struggled to a half-sitting position, cost what it did in pain, and pointed to the rocks overhead. He touched his son's shoulder and pointed and pointed and finally gave the boy another slight, weak push in the direction of safety.

Tomas stood up. He stripped off his shirt and pants and headed out to the edge of the cliff.

Immediately frantic, Nathaniel grabbed for his son, missed, and began gesticulating, crying, screaming for the boy to come back, to get back from the water. He barely noticed the pain that ate at his leg and grated his knee.

Tomas poised at the jutting edge. Outlined in the flame of sunrise, compact and wire-thin, he stood suspended at the water's lip, staring down. His body tensed. He seemed to change his very shape into something hard and lovely and sharp, a purposeful instrument. He dove. The swift, darting line of him shot across what seemed an immensity and disappeared into the sea's dark body without either ripple or tracery of bubbles to mark the spot.

Nathaniel gasped, his throat ragged and sore. He strained for a sight of the boy, but the rising tide slapped him back against the stones. He struggled against gravity and the earth pincer that held him down, but the tide bested him again. He gagged on salt and searched the heaving waves. There was no figure on the waters, no tousled head bobbing under the sun.

The warm sea rose, and rose. He was drowning; there seemed to be light, brilliant, yet then none, brilliant darkness. A roar of silence. Jagged pain in his ankle. Warm salty waters, thick and warm and soupy, floating, downward . . . and there, deep under water, he heard the singing. However impossible, there was a music with him, pure as clarity . . .

He touched a complete joy. It was a joy not his own but yet of him . . .

Then, warmth . . . heat woke him as the sun dried the salt on his face. He opened his eyes and coughed painfully, until he gagged up a mouthful of bile. Then he heard a crisp sentence.

I am not dead.

This was a wonder to him. He coughed again to make sure, took a deep breath. The air had a sweet taste, lightly sweet and brisk. He found himself atop the bluff, on a little sandy plateau, off which he remembered having fallen, ages ago. He could see the place where the rocky earth had given way. There was a new-made crevice at the plateau's lip.

"How did I—?" he murmured. His voice sounded bleak; his throat was raw. He sat up. The pain was stunning—he nearly fainted. Catching back his breath and equilibrium as the jolt subsided, he slowly examined the foot. Swollen purple, it was bent downward and to one side at an angle that wasn't possible for a foot to be in; torn, bloody, the flesh looked as if it had been gnawed. He was missing a toe. He could scarcely believe such a thing to be a part of himself, yet the pain connected him to it unbearably.

A whistling shriek drove the pain from his mind for an instant. Confused, he thought he, himself, had screamed again. Instinctively, he turned toward the bluff's edge, to see where the sound came from. Then, memory lurched into place—Tomas! Tomas, emblazoned by sunshine, poised at the rim of the cliff. The lovely, swift-darting line of his dive.

He struggled to move, but pain and a terror of falling again kept him pinned to the plateau.

What to do? Calling out was useless, there was no one to hear. He lay on the earth, panting and trying to will the pain into submission—somehow, he had to get down from this place.

He flipped over onto his stomach and began to inch to the downward face of the bluff, using his good knee and his arms. Though he tried not to, he wept. He kept seeing Tomas dive from the sunshine into the inky, roiling waters, the slender, brown dart of him streaking past and knifing into the foam.

Crawling, he made it to the brink of the rise and peered over. It was a long climb down to the beach. He could see his dirty-white sneakers tucked into the crevice where he had left them. They were an impossible distance way. Drenched in his own sweat, he put his cheek against the cool, smooth basalt and closed his eyes. His mouth was parched, the sun felt as a hammer at the back of his skull and he was so dizzy that the ground seemed to shift under him. He clutched at the grass to anchor himself to this uncannily moving earth; fragmented thoughts came and passed: had he imagined Tomas's dive? Maybe the boy was safe at home. Would he ever need two sneakers again, should he live through the climb down to them? Oh, that he would wake up in his bunk, his foot caught only in the footboard staves! Had mermaids come for him? This last thought took him into unconsciousness and his grip on the grasses relaxed. The earth stopped shifting and although the wild, piercing sound came again, he did not hear it.

Emily heard. As she strode along the beach near her home, kicking up small sand clouds and trying to frame a way to talk to Nathaniel about his son, she heard the cry. It stopped her. She looked around. Seeing no one, she trudged around the back of the hill, past the rocks and up the sand into the scrubby brush to get beyond the beach and high off the shore. From there, so far inland as to be nearly in town, she could see both ends of the cove.

Fog sat just off the shoreline and was lying flat upon the hill. Such fog was Monkar's nearly constant companion and so she'd supported George's campaign to try to make the ruin on the hillside above her house back into a working lighthouse—though she supposed there were no ships out there to see it.

As she came around the back of the bluff and eased herself down from the high scrub to the sand, she heard the cry once more. Loudly. Clearly. Whatever it was, was close. The sound shredded her mood. She ran to where she thought it had come.

At the water's edge, something moved—she stopped short. It was a figure too large to be a person and oddly mis-shaped, humped, ungainly. It was moving up the beach, away from the breakers. Nothing about it was recognizable. It, monstrous, limped along steadily despite its awkward bulk. It was so odd, she simply watched it for a few moments, unsure whether she ought to go near or run for help. She watched it crawl closer. Then the sun lifted up suddenly over the horizon and touched the humpback, illuminating—them! It was not some ungainly creature come slouching up from the sea, but two people—Nathaniel and Tomas.

Shocked out of herself, she still did not move but watched them struggle across the beach. Then she ran to them. Something was wrong. She called, but the wind carried off her voice. She ran harder, her feet sinking into the sand-shifts, her calves straining to propel her faster over the too-yielding ground. Gasping, she caught up with them.

The boy eyed her through a heavy veil of wet hair, threaded eerily with seaweed. He seemed naked but not exactly nude, for his hair was clinging to him as if in a grotesque parody of Lady Godiva, for it seemed plastered all over him somehow. His blank expression was hostile. She ignored him for the father, but Nathaniel did not seem to know her, or her voice, or anything at all—he was neither unconscious nor awake. His eyes moved to and fro aimlessly. He coughed.

She spoke his name. He did not respond. She could see he was soaking, as was the hairy boy. Both shivered when the wind came down. She stepped close. Tomas glared at her, tightening his hold on his father's waist. She made another, more cautious move, and the boy stepped clumsily away, dragging Nathaniel with him. He made a low call, which rooted Emily to the spot—she knew Tomas could make clicking sounds, but this was more of a growl. She hadn't heard such a sound since they'd driven away the wild dogs from Monkar. She gave up her advance and stood still. Looking them over, she could see that Nathaniel's hands were clenched and his lips blue. One foot was twisted in an impossible way, torn at calf and ankle, staining the sand bright red.

Her heart lunged with fear. Nathan looked as if he had met up with those long-gone dogs. She glanced down the beach, searching for a sign of a pack. Monkar hadn't been troubled by them in some time, but it paid to be cautious. Packs traveled wide. She took a deep breath and beckoned to Tomas. She smiled at him, but not too broadly, afraid her smile would shudder and slip from her face. She half-turned to her house and started walking toward it.

Once she had taken a few steps away from him, Tomas began to follow her. The three made slow progress to safety. When the boy staggered under his burden, Emily slowed her pace. Then she approached again. This time, the boy took no notice. She slipped her shoulder under Nathaniel's arm, helped Tomas lift him. Together they got him off the beach, into the house.

3

In Search of Someone Lost

(9:00 A.M.)

THE MORNING WIND rose. Sean felt dampness fingering its way through the layers of his clothing. He flexed his shoulders. They'd been on the open "road"—what was left of it—for about two and half hours, when Edward had stopped for a look at his map. He took them off to a small shelter of stubby conifer trees amongst dense scrub. In the unlikely event that a troll had come this far up the coast, they were hidden.

Sean glanced at Christine, who was leaning against a tree. Her posture was tense; she made a gesture of impatience toward Ed and JP, who were absorbed in the map. Sean shrugged. No one could rush Ed. You could argue, you could grouse, you could sigh loudly (Chris sighed loudly), you could sigh softly, you could sigh until you hyperventilated and still Ed would take his time.

Sean ground a black peel of corrugated rubber into the sandy soil, then dug it out with the toe of his boot. He stuffed his hands into his pockets and cracked a knuckle on the spine of Maria's book. He drew it out. It was very plain: chocolate boards and a black binding, clean lines, neat construction. He turned it over and flipped through the thin, empty pages, wondering why she'd chosen to give it to him. Ever since Emily had sectioned off part of the back porch to cultivate Maria's "paper" plants, he'd reacted to Maria—well, badly. He knew it. But he'd hated to lose part of Emily to something he couldn't fathom the use of, not when Monkar needed so many other, more vital, mechanical things—like farming tools or even fishing boats. If there were any fish to be had. Once the windmill was going and the crops richer and the rabbits and the chickens thriving, then perhaps he could think about things like books.

The sunlight grew to a wash of watery yellow over the misted earth, filtering through the brush of needles. Where the road curved away from sight, the mist thickened to fog. Sean stared into the opacity, trying to see farther than the bend, trying to see past the close stand of evergreens that hid them. He wished to have these trees behind him, he wished he was already at the bend in the road and staring up at Away Point.

He slipped the book into his pocket and turned his gaze back toward the just-visible wreck of the perhaps-lighthouse on the hill above Monkar, remembering that, when they'd gone to clean the place, they'd turned up plenty of old books and other such reading material.

Now, he thought, *there was a job! The trash we pulled out of dusty corners! Acres of paper. God almighty, Maria really didn't need to make more.* He half frowned, half smiled, and laughed quietly to himself.

"What's so funny?" said Ed.

Sean blinked. The sun was getting pretty high. He, too, kept his voice low when he answered. "You ready now?"

"Almost. Jay's gone for a piss." Ed shaded his eyes. "You see something to laugh about?"

"I was thinking about paper," he said, gesturing at the distant lighthouse. "All that trash."

"Nate went through every damn piece of paper, scrap by

scrap." Ed pulled up a wand of yellow grass and bit on the tender end of it. "A few days ago, he gave me some of it."

"For what?"

"For Sheila." Ed paused. "And maybe Nathaniel is getting to me, too."

Sean laughed quietly but outright. "What, about his seals?"

"Like I said, maybe."

"Well?"

"He'd saved a lot of that paper. He said it looks like a printing of some kind of a code to him. I can't tell. Sheila might, though."

"Might?"

"Be able to read it." He slid a flat, mashed packet out of his pocket.

"So you think it's not just scraps, huh?"

Ed shrugged again.

"Okay, I'll bite," said Sean, taking the papers and glancing over the first fold, to be confronted by a series of random, capped letters: GACCTACTTTTTTTTCAGAGAGAG-GAGAGAGAGAGAG. He looked up at Ed. "What *do* you think?"

Ed shook his head and then nodded toward the tiny bit of the distant ruin. "I don't think it was a lighthouse, anyway. Maybe it was a place for watching seals mate."

"All right. It could've *been*, Ed," said Sean. "Past tense." He handed the packet back and lifted his gear, settling it on his shoulders. "Why would people waste their time just watching animals fuck?" Tightening the straps and belting the waist buckle, he said, "Let's go."

Ed laid his hand firmly on Sean's shoulder. "Hey."

"What?"

"I'm not nuts."

Sean laughed. "I didn't say you were."

"Could've fooled me."

Sean cocked his head in surprise. "What's eating you? I

don't care if you and Nate want to chase ghosts."

Ed half smiled and blew out a deep sigh. "The truth? Emily's bothering me. Like I said before. She didn't look well."

"Not that again. She's fine, Ed. I wouldn't leave if I didn't think she was okay."

"I know, but listen—"

"Listen to what? You're getting me worried and it's too fucking *late*."

"All right. I'm sorry." He threw away the chewed grass stem.

"Yeah—" Sean glanced around. JP was back. "Let's go."

They followed the road until it suddenly dead-ended into a rock face—a long-ago landslide grown over into a bald hill. There, Ed detoured. Sean followed Ed, with Chris and JP behind. The land turned muddy. Footing became uncertain. No one spoke.

Sean was glad of this silence. He stared either at the terrain or at his booted feet as the land inclined upward and dropped speedily into a two-step rhythm that obliterated the present for him, a rhythm that took his mind off the journey and into memory, walking him back to the house he had just left, back into the night, back to Emily and his nightmares.

Whenever it rained, steadily, leadenly all night, he could never sleep. The rain seemed to harbor sleeplessness; sad and gently vicious winds would visit the shore, making the roof snap overhead. Emily would lie sound asleep beside him, riding out the storm, cradled (he imagined as he lay wakeful) by her vivid, opalescent dreams, the ones for which he so envied her. Whenever she spoke of her dreams, he got anxious. Once he told her she was foolish to remember them; they were nothing but leftovers, like sea-wrack. Not even as real. Truth was, though, he wished for such dreams; he only remembered his nightmares because they woke him, like those that throve on night storms and made his sleep as fitful as a tempest's fury.

Of Linda, of course, he dreamt of Linda always, never of anyone else and always the same nightmare, about that one night, when they'd both been so young, when, on a storm's wintry back, just outside of Monkar, he had first lost her— long before they'd known the town, long before they'd grown strangers to one another, long before she'd disappeared.

"Where are you?" Linda had whispered. It was so dark, he hadn't even been able to make out the outline of her near him. Still, he had felt her warmth.

He reached for her hand. "Here," he murmured, chafing her palm with his.

She made a low, nervy laugh. The wind blew down.

They had gone for a walk that night, venturing far from the others, trying, in fact, to get away from Edward, JP, Sandra, and Chris. Sandra had warned them to be careful, but they were tired of warnings—seemed as if everything they'd done or could dream of doing since they'd left the Area shouldn't or couldn't be done. Everything came tagged with a risk that would make the act, whatever it might be, more than simple disobedience. Since they had so much to risk, every way they turned, on this windy night they'd shrugged off the warnings, said to hell with safety.

As long as they could see the glow from their camp's brushfire, they believed they hadn't ventured all that far. Keeping the faint and wavering light in sight behind them, they walked arm and arm, hip to hip.

Sometimes at night Sean could still almost feel Linda's narrow waist beneath his fingertips, he could almost swear her small, upturned breasts filled the cups of his hands.

"This is far enough," she'd whispered as they scrambled down a small decline. "They can't hear us, now."

He sat in the sand and pulled her to him. "Finally," he breathed in her ear. The air was crisp. She leaned to him; he felt the warm, wet tip of her tongue as she bit his cheek gently and eased him against the hillside; he slipped his hands under her jacket.

A slight click-click-click made them both freeze.

Sean rolled into a crouch. Linda followed. They did not speak; tried looking, but could not see. His heart raced; terror made him nauseous, it impressed gold stress-stars on the darkness before his eyes. He reached for Linda's hand; his knuckles brushed her knee. He glimpsed a quick outline of her face as she turned her head, he heard her shortened breathing, but no noise beyond that. They waited, listening. At last, taking courage from the silence, he inched forward, straining his eyes, hoping to see past darkness.

As soon as he hesitated and stopped to listen again, an odd scuffling sounded loud and near. He held his breath, and reached for Linda. This time, he grasped only sand. He edged around. Nothing, no outline, no warmth. Her disappearance made him nerveless. Had she abandoned him? His legs melted. He moved slowly; any suddenness might bring whatever it was out there down upon him. It didn't sound like a troll, but . . .

For a few moments again, there was silence. The absence of sound reassured him, warmed his blood; he turned his head, looking for her. Where? He breathed her name, but even as he spoke, the noise awakened, it scrabbled—and now it was so near he could feel it—warm breath, warmer than Linda's had been, as warm as a fever. He had felt it. Hadn't he felt it? Hadn't he? Stumbling to his feet, he hit his foot on something. It cried out and he ran to outrun whatever, whatever . . .

Sometimes, this is where his nightmare would end—or not end exactly, but he would run and run and run until he ran himself awake. He would always be breathing hard, sweating hard, as if the dream-run were as vital as the real run had been. Yet, on that actual night, it had not been a long run. And on that actual night, there had been no reality to escape into.

He'd scrambled over the sand on all fours. He'd headed blindly back toward the family's brushfire. He'd thought he'd heard whatever horror it was behind him sobbing and screaming although later he knew that he'd been the one sobbing, he'd been the one screaming. In fact, his panic had petrified everyone in the camp. If there had been real danger his noise would have brought it straight home.

And then, the worst. In safe hands, he had to turn and face Linda—a perfectly calm and quiet Linda, who walked out of the darkness he had fled, shaken but not hurt. She came into camp with a man and a small child; Nathaniel and Tomas, on their way home. Nathaniel had gone out walking near Away Point, simply trying to get Tomas to fall asleep, when he'd spotted the family's campfire. Caution had kept them all speechless in the windy dark.

Nathaniel had then led them into the town they'd not known was so near, to Monkar, for shelter and food. But as they ate, Linda had eyed Sean. He felt more than just exposed under that glance. Later, when he tried to talk with her, she'd turned away. She'd played with little Tomas, instead of dealing with Sean. And the next day, although she would talk to Sean, calmly and sweetly enough, he knew he'd lost her. He knew, as surely as she did, that what he'd done was irreparable. He had been frightened, it was true, yet no matter how he tried, he could not accept that fright as legitimate. Neither could she. As far as she was concerned, he'd abandoned her.

"How's Emily?" asked Christine suddenly.

Sean flinched. The sound of Christine's voice wove into his memory. She sounded so exactly like Linda sometimes— the same lilting tone with a trace of a stutter. He stared at Chris, hearing her voice but not her question. He felt cold. It was as if Linda were calling him to account suddenly, out of the memory of his nightmare. But Linda was gone.

"Sean?" said Christine, looking puzzled. "Did you hear me?"

"What?" he said gruffly, slowing his pace.

"Emily—how has she been?" said Christine. "I haven't seen much of her lately."

"Oh."

"Oh?" Christine frowned at him. "I hope she's better than

that. The last time I spoke to her, she didn't seem well."

Sean stuffed his hands in his jacket and said, "Are you in cahoots with Ed?"

"Huh?"

"Ed asked me the same question. I'll tell you the same thing I told him. Emily is fine."

"To your eyes, maybe. What does Ed say?"

"Nothing."

"Has she been to Alice?"

"What the hell for?" said Sean. "I live with her. You and Ed don't. If she needed a doctor, I'd know. She's fine."

Christine stared at him and the corners of her lips went pale with anger. "Fuck you," she whispered. "I just thought—I thought maybe she was pregnant again."

"*What?*"

"Sean!" called Ed, soft and urgent. "Let's move it!"

Away Point loomed before them. There was no path; few from Monkar had ever climbed to the top; none of them had been so far away from any enclave of Monkar since they'd settled there and no one from the outside had come down it in years.

Sean stared up at the scrubby, untouched incline. He glanced to Christine. "Emily is fine," he said. "And she's not pregnant. I would know." He turned away. He had nothing more to say; there was nothing more to do but climb. Away Point waited.

Sean took several steps forward and braced his foot at the base of the hill. He glanced upward, shading his eyes, gauging how best to begin. He forgot, for the moment, Emily and Linda and even Christine. Breaking the undergrowth, tearing through a brittle snarl of brambles, he felt suddenly unencumbered. He took a deep, cold breath, nodded at Ed, and started for the top.

For hours, he kept his eyes firmly to the terrain before him—he had taken the lead and was path-breaker for the rest. His hands, even gloved, were beginning to pain him from the surprise attacks of the thick thistle bushes they met at every switchback. As the sun gained full the sky and made day, Sean sweated his damp shirt wet; behind him, JP's labored breathing reminded him that his sort of brother-in-law was going to slow the rest of the party down; he always did. Sean glanced back quickly. At least JP was still pulling his own for the moment. Christine noted Sean's glance and gave him a frown of annoyance.

Sean gritted his teeth and put his mind on the climb and soon, the four gained the top of the ridge—Away Point. Stopping so that Ed, last in line, could catch up, Sean scouted out what now lay before them. JP sat down and Christine took off her climbing gloves.

It was hilly land beyond the Point, gentle hills, brightly given to spring growth; even the grass, which would soon turn gold, had a pale, verdant blush, making the distant, rolling fields look new-made. About ten yards from where they'd mounted the Point, Sean found the road again. Heaved up and cracked in places, it had once run through this part of the land in a neat zigzag connecting the coastal towns. No one knew exactly when or why it had been, except for trolls, abandoned. Grass had made islands in it and earthquakes had separated good-sized stretches from one another. Sean crouched to examine the grayed asphalt, with its faded paint marks. He tried to picture what the road might have been like, with "cars" and "trucks" on it. He shook his head. These were just words to him. His father and mother had remembered. Emily's great-grandmother, Aretina, before she'd lost much of her memory, used to tell stories about how she'd ridden on the highways as a child, in the once-massive deecee relocations. She'd said,

Wherever it was possible, they used trains. But the tracks here were wrecked, blown apart years ago by greeners. So the deecees used trucks—until the fuel was gone. My father said we had been moved three times before I was six; my youngest sister was born in the relocation camp that swelled and swelled with people until it became Vanseaport. When I was sixteen, the dying started all over again. I didn't understand what "all over again" meant, but my father did; we wore face masks and gloves any time we left the allotment, burned them when we came back. Washing became a fiendish activity. Many people took to the road then but it wasn't an organized relocation, it wasn't like the trucking I remembered. People just left on foot until the deecees shut Vanseaport. If you got sick after that, you were dead.

Ed called, "Any more climbing today?"

Sean stood up, glad to have the interruption. "You winded already?" He kept his eyes averted from Christine.

Ed pointed down the road. "If we make a quick and dirty march to Sheila's," he said, glancing at JP, "we will have a hot meal and a safe place to sleep. Providing the trolls play with us, of course."

JP got unsteadily to his feet. "I can do it. Which way?"

"South," said Christine.

"Southwest," corrected Ed. "Jay?"

"Let's go," said JP.

They went to the wrecked highway in silence, two by two. And they went along for a mile or so without speaking. The sky was nearly cleared of cloud and fog, though they could still see patches of white hugging the coast, collecting in the low spots, swathing some of the dense, bluish firs. Those few deciduous trees they saw were still barren, though tiny buds blushed green.

Ed broke the silence first. "Sean? What did Maria want with you this morning?"

"She gave me a book—do you believe it?" He shook his head.

"What sort of book?"

"It's blank. To write down what we see, how things are."

Christine broke in. "What?"

Both men paused until Chris and JP walked abreast with them.

"Maria gave me a book," said Sean.

"A book? One of hers?"

"That's right."

"She *gave* it to you?"

Sean pulled the pamphlet from his pocket. "Ta-da!"

Christine took it from him and looked it over. Sean watched her narrow face, reading jealousy there. She handed it back.

"It's lovely," she said, blinking. "Maria works hard."

"When she wants," said Sean.

Christine frowned. "What does that mean?"

Sean shrugged. "She likes people to do for her."

"I know Em does stuff at the house for her," said Chris. "Is that what you mean?"

"Emily's done more than just stuff for that shack Maria calls a house," said Sean. "I used to be down there plenty myself a few years back, to try to keep that architectural feat from sliding into the sea."

JP laughed. "It leans."

"She's a hard worker," said Christine.

"Look," said Sean, "she's not lazy. I just think, you know, after Carlo died, that she lost track."

"Oh, give it up, Sean. You just don't like her."

"Maybe. To you, she's a hard worker. And hey, I know that she can be. I've seen her go at things like demons were after her. She can be single-minded. All I'm saying is that her energy is convenient; she works hard when it suits her."

"She's got reasons," said Ed.

"Ha," laughed JP. "We've all got reasons."

"Don't I know it," said Sean, pleased that JP took his side. He reset the shoulder straps of his pack and picked up the pace, tired of arguing. He didn't want to discuss Maria anymore, because Chris was half right; he just didn't like the woman. Still, he also thought that she wasn't well in her mind—not since the death of her son, at any rate. She'd become distracted, unreliable.

Yet she had given him the book. He smiled to himself. She had seen him as the responsible one. He decided he would keep the journal. And, should he ever have a child, that child would know him better through such a book. It was the one thing he thought books suited to—autobiography.

Was Emily pregnant?

He frowned, trying to make out whether Chris could have noticed something he had not. Emily had seemed quieter of late. He wouldn't have called it "doing poorly" as Ed had put it, or "unwell" as Chris had said. Just quieter, easily lost in her own thoughts. She often seemed adrift. He tried to recall how she had behaved during her previous two pregnancies but they'd been a long while ago. What he did remember was her desperate morning sickness—she woke him getting up before sunrise. Her queasy restlessness had become his, too, light sleeper that he was.

But had she been quiet, adrift? He shook his head. He just couldn't remember. To avoid worry, he spoke to Ed. "Sheila still alone?" he asked.

"Yeah. At least, last time I saw her she was."

"Nobody bother her?"

Ed chuckled. "Trolls don't know she's there."

"So you say. I'd like to see how she manages it."

"You won't be disappointed."

It was Sean's turn to chuckle. "Sheila, so far as I've heard, never disappointed anyone, really."

"True, true," said Ed, musing. "Except maybe Maria. But that's another story."

"You think Sheila can read that stuff Nate gave you?"

"Yeah. You know, sometimes, I wonder if I shouldn't go out there and live with her, just for a while."

Sean laughed. "From what you've said about her, you'd last three minutes."

"Break," called Christine. "Let's take a quick break." She was short of breath and her face was beaded with sweat. "Please."

Sean halted, surprised. He hadn't realized they'd come so far. He threw a glance back at the gentle but persistent rise they'd ascended and was impressed. They would do all right, if they kept this pace up.

"Okay," said Edward, pointing to a wide-spreading fir tree nearby. "Let's have a sit and some water. I want to check the map again anyhow."

The group trudged off the road and collapsed in the shade; there, the mattress of spongy needles gave underneath the collective weight as they walked upon it. The sweet tang of pine flavored the warming air. Christine spread out her rain slicker and lay down on it. JP joined her and they passed the canteen between them.

Sean squatted to take off his pack. The sun was high, unobstructed by even so much as one cloud now; there was no wind. He judged that they were pretty far inland; they hadn't seen water or the shoreline for a few miles.

He eyed the land. It had been more than a decade since he and Edward and the Nottages had come this way, with death at their backs. His parents dead, his brother Terence killed—the flight from that had been bad enough, but then, to have that journey capped by his own shame and fear on that night that would not let him be, and afterward, to live with the persistent, nagging horror of what he'd done that night he'd lost Linda, combined daily with the horror of knowing what he'd become, a dead-townie, to where he'd been driven—a dead-town.

He sighed, sweeping the land with a second glance, looking for some sign of familiarity. He didn't recognize any of it, not a leaf, not a hill, although he knew they had camped up this way, so many years ago.

"Look familiar?" said JP.

"Nope," he replied. "To you?"

"Nah—thought it might. But no."

"JP," said Christine, "You were only ten years old!"

"Yeah—so? I've a good memory."

Sean took a sip of water and then sat down to make notes in Maria's book.

ROWD CLERE
NO RAYIN

He stopped. Was that right? What else should he say? He stared at the page, then shut up the book.

Ed stood near a hunk of displaced asphalt, checking the area against the map. He frowned and knelt, smoothing the paper. He ran a finger along a part of the map, frowned again, lifted the map from the ground, shook a few needles off, and folded it.

Sean stood. "Something wrong?"

Ed shrugged. "Looks okay. Maybe we'll get to Sheila's by dusk." He snapped a pine needle in half and sniffed it. "We shouldn't stop again until we get there."

"What?" said Christine. She took a mouthful of water and passed the canteen to her brother. "Do you mean to travel at night?" She looked up at Sean. "It's a bad idea. We should camp."

"I'd like to," said Sean, "but I think Ed's right. More trolls romping after dark."

"We camped out this way once."

"Please, Chris," Sean spoke brusquely. "It wasn't yesterday. You just said yourself, JP was only ten."

"One night—"

"Is one night too many," interjected Ed.

"He's right," said JP quietly. "Let's go."

Sean nodded. He did not look at the brother and sister as they gathered themselves and came out from under the trees, because he was afraid he'd snipe at them, say something uselessly cutting, only to get reprimanded for it.

He let Ed take the lead and it wasn't long before JP began to lag behind; Sean pretended not to notice when Christine dropped back to keep her brother company. Ed kept pushing the pace, his concentration on the terrain and the asphalt, and so Sean felt pressured into keeping an eye on the Nottages, as they lagged farther and farther behind. He didn't want to slow Ed—and he didn't want to be saying to him, *I told you so—Chris and JP should not have come.* He hoped that maybe they'd catch up.

Soon, though, the gap between the four of them widened to the extent that Chris and JP became black moving figures, half obscured by a new fog. A moist wind began to blow, beating the fog thick and, as it grew denser, rain fell. The gap between Sean and the Nottages was too wide.

He waved at the small figures. The Nottages waved back.

Then he called out, cautiously, "Hey, Ed—Ed!" He had to run forward a bit to make his voice heard.

Ed turned around, scowling. "Quiet."

Sean nodded. "We've got a problem."

Ed squinted. "What—" he said, then, "Where the hell—?"

"Not far behind. I've been keeping tabs."

"Not far? Suppose you show me."

Sean took a few steps back to point out the laggards.

But they weren't on the road anymore.

4

Connections

(11:00 A.M.)

"CALM DOWN," SAID Sandra.

Maria laughed uneasily. "I *am* calm," she said.

"You don't look calm. You don't sound it."

She nodded and tried to slow her breathing.

"Tell me now," said Sandra. "Again. Exactly what you heard."

"A scream." The more she thought about it, the more convinced she was that something terrible had happened. She'd jogged along the shore, looking, searching, and then up into town. She'd seen no sign of trouble—she'd come up from the beach to the Rows, stopped in at Alice's—only to find the doctor gone. Ki, who was trying to nap, didn't know where her mother was. So Maria headed on to council. Alana, Gia, and Ty were there but they'd not heard or seen anything odd. For a moment or two, this calmed Maria. But now, at Sandra's, every minute that passed made the cry Maria'd heard seem louder, full of agony.

"Come on. What did it sound like?" asked Sandra.

Maria stared resentfully. While George had told his eldest, Lindi, to get some help at council—to roust Gia, at least—as he set off to search the cove himself, Sandra hadn't really budged since Maria had come to the door.

Sandra sighed and got up from her metal kitchen stool. She was a large, well-built woman who moved with deliberation. She stepped over to a steel bread box etched with fading numbers and brought out a seed cake. As she cut a wedge, she asked again, "What did this cry sound like?"

"It was shrill," said Maria. "Almost a screech. A long, high wail. Then it stopped." She scratched at her eyebrow nervously. Tapped her forehead with one finger. "A scream. A cry. Pain. I heard pain," she said.

"Here," said Sandra, setting a glass plate near Maria's hand. She cut a wedge for herself and set another plate on the heavy table. Then she lifted her newborn, Jett, from a basket on the floor, to nurse; the baby suckled with tiny slit eyes closed. Although they'd managed to have live birth, she and George had worried about this one; the child's weight had remained low, lower even than Lindi's, the first-born, had been.

"Jett's got quite a head of hair," said Maria.

"A handful. Don't I know it," said Sandra.

Maria smiled, though anxiety still needled her stomach. She admired Sandra—her broad shoulders and muscled arms radiated strength, while her long legs carried that strength with grace. She wore her copper-gold hair, oiled to a glow and brushed so smooth it seemed a hammered bronze, in a heavy twist at the nape of her neck, just as her younger sisters, Linda and Christine, used to do. Her features were large and her dark face broad, unlike the twins, whose petiteness, next to Sandra's solidity, looked almost like illness. Yet, Maria reminded herself, Linda hadn't really been delicate, at least not as delicate as Chris; she'd only appeared so.

"What's *that* I see in your eyes?" Sandra asked.

Maria smiled briefly. "Thinking about Linda."

Sandra shook her head. "I wish they hadn't gone after her."

"I know."

"Lindi's been asking me questions."

"Not surprising—her namesake."

Sandra nodded. "Lindi's nearer a woman than a child, and has been since she stood up on her own legs. She's more and more like my little gone sister every day that passes by."

"Oh, San. She's only eleven."

Sandra sighed. "Only? But they *got* to grow up fast. If they grow up at all. I've been lucky with that one."

"Yeah," murmured Maria. She glanced around the cramped kitchen, trying not to catch Sandra's eyes, trying to distract herself. (Carlo would never grow up.) Parts of this house were much like her own. (Neither had Sandra's last two boys. They'd both died in their first year.) Except that this place was large, stood smack in the center of town, which suited George and Sandra, and had a crazy-quilt appearance because they'd built on to it little by little. (Emily had lost two, in stillbirth.) They could have taken one of the even larger abandoned places at the outskirts of town, like Emily's, but they'd preferred to be at the center, to have the community fanning out all around them. (Linda's child had lived only a year.) And, as time had gone on and they put in extra rooms, fashioning adobe floors and walls to replace wooden ones, the house had become almost as much a center for the community as the council. (Why couldn't she stop counting? Monkar had lost too many to keep track. Why couldn't she stop it?) Sandra's did look awkward from the outside, but it was a solid home, a place where people liked to gather (but for how long? How many would be living in Monkar, when her generation died?).

"You *sure* you heard something?" said Sandra. Her child had fallen asleep at the nipple. She rocked the baby back and forth on her knees. "Maria? You sure?"

"Of course not," she said, reluctantly. "I thought I heard a cry. I'm sure I heard—something."

"Mm," said Sandra. She set her newborn back in the basket.

"Not a ghost, San," said Maria quietly.

The back door opened and Lindi poked her head in. "It was Nathaniel—"

"What?" said Maria, standing.

"He fell—"

"Fell? From where? Is he—"

"Emily found him and took him on up to her place."

"How bad?" said Sandra.

"Alice is up there already. I think he's hurt bad." Lindi's long face was heavy with worry as she came inside the house. Maria could see she was trembling, so she made the girl sit in her chair. Fighting her own panic, she asked, "Did you see him?"

Lindi shook her head. Staring at her mother, she leaned across the heavy, black-topped table, lifting her whole body on her elbows. "If Nathaniel dies, what will happen to Tomas?"

The callousness of the question startled Maria. Sandra frowned, obviously just as surprised. She took up her daughter's hands in both her own and smiled. "Why, then, honey, we'll take care of Tomas. What makes you think Nathaniel will die? Alice is a very good doctor. Remember how she took care of you when you had that fever?"

Lindi nodded, but she did not look relieved. Sitting back in her chair, folding her arms, she said, "Promise me, Mama. Promise me right now. He can have my bed."

Sandra gazed at Lindi with a quietly persistent frown. "I promise you. But I wouldn't worry about Tomas—Nathaniel's the one who's hurt. I think you might worry about him first, don't you? Look at Maria—see what a scare you've given her? Huh? And I don't suppose Tomas would take so kindly to your making out his father to be bad off.

Before you start moving that boy in here, why don't you get on up to the house and ask Emily how Nate is?"

Lindi looked down at her hands and nodded. "I'm sorry, Ma," she mumbled and then bolted for the door.

"Wait," said Maria, following the girl. "I'll come with you." She hurried after Lindi, who slowed her pace only as she came abreast of the council house, about a block from the door. Maria caught up with her and said, "Where did Nate fall from?"

Lindi shrugged. "I don't know." She glanced at Maria. "Mama keeps her promises."

"Yes. I know," she said; her voice shook. She glanced in the open shutters of council as they went by it, to see if George had come back there, but the house now looked empty. The women seemed to have left. "Do you think Nate will die?"

The girl shrugged again and frowned. "I dunno," she said, as she fast-marched along the rutted street, across the square, her thick braid jumping from side to side, her hands mashed low in her baggy pockets.

Maria strode at the girl's side, her long arms swinging; she almost wanted to shake Lindi for more information, but she knew it was best to let the girl take the lead, so she didn't break the silence. They hurried past the broken clock tower that Sean had never been able to fix, and up along the crescent of tented swap huts; few people were about. The ragged coast pathway to Emily's only had two other buildings on it—an empty cinder block, one-roomed and roofless, that was used to store rain barrels, and a toolshed in which Sean had spent a lot of his time of late. Maria glanced at it, thinking briefly of Sean and Christine, when Lindi said, in her high voice, "I heard them say it. You can't tell me they didn't."

Maria frowned. "Who?"

Lindi glanced sidelong at her companion, her heavy lids dropped low. "I know about the broken ones." Her pace increased. Her face had an angry set to it. "I had to wait all night, when Jett was born, to see that everything be okay."

"Jett is fine," said Maria soothingly.

"I won't let them do anything to Tomas." She stopped and turned to Maria, with tears in the corners of her greenish eyes. "I'm saying it—you don't have to hide. I know they did it to you. I heard them."

"Lindi, Lindi," said Maria, confused. She knelt down in the middle of the dirt pathway and hugged the girl. "I'm not trying to hide, but I truly don't understand. Why do you think someone would hurt Tomas?"

The girl drew back a little from the woman's embrace. She put her hands on Maria's cheeks. "Didn't they take your broken baby away from you?"

"Oh," murmured Maria. The question rattled her.

"The broken ones get taken away," said Lindi firmly.

Maria shook her head and gave Lindi another hug. "No," she said, "no one took Carlo away. He just wasn't strong. He died before he could grow up."

Lindi stared at her. "Really?"

"Yes. Really. Who told you he was taken away?"

"Nobody . . . I mean—" She wiped her face roughly. "I just thought, when I heard—" She stared at the ground. "I overheard . . . people . . . talking. They said Tomas really wasn't right. That he'd never be able to take care of himself, though he does, you know . . . and then they said that so many of us kids were, you know, sort of broken . . . or just kind of . . ." She frowned. "Hurt? But then, when they talked about Carlo . . . they said he was really broken and that . . . and that . . . well, I thought they'd made you . . . I thought they'd . . . made you . . ." She trailed off and kept her eyes averted. "I'm going to take care of everybody. Even if we are as broken as Carlo."

Maria had nothing to say. How many nights had she listened to her baby's labored breathing and wondered if she hadn't been wrong to go against the advice of council? She rocked the girl in her arms and held back her own tears of rage at the whole of things that had made such talk common. She kissed the girl's cheek and rubbed at the tear tracks on her face and said, "Listen to me. I promise you I will always help. And everybody, okay? Tomas and you and anybody. People listen to me. Okay? The next time you hear bad things, you come and tell me."

The girl smiled and coughed out the end of her tears. Then she pointed up the path to Emily's house and said, "Race?"

Maria stood. "Listen to those creaky knees—I don't know, Lindi, you've got an unfair head start—years' and years' worth."

The girl hopped from foot to foot. "Please—" she coaxed.

Maria posed in an attitude of racing, one foot forward, arms held stiffly. "Get ready," she intoned, "get set—"

Lindi set herself.

"—go!"

The woman and the girl veered up the track neck to neck. Lindi laughed wildly, until Maria lagged behind on the incline. At the top of the rise, she stopped and, panting, watched the girl race on, the sea wind loosening her braid, her bare, tan soles dusted white with the dry, sandy earth, her legs taking her easily up the rise. Emily's house sat at end of the path.

Hot, Maria rolled up her sleeves. She was calmed a little by the sight of the familiar house. She glanced back toward town but saw only the peaks of a few roofs and chimney smoke. She headed doggedly after the sprinting figure of the girl. As she walked, though, her heart started pounding again.

Nathan, Nathan, she called to him inwardly, trying not to imagine the worst and yet imagining broken legs, perforated lungs. Would Alice's skills be up to the challenge this time?

"Damn it," she muttered aloud.

Nathaniel was broad, sweet shoulders she could rest against; Nathaniel was narrow hips, so narrow she'd giggled. And he'd laughed with her, telling her with his speaking hands how the curve of her hips pleased him.

She clenched her fists, warding off the remembrance of his

skin under her palms. He had a pungency of his own she could never quite place . . . it made her taste spice yet not spice, something deeper, richer. That body she had held with and in her own, so safe beside her, how was he hurt? Would he mend? Or would she lose him, too, like all the others. . . .

She looked up at the porch. Lindi had already disappeared inside the house. She held her breath an instant, her gaze traveling over the low roof and graying shingles, the open windows along the side of the house and the screened back porch door—and, mounting the sagged steps, she held her breath tight against the possibility of loss.

"Nathan?"

The woman's voice tugged at the raveling edge of his dream—it was Cait, that was her voice. . . .

"Cait?" he mumbled.

But Caitlin was dead . . . he tried to lean forward, to see her . . . was she really there? He squinted. He couldn't focus. He pushed against the sense of sleep stealing over him. The small woman's face drifting nearby became yet smaller and rounder; her eyes grew enormous. She resembled Tomas—or Tomas resembled her—or maybe he wasn't seeing Caitlin at all, maybe it was Tomas instead? That large, too large gray-green glance, narrow chin, flaring cheeks—

"Cait?" he said.

But it couldn't be Cait.

She was dead. She'd fallen at the dock. Cut her foot on a rusted nail. Accident.

How absurd she looked now, not quite herself, not quite Tomas either. He squeezed a tighter focus and, as he peered at her, her face elongated and the short hair flattened out on her head. It spread thin, coiled down her neck, and smoothed, in neat tight waves, unfurling as if heavy fabric, then into a furry coat, a pelt. She pushed her snout so close to his face that he jerked backward—

—and nearly rolled off the bed. Clutching the sheets, he

blinked and found himself looking up at a round, heavy, familiar face—Alice Rey.

"*Alice?*" he said. "Where's—" He stopped himself. Stupefied by Cait's dream appearance from the dead and multiple transformations, he lay quiet. Where was he? What was Alice doing here?

"Alice," he said, "I thought—" He coughed. His throat was sore. "What happened?"

The doctor sat back on the stool that she had pulled near the bed. "You tell me," she said. "What happened?"

"I don't—" He tried to sit up—no go.

And then, suddenly, he bolted off the bed—or tried to. Pain, and a peculiar weakness in his legs, restrained him to a shuddery movement forward.

"Tomas!" he cried. "Tomas—"

"Here, here—" Alice put a gently restraining hand on his shoulder. "Tomas is downstairs. I'll go and fetch him, now that you're awake. But mind you don't move that foot. It's taken me a good while to clean and set it."

"Alice—" He caught hold of her wrist. "Alice—is Tomas—was he—is he hurt?"

"He's fine, except for the shock you've given him." She patted his hand and he relaxed his grip on her wrist. "Why?"

"Tomas was in the water the last I saw him . . . and I thought he'd—I was afraid he'd drowned."

"In the water? What was he doing in the water?" Leaning forward a little, she clasped his hand in hers and asked, "What happened out there?"

"I fell." He laid himself back against the pillow.

"Looking for seals," she said. "No more seal hunting, Nate."

He gave a dry laugh. "How can I, crippled?"

"Crippled?" She stood and rolled down her shirtsleeves. "I see you don't have much faith in my doctoring."

He glanced up. "I saw the foot, Alice. Don't lie to me."

She stared back at him, her face holding quiet anger. "I

don't lie. If you let your foot heal properly, and you want to walk without help, you will. You won't be running any races with that boy of yours, but I'd hardly call you crippled." She folded her arms. "If it sets properly, mind. Now, I'm going to take my hurt pride off for a cup of tea. I'll send Tomas up in my place." She headed for the door.

"Alice—I'm sorry."

"Well then."

"I'll stay off it and let it heal."

She smiled. "In two weeks, I'll remind you of that promise." She closed the bedroom door after her.

Cautiously, he levered himself up on his elbows. His foot, dressed white, elevated, was an alien thing. It scarcely seemed possible that it was still there, attached to his leg. He felt no pain, just a muffled throb—Alice must have given him a good dose of something from her small hoard of supplies.

He looked around the room. He had never seen it before; it was a close room, with one window and, strangely, three doors—one to his right and a set of double doors on his left. Comfortable though, even if barren. A clean bed, a three-legged stool at the bedside, a trunk at the foot of the bed. The walls were papered, but the pattern of fanciful animals in blue and pink had faded almost entirely away and the paper itself had buckled at the seams. He was upstairs somewhere; Alice had said Tomas was downstairs.

But upstairs where? He should have asked. How had he gotten here? Who had helped him? He listened for sound downstairs, but heard nothing besides the distant murmur of the sea through the open window. A breeze blew steadily and touched his face. He sighed. It was all so comfortable, so calm. His mangled foot was quite numb. He, too, was going numb. He folded his hands under his head and settled deep into the soft bed. He was safe. And Tomas was safe. He thanked the air, his luck, or whatever and whomever else he could think of, and drifted back to sleep.

*   *   *

Downstairs, Emily watched Tomas, who sat in the middle of the kitchen floor, beside the woodstove. He stared into the living room at the mantel clocks. He'd donned an oversized sweater of Sean's and his hair had dried into an amber sponge about his face, hiding his eyes. His spatulate-fingered, thin hands rested on bony knees, and he sat in so much stillness that Emily found herself fidgeting, just to make some small noise.

She had already offered him a bowl of soup, which he had taken and finished before she had fed herself, so she gave him her portion and, opening the bread tin, found him corn bread.

He seemed to be starving. He ate everything she'd offered.

At intervals, she heard Alice moving around upstairs where they'd carried Nathaniel. Listening to the floorboards creak, she prayed that he would recover. She was no doctor; she couldn't tell and she didn't know whether only his foot had been broken or whether he'd suffered internally.

She was no nurse, either. The sight of his foot had so sickened her that, as soon as she gave Alice everything necessary, she'd crept downstairs.

Tomas had followed her down. Moving as slowly as one of Maria's two ratters on the hunt, he had approached her and held out his hand. Still spooked by his silence, yet feeling guilty, she gave him hers. The whole of that long morning had scared and unsettled her; even this, a simple gesture, seemed odd. He'd held her hand for a few moments, long enough for her to think his hand ugly, long enough for her to feel it a strain to be so close. Then he let her go and sat himself on the floor.

She glanced from him to the mantel clocks and found herself thinking of Sean. And . . . what of Linda? She made a small noise of self-disgust and drummed her fingers on the table top—why could she not stop thinking about the past? Was Linda alive? Ed might have been mistaken. She laughed to herself, short and bitterly. *I tire myself with foolishness,* she thought and laid her head on the table, just as Alice came down the stairs.

Tomas shot to his feet and ran past her, fleet and soft. Watching him, Alice shook her head. She sat down at the table, saying, "He even moves silently. . . ."

"How is Nathaniel?" said Emily, lifting her head.

"Thank God, not too bad. Nothing internal," said Alice. "Any tea?"

"Of course!" Emily stood. "He'll be all right then?"

"I expect, more or less. A bad break though. Nasty. And—" she gave Emily a quizzical glance. "Did you take a good look at his foot? It's all torn. It's as if he'd been bitten."

"No. Blood makes me sick." Emily set the kettle on the stove top and moved the soup to the counter. "Did he say what happened?"

"Only that he fell. Looking for those seals."

"He's lucky Tomas was with him."

"Very." Alice glanced toward the staircase and sighed. "It's damn lucky Nate wasn't killed, or hurt worse than he is."

Emily bit her lower lip and put her hand on the kettle's arm. The water wasn't even tepid yet, but at least tending the tea, she wouldn't have to look at Alice with shame burning her cheeks. She spooned tea leaves and said, "You mean Tomas is lucky, don't you?"

"Well," Alice said. She sighed. "He has never exactly warmed hearts, has he?"

Emily checked the potbellied stove and poked another piece of wood in the fire. "When I was young, Alice, and my father was alive, I thought different than I do now." She slammed the stove's iron hatch shut, flipped the lever closed. She rubbed her face and brushed away an angry tear.

Alice reached out. "Hey," she said, "I'm not blaming you. Most of us have had some of the same troubles—and not just with Tomas. With all the kids. Our grandparents may have survived the first onslaughts with little damage and our parents braved both red wave and zoning. So we thought to be clear of disease. But now our children are paying for our survival—or maybe we are paying for survival by suffering to bring them into this world, burdened by their deformities?" She shook her head. "They are all damaged. You aren't alone in your concern."

Emily took a deep, shuddering breath. "I know, I know. But I blame myself."

"For what? You're talking nonsense."

Emily shook her head. Tears thickened her voice. "It's not that," she managed to say. "Earlier—" she stopped to clear her throat. "Much earlier this morning, Tomas tried to get me to help. Hours ago. Hours. Nate must have just fallen, you see. But I didn't understand. I thought—I don't know what I thought. Nothing, I guess. I was just annoyed. Tomas makes me jumpy."

"He spooks everybody, a little. Nate's the only one who can get to him—and Maria, I guess. Maybe some of the other kids. Anyway, that's not your fault."

"I should have known something was wrong."

"Oh, Emily, really—"

"*Really,* Alice. You should have seen his face."

"Stop it right there," said Alice crossly. "You didn't know Nathan needed help and when you did know, you acted quickly, with a level head. That's all that matters. *All.* It's nonsense to think otherwise and besides, I won't listen to it."

Emily laughed shakily. "All right, doctor."

Alice grinned. "Why don't you go upstairs and take a quick nap, eh? I'll wake you when it's time to go—you still want to work the sowing today?"

"Oh, yes—thanks. I nearly forgot." She frowned. "Won't Nathaniel need—"

"Sleep. That's what he needs. Tomas will be here, for anything else."

Emily nodded and went upstairs, unable to let Alice know how reluctant she was to leave Tomas alone in her home. She was sure he would do something troublesome—perhaps take Sean's clocks apart again maybe. But she was too worn out to talk about it, and, after all, she was a little afraid to talk about it. She didn't want Alice even to suspect just how often she had wished that Tomas would wander off from Nate's protection, to toddle on after his poor mother to some quick and deadly disease, or into the sea, where he would tragically, unfortunately, sadly drown.

That was a long time ago, she told herself as she passed by the closed door of Nathaniel's room. *Before we knew all the children would be affected.* She paused for a moment to listen. Hearing nothing, she went to her bedroom. The sight of her leather pouch nestled in the center of the bed made her freeze with dismay. Instantly, she assumed that its appearance had something to do with Tomas; then, just as quickly, she remembered having taken it out of the sea chest herself that morning. She sat on the bed next to the pouch.

Why, she thought, *why do I dislike that boy so much? Has he ever done anything, anything at all, to be suspected for every little thing? No. He's just alive.*

She touched the pouch's clasp, reattached it, and stored the bag away. She leaned against the sea chest and stared out the window. The beach was deserted, save for driftwood and the drying husks of bullwhip seaweed, tangled in clumps near the water. The bedroom felt stifling to her. She closed the frayed curtains and opened the window to catch the breeze. Undressing, pulling the comforter to the foot of the bed, she lay down.

But sleep was as aloof as a wary cat; it could not be coaxed. She lay on her side, staring at the lightly shivering curtains, watching them ripple and stir. Whenever she had not been able to calm or nap as a child, her great-grandmother would tell her a story in which she . . .

. . . was a lovely young girl. Everyone said so. Dark, sleek hair and seeking gray eyes. But more, wealth attended her

birth, and health sat upon her cheek. She was flush with youth and the blood in her veins seemed to run as rich as a dark red wine. Her mother was no longer, though before the babe was born, she had been as ravishing as her child, and indeed, many thought that the young mother had somehow found a way—a forbidden procedure, a conscripted physician—to transfer all her bodily treasure into the making of the babe, as if the marrow of her being had been wrung dry. Her father had been a deecee, and many knew that he had taken on the power young, held it strong, until he'd met the mother of his child and then, mysteriously, he had died.

But the lovely young girl knew none of this, for both parents were gone before she could know. Yet if she could not know, and if she fed you beauty with her very glance, what she fed you was never the serenity of still loveliness but rather a voracious, ravening challenge, a longing so intense people swore that the girl pined for those whom she had never known, and did not know she had lost, especially for the one she so resembled.

She grew to womanhood, beloved by her father's sister, who raised her with all the privileges accorded to deecee offspring. She was praised and held as a particular treasure by everyone and anyone who set eyes on her. Yet should you have taken time to ponder the seeking depths of her longing glance, you might have seen her hollowness, for she did not, could not, herself, give love. She knew only herself beloved, until one eve of a new year. On this eve she went to bathe before the dancing and mating began. Her aunt's house was full of guests and she went to the bath to escape the jolly noise, slipping into the room with a sigh of relief, only to find someone there before her, flush and hot from the water, with dark, sleek hair and seeking eyes. Ashamed of her indiscretion, she fled, but her flight was short—just out the door. For, as if her ankles had been enchained, she swiftly returned and without speaking simply threw herself at the beauty—who screamed. And screamed, a murderous fright, as they both tumbled to *the slippery floor. And it would not stop, though the young woman begged, trying to eat away at the other's terror with clumsy, hungry, hungry, and then hungrier kisses that became frantic until the other beauty's unseemly terror shifted entirely and in one lunging, horrifying instant, the two embraced so forcefully it carried them together into the bath.*

This is the story the naked and bedraggled girl told when her alarmed aunt found her half-drowned in the foam and steam; this is the story she clung to, all through the days of illness that followed, until the new year was nigh half over. Still no sign of the one whom the girl claimed so loved her could ever be discovered. Yet before she died in the early last months of that new year, she did bear a child, a lovely babe with dark, sleek hair and seeking eyes.

Emily turned over on her side, shivering at the remembered thrill with which she had always heard this story. She found herself staring at the sea chest below the window. The leather bag, hidden inside, seemed suddenly visible through the tight staves. She saw it distinctly; it was as lovely as it had been that night when Sean had given it to her.

"I made it," he'd whispered. "For you."

She'd laughed quietly at that. "Oh, no you didn't," she'd said. "But it's a nice lie."

That was in spring, an early evening. She and her father had been invited to supper at Sandra and George's.

"Hello, George. Sandra. Hello, Nathan," Andros had said as they crowded into the small, unfinished, and steamy kitchen. He was using the brusque voice that Emily knew as one to beware. She'd smiled tentatively at Nathaniel, to make up for her father's tone. They were led into the next room, where Sean, Ed, Linda, JP, Christine, Cait, and the child, Tomas, were already eating supper.

How shy she'd been that night! Except with Sean. Somehow, from the very first, she'd not been shy with him.

But with the others, these ones who were still strangers,

these people from the far-off Area whom Nathaniel had found camping on the beach a year earlier, with them, the Nottages, Ed, she'd been quiet, afraid. Instead of listening that night, or hearing much of what her father said, she'd mostly worried that the three young women with the lovely coiled-up hair didn't like her. Halfway through the dinner, when Andros was warming to questions, Emily found one of the women looking her over; that woman had been Linda. She'd been caught, even then, by Linda's beauty, by her steady gaze.

I wonder, thought Emily, *how she knew that I'd love her so?*

Later that night, Andros had been furious.

"They're trying to buy me," he'd said, turning on Emily as they sat in their own kitchen. "And you. Through you."

She'd stared at the gift Sean had given her. "It's nothing," she'd said, pushing it to the middle of the table. "Look. It's just a little bag."

"It's favor," said Andros. "You like them."

"I'd like them anyway."

"Would you?"

"Yes," she'd said, looking up calmly at him. "Papa. You know it's about Nathan and Cait."

"What?"

"It's not about those new people, is it? You're angry because Cait hopes we'll argue about the new people and forget her baby."

Andros had nodded. "Tomas isn't a baby, anymore."

"No," she'd said and sighed. She touched the bag on the table. "That's what Sean said."

"Did he?"

"Yes. He said he was sorry to see it here—"

"My voice might swing a decision, you know."

"Yes, Papa. I know." She'd stared intently at the twill of the tablecloth. She'd not said anything more. And, at the next council, Andros had suggested a trade—as she'd known he would, and as he would do again, in a slightly different way, when Carlo was born.

Let the newcomers stay, he'd said, *if the baby goes.*

Thank God, she thought, *it hadn't happened.*

Both times Sean had been furious. Nothing could persuade him that Tomas or Carlo should be allowed to live. He'd thought the decision cruel. He'd thought it better that they die before understanding themselves crippled.

It was a long time ago, she thought again, closing her eyes and turning her back to the sea chest. She wanted Sean out of her mind; she wanted his presence washed away, until maybe she could see herself, without his face blocking everything. She wanted to hear without always hearing his voice. She wanted to breathe without tasting something of him, his words in the air, his sweat, the odor of his hair.

But Sean would not leave her—not then, not now.

And after years of sharing his life and his loves, after years with the pain of him and Linda, and the confusions of her own wandering desires, she knew, lying too awake on the bed, that she had been waiting for him that night, waiting from the start, from the moment he'd given her that gift and whispered to her that the deaf boy shouldn't be allowed to stay, and held her hand so gently—waiting, caught in the vagaries of lust for the sound of his step on the porch.

Nathaniel woke abruptly. Confused, he stared at the blank ceiling and wiped his wet forehead with the back of his hand. The room was hot. He was sweating the sheets damp. He tried to turn over, but pain had snuck back into his foot.

A clicking sound came from the end of the bed. He looked up. Tomas sat on top of the chest there. He'd been leaning over his father's wounded foot, doing something or other, but now he sat back, his legs crossed and his whole face brightening in a way that made Nathaniel's pain simply vanish. At his father's movement, the boy left the chest and knelt beside him.

Tomas's slightly salt breath, the touch of his cool hand, something of his sheer physical presence, alleviated the press of Nathaniel's injury and the stifling heat of the unknown room.

A knock on the door broke the peace. Tomas started up.

"Alice?" said Nathaniel.

But it was Emily who poked her head in the room. "Do you need anything? I thought I heard you moving about in here and Alice told me you weren't to move." She yawned. "Just got up myself," she said.

"I wasn't moving," said he, smiling awkwardly. "That was Tomas. Is this . . . am I—this your house?"

She walked in, nodding. She kept her eyes averted from the bandaged foot. "You don't remember getting here? It was quite an effort."

"No. I don't. I can't. Did I walk here?"

"You tried. Tomas did most of the walking." She glanced over at the boy, who'd climbed back on the chest and eyed her warily as she spoke. She pulled the stool that Alice had used up to the bedside and sat down. "What do you remember?"

"Watching the tide get higher and higher, mostly," he said. "I slipped off Gideon's Point, near that dead tree—you know the place? Got caught halfway down. Stuck fast." He shook his head. "Somehow I got out."

"How?"

He frowned. He could remember Tomas diving into the sea. Had the boy loosened the rocks that had vised his foot? The tide had been so strong—and besides, Tomas had been swimming out, away from the bluff. He shrugged. "I got off the Point. After that—I don't know." He smiled weakly. "Probably best I don't remember."

"Mm," said Emily. She leaned over and touched his forehead with the back of her hand. "You're burning!"

"This room's hot—"

"Hot? Not that hot. There's a good chilly breeze. It's *you*." She left, only to appear a moment later with a tall glass pitcher and a lipped, handleless cup. She helped him sit, to drink.

He sipped gratefully. As she eased him back down on the pillow and dried his forehead, he watched her silently, closely; she felt quite small to him. Her arm was as thin as Tomas's, her hands no bigger than a young girl's. He had scarcely ever been this close to Emily Zafieras, and had never noticed before this minute size, this seeming frailty. For some reason, it intrigued him just then—that an adult could be so . . . so graspable. He had a sudden urge to touch her arm.

She caught his gaze and blushed, jostling the narrow water pitcher against the metal bed frame as she put it down on the floor. She looked so discomforted that he felt guilty, and turned his gaze elsewhere. The water he'd taken had reminded his stomach it was empty; he began to feel nauseated from the pain and the hunger, so that when Emily asked him how he felt he said, "Rotten," and asked if he might not eat something.

"Of course!" she said, standing. "Although—I'd better consult Alice, to be sure."

"Would you ask her for more painkiller or whatever it was that she gave me?" He gazed up again, trying to break the uneasiness that had crept between them. He felt himself thrown upon Emily's kindness and he didn't want to upset her or make her uncomfortable. He knew she was already uneasy with Tomas and he didn't want to make things worse.

She didn't respond. Instead she seemed to be watching his son, with strain in her face, as she headed for the door. She said, "I'll be back in a minute."

"Emily—" Nathaniel held out his hand, palm upward, and smiled. "Thank you. Thanks for your help."

She nearly backed into the door frame getting out of the room and stammered, as if terrified, "I—no thanks necessary." And she was gone.

"What the devil?" Nathaniel muttered.

Outside the nursery, Emily stood still to calm a jumping heart. *Shit,* she thought, *shit. Tomas will tell him.* When Nathan found out how she'd repulsed the boy, that she'd been worse than rude, he wouldn't be so warm to her.

Voices in the kitchen—Alice and ?—cut short this second dose of guilt. She hurried toward the sound, relieved that others had come. Listening as she went she was surprised and pleased to hear Maria's voice. She stepped into the kitchen.

"You're awake," said Alice, sitting back from the table.

"I didn't really sleep." She joined them. "Maria?"

"Em. You okay?"

"I'm fine."

Alice glanced at the ceiling. "How's the patient?"

Emily shook her head. "He seems feverish."

"What?" Alice stood.

"He's in pain, too," said Emily.

"Alice?" said Maria.

"I thought I gave him plenty." Alice rummaged through her canvas sack.

Maria stood.

"Hang on," said Alice. "I've got a smoke here."

Emily peered inside the cornbread tin. "Can he eat?"

Alice chuckled. "He'd better, if he smokes. He'll be chewing at the pillow otherwise. But I don't like the sound of a fever. Let me check on him before you go up there, Maria." She ladled out a cup of soup and sliced off a chunk of cornbread. "You didn't sleep?" she asked Emily.

"Not much. Overwrought."

"You want to share the smoke?"

Emily shook her head. "No, no. Go on."

"Alice," said Maria. "When can I see him?"

"I'll be down in a moment." She left.

Emily turned to Maria. "He seems all right. Just feverish."

"Thank God." Maria closed her eyes. "I heard him."

"What?"

"I heard him—out on the bluffs. Must've been him. I heard him cry—this scream."

"Why were you out—" Emily began. "Oh. They're on their way then? Sean and Ed?"

"Yes," said Maria, staring absently at the staircase that led upstairs. "Em, did you know Christine and JP went too?"

Stunned, Emily said, "*Went?* But Chris said—"

"Yeah." Maria kneaded one hand with the other, then spread them in front of her; both index fingers were crooked. She sighed. "Chris changed her mind. I wish she wasn't so bullheaded. But," she said quietly, changing the subject slightly, "it'll be good to have you all to myself for a change."

"Yes . . ." said Emily in so small a voice that Maria wasn't sure she'd heard it.

"Em?"

"Damn," said Emily. "I can't believe it." She stood and began to wash the teacups.

Maria said, "I spoke to Sean."

"Oh? Bet he was in a tip-top mood. What did he say?"

"Not what you might think. I gave him a book to carry. A journal."

Emily turned around.

"We need to know. We need to know what he sees."

"*Sean?*" said Emily. "He won't see anything but his own two flat feet."

"I knew you'd be upset."

"Damn right."

"I'm sorry."

"You should be." Emily took three sudden steps to the door and out, before Maria could say another word. The older woman followed her to the doorway, calling, but Emily walked swiftly, shaking her head, "No, no, don't follow me."

To give a book, one of *their* books, to Sean! To give the work of their hands to the one person who would not understand the effort, nor appreciate the care. Had Maria lost her mind? Why hadn't she given the book to Chris? And Chris! Just yesterday she'd said she was glad she wasn't going—why had she lied?

"Why?" she murmured aloud. "Why, goddamnit?!" she said to to the air. Then, angry but ready to talk, she went back inside.

Maria was staring off into the living room.

Emily stood at the kitchen door and looked down at her folded hands, listening to the quick ticking of clocks. They sounded to her like an army of mechanical crickets, a droning, regular "chirp-chirp."

Finally, Maria said, "He'll learn from having that journal."

"You could have given it to Christine. Or JP. Or Ed . . ."

"No."

"Fine," said Emily, squeezing her hands together.

"Emily," said Maria.

"I said, *fine*. You gave it to Sean. That's that."

"You're acting like a child."

"Why not? You've hurt me like a child, right where a child lives—in my dreams. You know what I mean—those books, Maria. Our work. Now you've gone and ruined it all."

"Ruined it?" Maria stood up, her long arms akimbo, her afflicted hands half curled at her sides. Her short hair, a wiry mixture of white and brown, seemed a crazy nest in the top of a very tall tree. She said, "I wish you didn't feel that way."

"But I do. Feel that way."

"Am I so cruel a person that I'd set about hurting you? Is that what you think?"

Stung, Emily unlocked her hands. "Yes."

Maria turned away. After a few minutes of the tick-tick of the clock, she said, "It's time for us to get to work, isn't it?"

"Yes."

"Well I won't be along today. I promised Christine I'd go over to the seaweed harvest in her place. Tell them that for me, will you?"

"Sure."

A few more moments went by. Emily stood as if rooted to the kitchen floor. Maria seemed likewise rooted. Emily stared at the older woman's back, at her slightly rounded shoulders and at the two top knobs of her backbone, willing her to turn around, but unwilling to ask. Still, Maria did not move.

Alice, empty plates in hand, came down the stairs. "I'd fill that water pitcher again soon, Emily," she said. "Nate's asleep."

"And the fever?" said Maria, keeping her back to Emily.

"I don't like it but he will probably ride it out. I'm more worried about Tomas. He's been fooling with my bandages."

Maria frowned. "What? Why?"

Alice shook her head. "He had the bandage loose for some reason. So I scolded him. Nate should be okay for the afternoon. Anyway, I promised to stop in at Serena's and check up on her today. After that, I'll come back."

"How's she doing?" asked Maria.

"Three months along and so far, so good," said Alice. She set the plates in the sink. "What are you two arguing about?"

Emily laughed dryly. "You hear everything, don't you?"

"How could I help it? You were shouting—almost."

Emily shook her head, wishing both women would just leave. "Nothing," she said.

Maria folded her arms. "He's asleep?"

"For now," said Alice. "You should wait a few hours to see him."

Emily stepped across the kitchen and touched Maria's shoulder. "Have supper?"

"You sure?"

"Yes."

"Sundown?"

"Or thereabouts," she said, trying to smile.

Maria nodded and left, letting the screen door slam.

Alice tapped her foot. "That's an angry woman. What did you say to her?"

"Nothing," said Emily. "Nothing that wasn't true."

5

Safety?

To Sean, the forest, the fog, the glimpsed blue of a hide-and-seek sky, all of it became too present, too utterly distinct; the green went brilliantly flat, the gray to slate, as if made by a child's hand. Christine and JP were gone.

He hadn't heard a thing; there was no troll-mark. He tried to look for them, tried to listen. But the fog had come upon them suddenly, strange and cold, and in this thick stillness, Ed's breathing had amplified to the point of maddening interference. Sean backtracked slowly. Christine and JP were simply gone.

"Here," said Ed in a shaky whisper. He crouched to the asphalt. Close to the ground, the fog was less dense.

"What?"

"*Nada*," Ed whispered. He shrugged. "I thought I saw something."

Sean swore silently. Around them, the flat green trees seemed to be crowding together. The spaces between were narrow and dark and wet. Sean stared at the road again; this time, he thought he'd located the spot where he'd last seen the Nottages. He took a few steps and, like Ed, crouched low. But the asphalt was cruelly blank. He stood.

Ed pointed. Sean shook his head. And so, they continued backward—but for a moment only. All at once, Ed bolted. In confusion, Sean thought his friend had been sucked away; it was as if his nightmare about Linda had been repeated. Once again, he stood abandoned to silence. The road seemed to leave his feet and the living fog to smash against him like a breaker and he, too, was going to be eaten. . . .

"Sean?" Ed's voice. "They're over here—"

And so they were—safely sheltered by twin conifers welded together at the roots. The splayed trees, dense with live needles, had created a generous circle of needle carpet some five steps off the broken road. Sean remembered having passed up the very spot as a rest stop earlier.

Staring at Christine, he tried to speak calmly. His tone was gruff. "Let's go," he said.

"You wouldn't slow down," said Christine. Her voice was a thin whip of a whine. "So I did."

"Chris." Ed's dark, round face seemed elongated, the few lines in his skin drawn hard and deep. "Listen—the next time you want a rest, tell me. Say something, all right? Don't just lag behind. Don't. It's petty, and stupid. Do you hear?"

"It's my fault," said JP. He squinted up at Ed.

"Fine, okay, just *say* something! Do you know what I felt, when you were gone? Goddamnit, Jay . . ." His hands shook.

JP sprang to his feet and grasped Ed's hands. "I'm all right," he said. "I'm sorry."

"Jesus," swore Sean. "Come on already."

"Okay." Ed stooped to pick up JP's backpack for him.

Sean turned for the road again when a low rumble froze him to the spot. He could feel the sound, as if it came up from the damp earth into his legs.

"Troll?" said Chris, her voice dropped to a dry whisper.

"Down," muttered Ed. "Get *down*!"

Sean crouched, then inched his way backward, until he was flat behind the twinned conifers, wrapped still in the smoky fog. The rumbling came closer, but he couldn't see the troll—in a few moments, he couldn't even see Ed anymore. Pinned to the tree trunk, socked in like some stranded boat, he wished he could become the tree, pull its rough hide around him and disappear.

The rumble shifted to a burring roar, adorned with metallic bings. It shook the ground and the tree. He thought he could hear someone crying underneath the troll sound. He leaned closer to the tree and kept his head down. The troll sound grew, but it spoke to him only of size, since neither he nor anyone he knew had a clear idea what a troll really looked like.

Except for Terence, he guessed. His brother Terence had seen one—the last thing he'd seen.

Sean closed his eyes, his mouth bitter and dry. The troll sound taunted him with a perverse desire to just step out from cover, step out and see it, the sort of thing that had killed his family. . . . They must have come about midday, probably a whole fleet of them. He and Terence and Ed, along with the Nottage kids, had been sent off by their parents early, to food line. He remembered the weight of the knapsack, and how the tins he'd carried that day ended up feeding them for weeks on end as they fled the Area; and he still wondered if, somehow, their parents had guessed what was going to happen—what had happened; if his father and mother had known, somehow, that the trolls would come to that part of the bay, with a wickedly white, liquid fire that razed everything and everyone. The next morning those who'd survived found smoldering rubble. None of them had seen the ones who'd done it. He'd caught a glimpse—a brief blinding arch before he'd thrown himself into an alley. It was Terence who must have seen; Terence leading the way, Terence who'd shouted, "Troll!"

"Sean?"

He opened his eyes. Fog. "Ed?"

"Here." Ed materialized out of the white. "Jay?"

"Yeah—we're okay."

Sean stood up. "Too close."

Ed nodded as JP and Chris appeared.

No one spoke as they started off again, at a much slower, much more tentative pace. In less than an hour, Sean felt spooked and hobbled. A couple of times he tried to catch Ed's glance, to tell him without speaking to pick it up, but Ed kept to a cautious dogtrot.

The fog began to lift, shredding at last into thin banners or stretching to nothing as the sun burned it off. Glittering drops, residue from the damp morning, clung to the trees and furred the pine needles until the sun cleared the air. Watching the land change under the sun's hand and listening for the telltale quake of trolls kept Sean focused, and yet, every so often, a memory would dash out at him. He gritted his teeth on forgetfulness—a temporary victory since, for some reason, just at that moment, Chris was suddenly, inexplicably, too, too much like Linda.

He'd always been able to block out the extraordinary power of this resemblance—Christine and Linda were twins, yes, but he'd known them both so long that they had never been the same to him.

He gave Chris a quick, surreptitious glance, and shook his head. Right now, even her yawn reminded him.

As the day lengthened and the memories became denser than the morning fog had been, Sean tried to put Christine out of his sight. He walked in such a way that she was far to one side or the other of his peripheral vision and then he tried to look only at the broken road.

They climbed another rise. Ed stopped short; Sean stood beside his friend and, seeing what Ed saw, rested his hands on his hips in blank dismay.

The road was gone, entirely gone, sunk and swallowed by a fissure that loped wide and long across the valley. The land was scorched black and still smoldering, giving off an acrid smell. Stubbled trees, thin as toothpicks and nearly as smooth, dotted the plain. Sean kicked over a few rocks that had been welded violently to each other.

Christine whispered, "Trolls."

"Had to be," said Sean. "What else?"

"But what for?" said JP.

"Who knows," Ed muttered, and took out the map, as Christine crouched to stare at the ruined earth. Clumps of blackened brush rattled like exposed wires whenever the wind picked up.

Sean sniffed at the biting smoke.

"Why?" said JP.

"Just because," said Sean. Like so much of the destruction he had seen. He sat down next to Christine and took out his folio and pencil. Something had to be noted. Something ought to be said. He stared at the blank page. He even put the pencil point to it. But all it brought him was Terence's scream, Terence burning incandescent. No words. Sean stared down at the blank of the paper in his hands. He didn't want to look out over the ruined plain. He dared not move, because there was a distinct possibility he was about to be sick. He closed the journal and slid the pencil back into his pocket.

"We can go through or around," said JP.

"Through is safer," said Ed, folding up the map. "The troll won't be back this way. It's finished its job. Around will take us down this hillside, along the beach and I don't know about that beach, even at low tide."

"It should be low tide now," said JP.

Startled, Sean asked, "How do you know?"

"High tide was, oh, a little after sunrise."

"What time was that, do you think?" The nausea was going away. Sean stood and brushed off his trousers. He pulled at the heavy twine around his neck, revealing the pocket watch he had brought. He clicked open the case, and looked at the face.

"Where'd you get that one?" asked JP.

"It was Terence's, once," said Christine.

Sean looked up. "I'd forgotten I told you that."

"You didn't," she said. "Linda did."

"High tide was an hour after sunrise," said JP quickly. "Low tide should be now—or soon."

Sean glanced up. Why did Jay always seem so nervous whenever Linda was mentioned? "It's twelve forty-five."

"I think we should try the beach," said JP. "Even if we have to take a lot of sun."

"It might be a waste," said Ed. "We might have to go through this mess anyhow. Even supposing we do go along the beach, who knows how far this burnt patch extends? I say we keep to high ground. At least there is shade."

"No. I'm with JP," said Christine, standing up.

"It might have been a brush fire," said Ed halfheartedly. "Or lightning."

"Yeah," said Sean. He glanced back over the swath of black earth; troll blast or brush fire, he preferred not to have to walk through it, kicking ash. A detour might be dangerously exposed or a waste of time, but he said, "I vote for the beach."

To everyone's surprise, the trek to the shore was easy; once they cleared the trees, the land was rolling and sparsely covered with tall grass—not much scrub, no brambles or rocky patches. There was little shade, but they'd brought sunblock headgear and they could move quickly—until they hit the sand. It was white and very fine and there was a lot of it, making their progress slower but still not difficult.

Ed's spirits seemed to rise with every step, until he began to whistle into the rising growl of the sea. When they saw that the beachhead was exposed for a long, long stretch, leaving a wide path between sea and bluffs, they were all so relieved that their pace increased without discussion.

This ebullience took them about a mile farther. Then they broke for a quick meal. Sean chose a pocked stone contoured roughly by the water's insidious persistence, under the parsimonious shade of the bluffs for his perch. A tide pool, warmed and uninhabited, served to cool his blistered feet; the salt stung where a blister had broken, but he didn't care—he welcomed the sting; he had thought his feet tougher.

Each of the others went off on their own, not out of view or earshot, but separate. Sean ate and watched the sea and felt the sea's tangy breath dry his sweat, fill his lungs with its pungent, living taste; it carried off the sight of the scorched earth, cooled the sun's ferocity, and cleaned away the scorched memories. Again he took out the folio and pencil; he wrote down the time, checking his watch. Then he wrote:

AT SEE

—and stopped.

What else? He didn't want to record the burnt land—yet shouldn't he mention it? And what about how he'd felt when he'd been left on the road in the fog, alone? And the trolls? These things seemed important—yet if he wrote them down, he'd be sitting there until the next tide.

Annoyed with his own indecision, he scribbled,

LEFT EMELE

The sight of her name there, on the brown paper, pleased him. He rubbed his thumb over the script and wondered what she was doing at that moment. Strangely, nothing suggested itself to him. She could have been doing anything—her days had no particular scheme to them that he could ever find. One day he'd see her sitting on her porch, idle and bare-legged, watching clouds; the next day she'd be down at council, quilting with Sandra. She was so unlike Linda, whose ways had been even more regulated than his own.

He sighed, set the journal down, and began to tend his blistered feet. But sharp memory made him fidget—Linda, tough and strong and so greedy. She'd taken what she needed from him. How different it had been with Emily! She would cry, not willing to let him rest, wanting him to hold her. At first he'd been rather touched at how much she'd needed him.

He shook his head to clear it and stood up. But Emily'd expected *too* much.

Expectations! he thought. *She should learn to live without them. I have.* He glanced back down at Emily's name in his book. He picked up the pencil; looked at the curious black lettering on it—UNCDC-R&D-UBAS—put the end of the eraser over the first E he'd written. Then he dropped the pencil in the book, shut it, and packed it away.

Climbing off the honeycombed rock, he headed over to Ed, who was sitting on a bleached log, pouring over the map again. Sean sat next to him. The map's edges shuddered in the wind. A few yards away, Christine had gone wading, her hat pulled over her forehead, her pant legs rolled up to her knees. JP was asleep, his head cushioned against a windbreak rock, his long legs curled around his knapsack.

Ed glanced up. "Time to push on."

Sean stretched his arms over his head. "Will we make it?"

"I think so. Gotta keep the pace up, though."

Sean nodded toward Christine and JP. "Good luck."

Ed sighed. He put away the map, and went over to Christine.

Sean frowned. He couldn't hear his companions, but he didn't much care. Whatever Ed could say to try to persuade Chris to keep up the pace would make very little difference; she'd promise Ed and keep right on walking slowly.

Promises. Linda had made so many and broken so many, he'd almost ceased noticing until that one, that last impossible one, the one that had made all the difference between them. Just thinking about it made his back stiffen and his face flush. But she wouldn't say anything, wouldn't tell him, and then, she'd just out and out lied—

"Hey, Sean," called Ed, from the water's edge. "Come here and tell us what you see."

Sean got up and jogged over to his companions. Christine pulled at her hat's brim with one hand and then pointed across the horizon.

"What?" he asked, trying to follow the line of her hand.

"We thought we saw something. Something big," said Chris.

"Like what? A boat?"

"No, no," said Ed. "Swimming. Diving."

"Oh, come on. You both must have sunstroke."

"It was swimming out there," insisted Christine. "Take a good look. Your sight's the best."

Sean scanned the water dutifully. In the distance, where the sky met the sea, little bobbing flashes of light showed the surface unbroken; it was quiet except for the ocean's own undulations.

"Nothing," said Sean. He softened his tone. "Nothing's out there. I'm sorry."

Chris frowned. "But we both—"

"Could have been," replied Sean in as noncommittal a tone as he could muster. "Might've been—"

"Yeah," said Ed flatly. "Well. We'd best pack it up."

Later, as the group found their way to the end of the sand, they also found themselves stuck. A cliff, a shelf of green, jutted out over the beach. Large enough to bar the travelers from the rest of the coast, it looked fragile as well, for the sea was eating away at its base and would eventually eat out its heart so far as to make the whole shelf fall in. Such solidity so dangerously undermined made them hesitate to climb it. They stood and watched the sea rush in with a great noise, a wild spray.

At last, Ed pointed them upward. They had to climb, push onward. The terrain became difficult—brushy, slippery with slag and pebbles. But the earth held. They scaled the cliff and marched beyond it, to pick up what was left of the road again.

Ed was obviously relieved. The best route to Sheila's, the

most direct, was along the road and he'd thought they might have lost it altogether. Dusk was already filtering the light, making shadows thankfully deeper, but making the distances look unfortunately longer.

Sean despaired of reaching safety. He could feel the open blisters on his feet bleeding through the wool socks; he had the uneasy sense of trolls amassing in the dark. Hunger had come and gone again, leaving him lightheaded, and, so far as any of them knew, they could be wandering through ube territory. He could hear Christine breathing hard; he stole a glance at JP—his color had faded to a flat, almost greenish, brown.

Ed whispered, "There it is."

In that evening half-light, the patch of brush near some evergreens toward which Ed pointed looked like—a patch of brush. The trees backed up against a ridge in a row, and the brush grew in erratic bursts here and there between them. The slight wind riffled what little grass there was. Crickets sang. Here and there a cone had dropped among sun-dried, auburn needles. It was a lonely, empty place content with its loneliness.

Sean looked up and down, trying to make out what told Ed so surely they'd arrived. Nothing suggested itself. If he'd been traveling alone, he would have gone right past. But when Ed nodded again to himself, his smile of relief was so genuine that Sean relaxed a little.

"Okay," said Ed.

"Okay what?" said Christine, looking quizzically at him.

"Come on."

They made their way with caution across the road to the ridge of trees.

"Keep sharp," said Ed. "Sheila's got good defenses."

"Great," muttered Christine. "What kind of defenses?"

"Always a surprise," said Ed lightly.

JP stifled a nervous laugh.

Within a few feet of the densest brushy growth, Ed began

to hoot. JP gasped when the hoot was repeated, but not by Ed. He grinned and hooted again. In reply, from the edge of the brush, a hatch popped up, and then a head.

"Sheila?" cried Christine.

The woman seemed to leap up out of the earth. She strode briskly across the yard or so between them and grabbed Christine by the hand. "*You* girl! It is Chris?"

Christine laughed assent and the two women embraced.

"Hey," said Ed. "Leave a hug for me."

Sheila turned. "I been seeing you. You get your hugs. This one—well, now!"

Ed shook his head. "I don't rate?"

Sheila laughed softly.

Sean watched, with JP, from a slight distance. He took off his knapsack, dusted his hands, and folded his arms across his chest. He had never known Sheila very well. Like all the old townies she'd always been reclusive. He'd not been saddened when she struck out on her own, as many others were, because he'd always considered her difficult, if not incomprehensible. From time to time, Monkar would get wind of what she was up to, mostly through Ed. Sean never did understand what Ed saw in her. In fact, Ed's friendship with Sheila had become something of a joke between the two men. Now that Sean was faced with her reality, he felt awkward. He wondered if Ed had ever mentioned their jokes.

Unsure, he stepped back and glanced over at JP, who seemed to be as uncomfortable as Sean was—he hadn't made even a tentative move toward saying hello.

Sean watched JP's discomfort as a mirror to his own; he was about to say something, anything, to break the tension, when his lungs were emptied in a burst of excruciation. Weight and pain drove him to his knees. Struggling for breath, he felt a line, a thin slice of cold, press against his windpipe. He'd never felt anything like it before, but he knew, some-how, not to move; fear drove the blood from his head. He tried to steady himself but he was carrying a load on his back that bowed him over.

His attacker's breath was hot against his ear.

"Ona!" cried Sheila sternly.

Sean did not move. The breath on his ear became hurried. "Ona."

The weight on his back shifted. The thin wire of pain at his throat was released. He sat down heavily. The sweat on his face turned icy. He had to rub his eyes to clear away the panic stars.

A figure came round from behind him, a youngster who seemed oddly familiar. She was small, but sinewy—

"Ona!" said Sheila again.

The knife lowered.

Sheila pointed to Ed. "You know him. Remember?"

Ona nodded and sheathed the knife.

"She does?" murmured Ed, clearly shocked. "Who is she?"

"My child."

"*What?*"

Ed's surprise seemed to amuse Sheila. She laughed.

Ona, meanwhile, had turned toward Christine.

When Sean saw the weapon disappear, he stood up. He said ruefully, "Ed, you weren't kidding. Sheila has great defenses. More than you bargained for, looks like."

Sheila laughed harder. "And more than you did, clearly." She held out her hand. "Sean Rider, isn't it?"

He shook hands with her.

"Hello," said Christine, leaning toward the strange child, who was staring at her steadily and hard. "I'm Chris."

"Ona?" said Sheila softly. "Ona was only protecting me." She gestured toward the road. "Ona? It's all right. Go on now, go on, it's all right."

Ona jogged off.

"Your *daughter?*" Ed asked.

"Well, not exactly," said Sheila. "Come on—let's go in and rest. You all look run out." She touched Christine's shoulder. "Don't worry. Ona can take care."

"So I gather," said Christine. "Wish I could do as well."

"I wouldn't like to meet up with her," said Sean, grimacing, "when you weren't around to call her off, Sheila."

"You were at a disadvantage."

He laughed. "Yeah, right."

Sheila frowned. "Remember, Sean. Ona's just a child."

"Oh, yeah," said Sean. "Harmless."

"I didn't say harmless. I said a child." Sheila took them over to the hole in the ground from which she had appeared. It had a lid, a ceramic trap door, rounded and heavy. It had been fired matte and covered with shreds of tumbleweed and tree needles. A rope ladder led downward.

Inside they found a labyrinth—or rather, it seemed one at first, yet it was only five rooms, clustered around a central, open area, off the entry. The entryway itself was dim and bare; but the area beyond it was bright. The steady, even lighting surprised Sean, until he realized what it was—electricity! He stood under the central lamp in sheer pleased amazement. He hadn't seen electricity since he'd been a teenager.

"When I first got here," said Sheila, "the place was a wreck. Looked like it must've been a big building once, but all that was left was this basement. So I camped and excavated. Put a roof on it; wired it to a generator, well, you see—" She gestured around. "Got a lot a help from people in the Area. They don't tend to think of me as a townie, least not the ones at the north end of the bay. Ed helped, too."

He waved a hand. "Only a little and late in the game."

"Help is help."

"But how did you get help from the Area?" asked Sean. "I thought anyone without deecee i.d. was—"

"By careful trading. I've bribed the deecee introduct unit at North Bay Ridge—I bring them things that are hard to squeeze off rationing restrictions, odd things they want. For that I get supplies and little questioning. I got the generator, wiring and learning, tools, and the kind of mechanical stuff you can't just find by poking round the abandonments."

"Right," said Ed, "but what you do is real risky, my dear. One of these days that introduct unit's going to get worried about you and then—" He made a cutting gesture.

"What—" asked JP. He glanced over to Ed. "What was all the hoot-hooting about?"

Sheila smiled at him. "You've grown, Jay."

He nodded shyly.

She flipped a small, metal switch on the wall. A tinny sound of distant crickets filled the room. "No owls left around here—except Ed."

"But how—" said Sean, staring at the wall switch. He swung around to Ed, his voice taking on both urgency and frustration. "You knew about this? Why haven't we done some of it up home? It can't be that hard—"

"You must be hungry," said Sheila, breaking in on Sean's confused excitement. She led them away from the mystery of the wall switch into a small kitchen. Two rickety folding chairs, a few cushions on the floor, a table, a tall Formica counter that ran the length of one wall greeted them; pots and other utensils were hung above the counter. There was a low, wide pit stove in the center of the room. A funnel pipe hooded the stove and narrowed upward until it disappeared into the roof. Sheila stirred the fire and took the wok off the wall peg. Opening another trap door in the floor, she collected vegetables, roots. She glanced at her visitors and said, "Well? Relax—sit down. Dinner won't take long."

Slowly, the four uncased themselves from their packs and outer clothes. It took a few minutes for Sean to tear himself away from the various wonders of Sheila's home, already storing up ideas to bring back to Monkar. Why had Ed kept this all so secret? He'd believed that the Area was closed and deadly, but Sheila made it sound pretty accessible. Reluctantly, he sat down, peeled off his socks to inspect the bloody patches that had been blisters earlier in the day. He noticed that no one's feet had escaped; all of them were taking off socks with such a grim determination, one might have thought they were removing a layer of skin.

"Here," said Sheila, handing Christine a basket. "Stick the socks in this. We'll wash them tonight. And anything else." Christine threw her socks in, while Sheila took down a good-sized knife and began slicing. She said, "Let me tell you a few things you need to know about this place."

"Hold on," said Ed. "First—why the hell've you been hiding that child?"

Sheila shook her head. "Ona's the one been hiding. Been with me now for about five years—"

"She's not your daughter," said JP.

"Not by blood, no." Sheila turned her attention to the food as she spoke. "I met this woman in the Area waiting for introduct. She'd come from a dead-town, I could tell, but of course she wasn't saying. Anyhow, she had Ona." Sheila turned to JP. "For trade."

"Trade," said Christine. "You mean like—" She fumbled. "What do you trade for a child?"

"I had something." Sheila shrugged and finished cutting the vegetables. "Ona ought be back. Ed, could you go check?"

"Won't she run from me?"

"Nope. Not since your redhead's been downed."

"Very funny," said Sean.

Sheila smiled. "But it's true—Ona won't worry, now." She turned to Ed. "Check the back way?"

"Great," muttered Sean, touching his throat.

"What back way?" asked Christine.

"Here," said Ed, taking them all from the kitchen into the central area again and then through to a room with a mattress on the floor, covered by pillows. There were two wooden boxes, one with drawers, one without. Beyond this room was another, smaller one and then, leading off that, a hall.

Ed went down the hall. It narrowed so that Sean had to

stoop. Finally they reached a door that Ed unbolted and they found themselves looking out from the back of a hill—or, Sean realized, the back of the rise they'd seen as they'd come into Sheila's place.

On the horizon, the thin line of the sea was visible—and so was Ona, jogging toward them with a bundle of small wood in one hand and a string of three dried fish in the other. She jogged right on past them up the hall, saying nothing.

"Talkative," said Sean.

Christine followed after the child.

Ed shook his head. "Sheila's holding out on us."

"What do you mean?" asked JP nervously.

Ed shrugged. "About Ona."

"Well, if you think she is, then we'd better find out what it is," said Sean.

"No. I don't think so."

"But you just said—"

"Yeah, I know. It isn't important—except to Sheila."

"Come on, Ed. We're going to stay here for the night."

"So?"

Sean frowned. "So I don't like mysteries. And I don't like being held out on." He gave Ed a long "meaning-you-too" stare.

Ed seemed to ignore it. "Oh, hell," he said, "Sheila's okay." He slapped Sean on the back. "Just forget it."

"Forget it? When that kid almost killed me?"

"Yeah. Forget it." He went inside, with JP at his elbow.

"Fuck," muttered Sean as he followed them.

In the confines of the underground kitchen, Ona seemed even smaller than she'd first appeared; small, unkempt, shy, and still peculiarly familiar, maddeningly inoffensive, as harmless as Sheila had claimed. But the more harmless she seemed, the more tense Sean became. He couldn't help glancing at the knives on the wall—and he didn't like it that, try as she might, Christine couldn't get the child to talk to her. Chris was good with kids—he had seen her make Tomas smile.

Sheila, however, was oblivious to the tension in the room. She served the meal, told them about the widely placed vegetable patches that she hid from trolls. These vegetables were among her special trading goods. She spoke to Christine about Sandra's newborn Jett, and finally ended up talking to Ed about the package of printed paper that he'd brought down from Monkar. He handed it to her.

"Pretty old stuff," she said.

Ed touched the edge of the printout. "Nathaniel—you remember him?"

Sheila nodded. "Came in right before Barbara died. Took up with Caitlin."

"Nathaniel's convinced there are seals in Monkar."

"Seals? Makes sense. There must've been seals all up and down this coast once. But they're gone now."

"Yeah. That's what I told him."

"And?"

"And I'm not so sure. Maybe they have come back."

Sheila shrugged as if at the packet. Christine stretched and left the room. Ona stared after her. JP had fallen asleep.

"Ed," said Sheila, handing him the paper. "This is just junk—"

"No—"

Sean got up and followed Christine. He didn't need to hear Ed try to persuade Sheila that junk wasn't junk. He laid out his bedroll, as Chris was doing, and put the rest of his equipment in order. When he'd finished, she was washing out the socks. Sean sat down with his journal.

"What do you write?" she asked.

He looked up. She looked more like Linda than ever. He took a deep breath and said, "This and that."

"Oh." She wrung out a sock. "Ona's quiet."

"Talkative, as I said before."

Christine inspected her washing. "These are going to be spotted. But at least they're clean." She put the wet things back in the basket. "I want some kindling, so I can dry this stuff—come along?"

"Wouldn't you rather take Ona?"

Christine smiled. "We're not on speaking terms."

Sean laughed, and followed her down the hall, out the back way. Night was just falling. The indigo sky had a cloud stain of pink and yellow rippling through it. Sean wrapped his jacket closer. Christine gazed overhead.

"Look—there," she whispered. "The evening star . . ."

"Venus," said Sean. "Always the first." He put his hands in his pockets. "I heard people went up there."

"Me, too. Heard it from the same place, I bet." She started to gather twigs. "Remember?"

"No."

"From my granddad." She glanced over at Sean with a quick, quizzical intensity. "You used to ask him a trillion questions whenever you could. Don't you remember?"

Sean nodded slowly. "Yeah. You and Linda teased me. You thought it was boring, boring, boring."

She laughed. "It was! Granddad just remembered about things—not about people. At least not about a person in particular. He used to say that people had gone to the moon. That people had done this or that or the other but when we'd ask him what those people had been like, he could never tell us. I remember him talking about 'agribusiness and orbiting habitats.' " She smoothed down her cropped hair. "Both Granddad and Dad believed in rumors, in conspiracy, and in business. If it had been good for business, then it had happened." She glanced up. "We used to bet those who went out there weren't people like us."

Sean nodded. "No kidding. They left us for dead."

"That's not what we meant."

"No. But it's true."

"True?" she shrugged. "We don't know that."

"It's enough to know what we know," said Sean. "Enough

to see what's been done here. Enough and more than enough."

"We're alive," said Christine stubbornly. "Monkar is still trying to survive—and we *do,* more or less. That's what I try to remember, when I look at Venus, or any other star. If people left the earth, they took problems with them."

Sean smiled. "Bravo, Chris. You're an optimist."

"I have to be," she replied.

"Oh? Why's that? We're on a plague ship and it's rotting."

"Everyone dies, Sean. Venusians will die. To tell the truth, I'd rather do it here than in some place I couldn't breathe air, or roll in the grass."

Sean stuffed his hands back in his pockets. "Fine. You want to die here. Doubtless you will get that privilege."

"Oh, hush."

"Hush? No, no—I'm not letting you off that easy. You still haven't told me why I have to be optimistic."

Christine turned on him. "If you're not, Sean Rider, why the hell do you think we can find Linda? The way I look at it, hoping for anything at all is optimism. Monkar is optimism. You can call it what you like, but that's the name I use for it."

"Touché," said Sean.

There was a moment of silence between them. Then, Christine said gently, "What is it with you? Is it Linda?"

He gazed at her all-too-familiar face. "Yes," he said softly. "Linda."

Her eyes bespoke sadness. "I remind you of her. I remind myself. But I'm not Linda, no matter how much I've sometimes wanted to be."

"I know," he said. "It's not just that, either. That burn we saw. It reminds me, too."

She nodded. "I remember," she said. "Terence. I loved him, you know. And Mom. Dad. Your parents."

"Stop," said Sean. "Please."

She sighed. "I'd like to. But being in the Area will bring it all up close again, Sean."

"I know." He folded his arms tightly across his chest.

"That's why I ask, isn't going back some kind of optimism?"

"Maybe," he said, thinking silently, *no. Optimism is your word, Chris, your illusion. We're living moment to moment on a bare thread of continuity that could snap at any time. The fragile thing we call Monkar, so small a group of us, that home you so hope on, so live for, is as uncertain as a spider's web, stretched between slender stalks of grass, easily destroyed by a careless hand, a hasty foot.* He listened to the speaking darkness. Living as they did was living on illusion—but for the moment, it was real enough.

When Sean and Chris returned, they found JP in his bedroll and Ona asleep on the pillows. Ed and Sheila were still talking—arguing; Christine got the fire going and strung the wet clothes nearby. Then, nodding to Sean, she turned in.

But Sean was jumpy. He reopened the journal. The few things he'd written looked silly. He shut the book and wandered into the kitchen. Neither Ed nor Sheila noticed.

"—nonsense," Sheila was saying. "If there had been some kind of work, or what did Nathaniel say? Scientific research, going on in Monkar years ago, Barbara would've known. She never spoke of it."

"Nathaniel says a pupping ground," Ed insisted.

Sheila shook her head and pointed across the page Ed held. "From *this*? It's just a bunch of letters."

"He says code. Besides this," he pointed, "UBAS—that's all over the place up home. It must mean something."

"What?" She rubbed her chin. "It could just as easily be a set of musical chords for all I know. Maybe it's a song."

"Would Barbara have known?" Sean asked. "Would she have?"

The two looked at him, both startled. Sheila seemed annoyed.

"I'd like to find out," said Ed slowly, "when, and for what reason, Monkar was built." He gave Sheila a long look. "Barbara did know, didn't she?"

"Ed," said Sheila evenly, "Barbara probably knew a lot of things. She wasn't much of a talker, though. *I* understand this: the whole coast was left to itself a long time ago. I can probably give you a dozen reasons why."

Ed nodded. "Still—"

"Still, *nothing*," said Sean abruptly. "What about Ona?"

"What about Ona?" echoed Sheila.

Ed interrupted with, "We should all get some sleep."

"He's right," said Sheila. "You've got a long haul." She stood and held out her hand. "Ed?"

"Shell?" he asked tightly, without moving. "You've told me everything I need to know, haven't you?"

"I think so," she said slowly. "Yes." She withdrew her hand and switched off the lights, leaving Ed to fold up his papers in the sudden pitch dark.

Frustrated, Sean had to feel out his way to his bedroll in the dark. He'd wanted to question Sheila about Ona. He'd wanted to know how to bribe his way into the Area, and about Sheila's generator, and about how she'd gotten wiring in the place or how she got the wall speaker set up. But he knew he wouldn't get anywhere without Ed's help and he couldn't figure out why Ed was being so private, or had kept such information from Monkar. Why had Ed been so secretive all this time? He turned over onto his stomach. And what kind of secret did those letters on Nathaniel's paper hold, if any? He'd wondered about the "UBAS" himself, especially since those letters were repeated on the pencil Maria had given him. He turned over again. Was Sheila asleep? And Ona? The windowless dark had closed in solidly. There seemed to be nothing across the black room. Nothing. Closing his eyes against the emptiness, he forced himself to breathe deep and even. The best he hoped for tonight was rest. Not sleep. Not sleep.

6

A Canticle for Spring

(4:30 P.M.)

MARIA SAT ON the rocky ledge at the end of the dock to warm her legs. From the knees down, her skin was puckered. Her shoulders tingled with sunburn and although she'd worn a thick long-sleeved shirt, she could still feel the weight of the harvest basket she'd been carrying.

Shrugging to loosen her neck muscles, she watched Lindi pass around a snack to the seaweed-harvesting crew. The six harvesters had taken a break out on the leeward of the dock; only Alice's daughter, Ki, and Ki's son, Jiro, were still in the water.

Maria yawned and stretched. She felt lightheaded. She pushed her headgear forward to shade her eyes.

The tide was turning again. The sea crept slowly out and the sun dipped, as if to signal the water's retreat. The ruin of the dock on which Maria sat, and the jutting bluff behind it, formed a shelter within the larger cove where seaweed grew. Here and there along the cove's lip, shrinking tide pools glistened between the dry rocks. Anenomes, closed tight against the day's withering heat, waited for the relief the warm sea would bring. Stranded starfish waited there, too, as stoic as their brethren.

She glanced over her shoulder. The intensely yellow light of the late day struck the peeling walls of the distant building on the hill, making the whole place into a mild amber beacon that seemed to shed extra warmth on the town and shore below it.

Suddenly, Lindi sat down with Maria. "Hi. Want some apple?"

"You bet," said Maria.

The two ate dried apples and watched Ki work with Jiro. Ki waded, holding herself stiffly against the undertow, with the harvest basket in her arms. A leather strap looped around her neck anchored the basket. Jiro scurried ahead of his mother. Bent double, he hacked at the seaweed, slicing it off at its roots with a sickle and dumping the pulp into the basket. Harvesters always worked in pairs that way, child and adult; Lindi had paired herself with Maria since Christine had gone.

Maria chewed thoughtfully, pleased with Lindi's company and also grateful for her silence. The argument she'd had with Emily that morning had unstrung her—she felt abused, guilty. In the course of harvesting, she had decided three times to skip supper at Emily's house, and then thrice undid her decision— she wanted to see Nate, and she still wanted to explain herself to Emily. Yet, at the same time, there was no explanation. She'd simply felt that Sean was the one to have that book.

What could she say? Worst of all, she understood Emily's pain only *too* well. "Damn," she whispered.

Lindi glanced up, quick as a mouse. "What?" she said.

"Ever argue with a friend?"

"Sure. All the time. Mostly, I'm right. Except with Tomas. He wins, every time."

"Oh?"

"Yeah, he's tough." Lindi grinned. "I bet you thought Tomas couldn't be tough."

Maria laughed gently. "No."

Lindi shrugged. "Everybody thinks he's weak, but they don't know anything." She bit into an apple slice, for emphasis. "They don't know."

Maria smiled and gazed idly back out at the harvesters. "What is he so tough about?"

"Oh," she said and then paused. "Well. Sometimes it's about our parents. Tomas thinks his father can tell a better story than my mom, but I say Mama sings a better song, and that a song is as good as any story." She shrugged. "I'll tell you a secret, nobody ever wins *that* one. We both win—I like his dad's stories and he just knows Sandra can sing best, 'cept maybe for Emily—and himself, of course."

Maria looked over at Lindi in surprise, but the girl was watching two of the other harvesters get ready to go back into the water for one last shift, so she let the talk about Tomas slide as she finished her apples. Everyone knew that Tomas couldn't speak; he certainly couldn't sing. Maria assumed Lindi wanted questions, but knew better than to jump at such bait—she'd be left flapping on the hook, gasping for answers.

Finally, Lindi wiggled the bait again, saying, "You think Tomas can't."

"Maybe," said Maria.

"Maybe!" Lindi sniffed. "Huh. Maybe." She reached over and absently pulled a ribbon of seaweed from the basket.

"Okay," said Maria, brushing crumbs from her lap. "I bet you made it all up. Tomas can't talk. He can't sing."

Lindi laughed and nibbled on the seaweed. Then she jumped down off the dock.

"You're a tease," chided Maria, jumping down after the girl.

"That's what Papa always says."

"Well, he's right." She paused. "Raw seaweed?"

Lindi glanced at Maria sidelong. "Tastes good."

Maria grimaced. "Too salty. It's better steamed—or pickled." She flung the basket's strap over her head. "Okay, tease, you win. But I warn you, I'm as tough as you say Tomas is. Tougher."

Lindi folded her arms. "Huh," she said. "Bet you just are—maybe." She pulled up the tails of her shirt, tied them in a knot, and strode into the water. Maria adjusted the strings of her hat and waded in after the girl.

It didn't take long for the strap of the harvesting basket to feel as if it were cutting her shoulder to ribbons, so when Lindi resurfaced, Maria insisted that the basket was full enough for the day. She was impressed by the girl's stamina—Lindi was one of the least affected of the children, but still, she did have hearing problems—she couldn't catch a certain low range—and her hands and feet were slightly misshapen, the digits overly long and flat. Yet she was very strong. Staggering a little, Maria moved up to the shore to a spot where the water was low enough for Lindi to stand easily, then they took the basket by its handles, the girl on one side, the woman on the other, and heaved it to the beach. Maria flopped down in the shade; stretching her shoulders, she took off her hat and rolled her head from side to side, wincing at the stiffness. Lindi crouched behind her and gave her a back rub.

"You're a little witch," said Maria. "That feels great." She closed her eyes.

"Me and Jiro will carry the basket to dry," said Lindi, "if you'll do something."

Maria grinned, her eyes still closed. "Okay, okay, anything as long as I don't have to touch that basket again."

"Come swimming—for a little while."

"Swimming?" She opened her eyes. "Haven't you had enough of the water?" She turned around. "Look at you, you're puckered all over!" She reached out to give the youngster a pinch, but Lindi was too quick and escaped.

"Won't I be a nuisance?" called Maria.

Lindi smiled and dashed off to fetch Jiro. Maria absently rubbed her neck and rolled her shoulders. She thought a swim might loosen her muscles. The sun was getting low enough to stop worrying about severe burn. Afterward, she would go up to Emily's to talk. She'd decided to begin with an apology but she couldn't say she'd done something wrong. Emily would have to accept that.

Lindi and Jiro returned, bringing with them another girl Maria didn't know well. Beryl had inexplicably wandered into Monkar one midday the previous summer. Malnourished, burned, tattooed with +xyy+, dehydrated, silent, and seemingly too small for her age, she'd been adopted by Sandra and George. Though shy or easily scared, she seemed to be doing well. The rest of the children had taken her in right off. But then, thought Maria, so many of them had their own difficulties. . . . Maria smiled, particularly at Beryl, to try to put her at ease. The girl smiled briefly back but held tight to Jiro's hand.

"I told them," said Lindi proudly.

Maria nodded cautiously. She had no idea what Lindi had told them, besides the fact that they were going to take a swim.

Jiro eyed her as if he wasn't convinced. Beryl stared. Maria began to feel a bit awkward under the silence and scrutiny.

Lindi frowned. "I told them you promised."

Maria nodded, electrified by the tension in Lindi's voice—and then she remembered. She said softly, "I keep my promises!" She looked at each child, making her face as solemn as theirs. These, she thought, were the lucky ones. They were alive. "I will always help you. Every one."

Nobody answered her. Not even Lindi.

"Well," she said. "Okay?"

Lindi said, "Let's swim."

As she spoke, the children ran, as if on cue, down to the cove's beach, past the ruined dock. Maria trailed after them, too tired to run. Jiro, Lindi, and Beryl made a beeline for the water, diving like darts. Maria simply waded in after them.

Several neat strokes in the warm water brought her among her companions; for a few moments they all played tag. Nearsighted, she lost miserably to them and although she was a strong swimmer, she wasn't nearly as swift or as flexible as the children, who were all astonishingly quick.

When she managed, at last, to tag Jiro and relieve herself of a third term of being "it," she took a back dive away from them and cried out, "I give up, I give up. You're too fast—the fish must be giving you lessons!"

Lindi leapt far up out of the water and, tossing her head from side to side, said, "They are!"

"What?" said Maria.

"Nothing," said Jiro, interrupting. "Lin—"

Lindi shrugged, laughed, and disappeared. In fact all of them dove below and left Maria bobbing on the surface alone. She waited for them a few minutes and then began to swim toward the rocks. Halfway down the cove she turned and headed inland, and let herself be propelled onto the sand by the waves. The children were not to be found.

A lot of pebbles had been washed up in this part of the beach—black, smooth pebbles, from as small as an insect to foot-sized. The water made them chuckle whenever the tide pulled out. Glistening black, when dry they turned gray. She picked her way over them and sat on a driftwood log to rest and watch the pebbly bed and listen to the wet stones laugh.

Meanwhile, the children had now surfaced near the wreck of a dory Nathan wanted to salvage. Their game of tag went on, and so they didn't see her wave at them. Finally, she sat down with her hands clasped around her knees and waited; eyes closed, she let the sun dry her face. When she opened her eyes, she saw the kids haul out and sit like a line of fuzzy birds on the dock.

Watching them, she thought of Carlo. He had never been able to play or swim—his handicaps, unlike the other children's, had been too debilitating. Jiro might have a severe speech impediment, Beryl's growth might be stunted, and although Sandra's kids all bore some burden, almost none, except Tomas, had lived long with so much, well, wrong with them. Alice had tried to help Carlo and Tomas but . . . Maria felt her mood sinking, so she stood and stripped off her wet clothes, dragged the log around vertical to the water, and lay down in its shelter.

She dozed into a half-asleep haze. The idea of supper became a pleasing, dreaming diversion when a loud splash nearby woke her; jerking upright, she grabbed for her shirt, thinking Lindi had returned.

Frowning, she looked around carefully. No kids. Had someone else come for an afternoon swim? There—two heads popped up from the chopping waves. One shook hair back from its face. The other was motionless.

Maria was so surprised, she didn't do anything but clutch her shirt over her breasts. Who—? She called to them, but they didn't answer. Who? She just couldn't make out. For long moments, the three watched each other. The motion of the water and sun, the small, drifting heads, bobbing—Maria leaned forward. She squinted. Who?

The swimmers dove, breaking the enchantment of their silent gaze.

Quickly she slipped on her clothes and walked down to the sea's edge. She waited, searching the waters impatiently for another glimpse of the strange swimmers. And waited. Whoever was out there stayed submerged for what seemed to her an impossibly long time. Her eyes stung a little from the salt and the sparkle of sunlit waves. She was just about to give up, when a swimmer breached, close by.

Tomas!

She waved at him, wondering what he was doing out there; it was unlike Tomas to leave Nathan. And where was the other child? She waved again, beckoning the boy to come to shore. But he either did not see, or chose to ignore her, and dove off again. This time he was gone only a moment from her sight but when he reappeared, he was much farther out, and had his back to her. He seemed to be looking to the horizon at something. She waited for him to turn, but instead, he began to swim. He dove and rose, dove and rose, cleaving along the surface like a quilting needle running through cloth, up and down, up and down, leaving a tiny white trail of foam.

Maria sighed as the boy's feet dipped below the water. She folded her arms, waiting once again for him to surface and go on with his quilting swim toward the horizon. She hoped to catch his attention.

He appeared, now even farther offshore. She waved frantically, but again he did not see. The other swimmer, whoever it had been, was gone. How could she bring him back to shore? Maybe send Lindi after him? She considered. Tomas was even more like a fish in the water than her tag companions had been. Glancing down to the dock wall, she saw the children still perched there. Good. She shaded her eyes, began to wave at Lindi, and took a deep breath to call out to the girl, though she doubted her voice could reach so far.

Wetness touched her arm.

Starting, turning around, she nearly shrieked. Standing in the pebble bed next to her, Tomas. He was dripping and apparently naked. *Though was he? Yes, but so much hair! When? And how had he gotten to her so fast?* she wondered, both startled and embarrassed to be staring at the boy so. Tomas smiled at her through the weedy length of his hair. And before she was able to respond, he ran from her—an amber streak on the sand, a quick dart, a splash into the sea. He surfaced and swam to the group on the wall. Hauling out on the dock, he crawled in among the children and they nestled close, holding him, holding each other.

Maria regarded them nearsightedly for as long as they stayed on the dock. Tomas and the others were giving her a glimpse of something they shared—but only the merest of a glimpse. She shook sand from her clothes, her hair, her arms and legs, keeping an eye out for her elusive companions and wondering how she might prove to them that her promise wasn't idle talk. They'd all been teasing her and testing her—especially Lindi and Tomas. She turned toward Emily's house. She would have to wait on the children. She couldn't rush them. They would find their own trust for her, in their own time.

Emily cut out from the group of planters to stand alone beneath a tree. She took off her sunblock hat and gloves, and waved to her friends, her black hair tangled by the light evening wind. Suddenly, she lowered her hand.

An odd, dipping movement near the edge of a newly plowed area had caught her attention. Evidently the day's planting had attracted a flock of six birds. It was a motley group—two skinny ravens, a seagull, and an active triumvirate of noisy Steller's jays. Emily didn't chase the birds; they couldn't possibly eat all of the seed, and it had been a long time since she'd seen so many birds so close. Slowly, she squatted. But even this careful movement frightened the flock. They scattered into the nearby woods. Emily dropped her hat and stood up, shading her eyes.

If only I might just fly off! she thought. Escape would be better than trying to figure out what to say to Maria. All that afternoon as she'd hoed and weeded, she'd found herself inwardly repeating the short, bitter conversation they'd had that morning.

She walked out from under the tree. It was still warm; the earth was baked dry in spots. To her left, far down where the field was edged by the forest, Matty sprinkled water from an old watering can, left and right, left and right, left and right, in a rhythmic pattern, moistening the seeds. She turned toward her low-roofed house above the town. Its wooden shingles were bleached, the faded blue paint on the sills chipped, and the chimney was missing a few bricks, but it looked solid—and then she saw Maria, standing in the town road, just below the house, waiting at the bottom of the hill.

Emily waved a slow greeting. Was it suppertime already? Her heart pounded as if she'd been running, as if Maria might have heard what had been going on in her head—she felt as

awkward as if she'd found an eavesdropper. She bent to collect
her hat and gloves. The air was heavy with the odor of the
earth and the heat of the day had brought out the taste of
the honeysuckle that was twined about the solitary tree. She
plucked a sprig—when she was young, she'd come out here to
sip the first honeysuckle sap. The field there had been half
the size it was now. Monkar, too. In those days she'd liked to
sit by the tree and watch the lazy movements of the half-
inhabited town, wondering what it might have been like when
it was first built, long before anyone could remember. What
had those people done, living all in neat rows that fanned out
from a hodgepodge center of a clocktower square and the
wide half-circle of a road? The council house must have been a
place for those ancient people to gather as it was now, judging
from the mass of chairs stacked there, all marked with bold
capped letters UBAS; but then, so many of the places had been
piled with chairs you got the sense, said old-townies, that the
only thing people had done in this place in the long ago was
sit.

She sighed. Maria had to be faced. She cut directly across
the grass onto the dirt road and then to Maria. What was she
going to say? She gave her friend a brief, uncertain smile.

Maria said, "Hey!"

"Hi."

"Listen, I—I'm—do you mind if I run down to my place
and get a quick wash? I'll be back soon."

"Oh, sure, *sure,*" said Emily. She hoped her voice did not
betray the depth of her relief. "I'm going to make a stew. That
takes a while. You needn't hurry."

Maria nodded, gave Emily a glancing kiss on one cheek,
and jogged off toward her home. Emily touched her cheek,
watching Maria go. Tears started to her eyes. Determined not
to cry, she walked swiftly home. But once there, she stood in
the kitchen dazed. What *would* she say tonight? How could
Maria just kiss her like that, as if the morning had never happened?

She sighed and rubbed her cheek. The house was silent except for the ticking of Sean's clocks. Irritated by the lonely sound, she threw her gloves into her hat, tossed them in a basket by the sink, and headed for a shower. But just outside the room where Nathaniel lay, she paused and put her ear to the door—it was so quiet, it made her uneasy. She knocked. No answer. She knocked with a little more force, leaning her ear on the door again. No sound came from within, not a stir— were both father and son asleep? She eased the door open and peered in.

The room was warm and close—a sweltering mixture of maryjane and sweat, musky and rich. Nathaniel lay on his back, one arm across his eyes. He breathed slowly, with a slight catch in his throat. Sheets had been thrown or kicked to the floor, and the pillow elevating his wounded foot had fallen onto the chest at the bottom of the bed. The water pitcher was empty.

Tomas was gone.

Emily crept in. Nathaniel coughed but didn't move. She stood still in the stifling room for a few minutes, afraid to wake and startle him. He seemed to her very long and very thin, stretched out there on the bed, naked; his rib cage showed faintly under light, curly hair. Hastily, she got the water pitcher.

Outdoors, she breathed deeply of the salty air and filled the pitcher from the pump in the yard, seeking the freshest and least acid-laced of the household's water. She splashed her face and wet her wrists. Then she took the pitcher back upstairs.

Nathaniel still slept. She tried to be what she imagined was nurselike: brisk and effective, cautious and gentle. She slid the pillow back under his wrapped foot, folded the sheets, and laid them within reach. She lingered to look at him again; the lines of him, the half-moon scoop of his hips, the gentle graceful languor of his penis, the flat expanse of his sweat-damp chest, his violet nipples nearly hidden, and his shoulders bent forward, even as he slept.

She swallowed and found her mouth a little too dry, her heart beating a little too fast. She shut the door, crept downstairs to the kitchen and drank a glass of water, staring out the window over the sink at the cove below the house. The beach was empty, the sky blank, and the sea as unhurried as lake water.

All was quiet, no one was about.

She frowned. Where had Tomas gone?

After a few minutes, Sean's clocks seemed terribly loud. There were four. They did not speak in unison; each one had its own pace. The biggest three sat on the mantel; one had a pendulum and a ponderous tick, tock, tick, tock, while the other two tripped along at a much jauntier speed, one tick-tick-tick-tock, the other tick-ticking. The fourth musketeer, a chimer, sat in the window niche, its click-clicking nearly silent.

Emily fetched the clock keys. Looking at the faces of the clocks as she wound them, she kept seeing Sean's face. Dropping the keys on the mantel near the biggest clock, she hugged herself, wishing another's arms, imagining someone else's arms around her shoulders, someone else's hands against her back.

Trembling, she wandered down the hallway, into the large storeroom; the long, wide, substantial table there held Sean's unfinished repairs. She let herself into the porch garden where the "paper" plants grew, and the discarded clocks rusted away. The warmth there was deep and moist, especially in the section she'd tented in sheets of plastic scrounged from the old lighthouse. She was particularly happy with the tomatoes, which she'd had little luck growing outdoors. And, as she went up and down the planters, watering that, tying up this, peeling off dead leaves, her restlessness eased away.

Nathaniel woke. He sat up. He was alone. His mouth was parched, he was hot, dizzy. He took a sip of water and was surprised at how cold and crisp it was. As he drank, he wondered where his son had gone—home? The boy's absence worried him, because he knew that Tomas had sensed Emily's discomfort with her guests—and Tomas was a prankster.

Nathaniel, spurred on by the memory of pranks past, inched to the end of the bed and eased on his trousers. Buttoning them, he regarded his mummified foot as it sat quietly on the braided rug next to his other untouched foot. The wrapped foot throbbed, but the edge of his pain had been dulled by marijuana, sleep, and by whatever else Alice had given him.

Still, he regarded his wounded foot cautiously, as if too much looking would bring the nerve endings into fiery life. Rocking back and forth to get enough momentum to stand up, he tried to forget that he'd promised Alice he would not move. If Tomas had gone home, fine. But if Tomas was planning mischief, he wanted to nip it in the bud.

Evening seemed to be well on its way. The room was dim, and beyond the small window, the sky was rose-gold. It was very quiet.

If he could at least get to his own bed, in his own Row house where he could hear the children shout in the square, where Maria's flute played to him at night (although she did not know she still had him for an audience), where Tomas would not have to sit as quiet as a trapped rabbit, frozen by Emily's disapproval, hatching plans of harmless revenge . . . if he could get home, where his child was free to laugh his silent laughter, Nathaniel was sure he would heal faster. This house of Emily's was haunted by a silence Nathaniel felt belonged, in part, to deaths—of children stillborn, of Andros and of Aretina, of Linda and of love, a quiet far heavier than his son's muteness. The more he sat on the bed, the more uneasy he felt. Bracing himself, he stood.

Pain stars and pinwheels made the room spin and vanish beneath their fireworks. The emptiness of the house was dispelled by a whining ring in his ears.

When the dizzy, noisy ride subsided, Nathaniel found

himself sitting back on the bed lopsided, panting and grateful that the spin hadn't carried him off. But it had kept him in thrall long enough that he did not notice when, in the midst of the ride, Tomas had returned. For a few moments Nathaniel thought the boy in the room was part of pain's mummery, or a fragment cut from the tail end of his earlier hallucinations, because Tomas looked exactly as Caitlin had, as if he'd been changed into a seal.

"Seals everywhere," he mumbled.

Tomas touched his shoulder and the room cohered.

"You're wet," said Nathaniel. He felt his son's matted hair, then his cheek. "You're cold."

Tomas shook his head "no" but his skin was dimpling in the air, and his thin-to-vanishing lips were drawn and white-rimmed.

Relieved of his solitude, if not of his pain, Nathaniel held his arm out for help.

Tomas eased his father back on the bed, pushing him down with enough gentle pressure to make it clear he should not try to move again. Then he sat on the bed beside his father with his back against the wall, a sentinel.

Nathaniel laughed weakly. He glanced over to the one door he'd seen open and then back at his son. *Home?* he asked silently. At this, Tomas looked perplexed. He blinked and glanced at his father's wounded foot. Nathaniel followed the boy's gaze.

The white bandage was dark with vivid red spots.

Wide-eyed, Tomas looked back to his father. Nathaniel sat halfway up off the bed, and, leaning heavily on one elbow, touched his son's cheek and nodded calmly. But his foot was throbbing. He hoped to hide it, *had* to hide it, if he wanted Tomas's help—and, if he'd already screwed Alice's good work, he decided that he might as well carry on through and go home.

But he'd never been able to hide anything from Tomas. The boy nearly growled, gave him to understand that he must not move, then leapt to the floor and left, slamming the door behind him. Nathaniel took a deep breath. Doggedly, he sat up.

"What was that thump?" asked Maria, unpacking the basket of new potatoes she'd brought up from her garden. She'd found Emily in the kitchen scrubbing vegetables and frying onions, which filled the air with their sweetness. "Is Tomas upstairs with Nate?"

"Not when I came in," said Emily. "Perhaps he's back now, though."

"Of course," said Maria, nodding and shedding a light jacket. "We went swimming."

"I wondered where he'd gotten to. Why did you take him off swimming? I thought you were working Christine's shift—"

"I was. I didn't take Tomas anywhere—he just showed up on the beach. Nate's okay, isn't he?"

"Yeah, he's fine. Asleep. But I was surprised to find him alone." She stepped over to the stove and gave the onions a turn.

Maria nodded. "Surprised me, too." She stretched and glanced over to the staircase. "I'd like to see Nate now."

"I don't know if he's awake."

"Has Alice been back?"

"No, not yet." Emily started paring a potato, shaving off more meat than skin. "But you know she *should* have been. I'd forgotten."

Maria nodded, frowning. "She didn't seem worried."

Emily gave her a dubious look and Maria glanced at the staircase. "I'd better see—"

"He's in the nursery."

"The *nursery*? Emily—"

"Easiest place to put him."

Maria headed up the stairs—only to find Tomas coming down them. He nearly threw himself into her arms, grasping her hand and pulling her; she followed hastily after him and—

"For god's sake, Nate!" she cried.

"Maria?" He looked up at her from all fours on the nursery floor and then looked away. "Damn."

"Charmed to see you, too," she said, stooping.

"Damn," he said again as Tomas tugged at him and signed to Maria. "All right, all right," he said, shaking his head. Under Tomas's arm, with Maria's help, he half staggered back to the narrow bed. She pulled the stool over to the bedside, sat down, and laid her hand flat across his brow. "You're sweating," she said in alarm.

"No kidding. I'm soaked."

Tomas took the empty pitcher and left. Nathaniel turned toward Maria.

"How do you feel?" she said.

"Hot," he said. "And hungry."

Maria smiled uneasily. "You're fine."

He sighed. "Feed a cold, starve a fever. I hope that's not what Alice has planned, because whatever's cooking downstairs smells great."

"Stew." She eyed his foot. "Should that be bleeding?"

"I don't know." He turned the foot over. "Hurts like hell."

"What did Alice say?"

He chuckled. " 'Don't move.' "

"And you promised you wouldn't."

He gave her a long, guilty glance. "Ah, Maria. You know me."

"Too well," she muttered, staring at the bloodied bandage. "Maybe I'll just jog to Alice's right now."

"Don't," he said. "Please. You know how Alice can get. I'm sure my guilt can wait to be discovered."

"For god's sake, Nate."

He sighed. "I know, I know, it was stupid."

"Jesus," she muttered, glancing around the room. She had caught a whiff of marijuana and soon found the pipe Alice had left. She sighed. "You scared me," she said softly.

"I've scared myself."

"Well, try to stay put."

He closed his eyes. "Truth is, I don't think I should stay here. If I could go home, it would be easier. Listen—speak on the sly to Alice about it, eh?"

Maria picked up the pipe. "Any left?"

"A hit or two. Shall I make you promise to speak with Alice before I say yes, take a hit?"

She laughed. "You're as bad as Lindi."

"What's that mean?"

"Blackmailing me. She tried it today."

"Maria?"

"All right, I'll talk to Alice for you. A light?"

"On the table. What was Lindi wheedling for?"

"A swim." She picked up a box of matches, lit the pipe, inhaled, and examined the matchbox. It was slim and flat, matte white embossed black, UNQC8. Exhaling, she said, "Where did these come from?"

"Alice."

She made a face. "That's not what I meant."

He yawned. "Of course not. But I don't know."

She put the matches back on the table. "Lindi said something odd today about Tomas."

"She did?"

Maria took a second hit, exhaled. "Claimed he could sing."

"What on earth—" Nathaniel said. "Sing?"

"Had me stumped."

"Lindi's got an imagination."

"So do you, Nate."

"Oh? Oh—but I'm not imagining the seals, Maria." He reached out and grasped her wrist, suddenly intense. "You walk the caves, the break. Tell me you haven't seen *something*."

Gently, she shook off his hand and said, "I've seen the children romping about."

"By the sea caves," he pressed.

"I . . . I don't go down there anymore—much anymore."

He nodded and turned over onto his back, flexing his hand and staring at the ceiling.

She stood up. "I don't go there anymore," she said again, though it was a lie.

"No."

She got up abruptly and pulled open the double doors that separated the main bedroom from the nursery. A few brisk steps took her over to the window. She slid aside the frayed curtain and gazed out, down across the cove.

Their little boys used to sleep on the floor of her cottage in the summer, while she and Nate had curled up together, quiet in the dark canyon of the bed. The comfort of Nate's arms and the passion of his legs about her had washed older sorrows out with the tide. Theirs had always been a wordless and nocturnal love, but after Carlo had gone, their love slipped into twilight. When Carlo went, the voices of her past that wept in the wind never seemed quiet and something in those silent nights with Nate grew frostbitten, left her nipped, amputated, afraid.

And then came jealousy. His living child with the beautiful gray-green eyes hurt her and took away her breath with the horrid question, why had Tomas lived, and not Carlo?

She leaned her forehead on her palm against the glass. She loved Emily's bedroom far more than any other space in Monkar, although she had been in it so seldom recently—too seldom. She loved it for its peaked ceiling, its frayed white curtains, the blue spread, and the vision of the cove from its windows.

The sun had still to set, but the moon was out, and the evening star. The sea wind shifted the scales of the water, the skin of the sea moved, and it made her think of the movement of her life, the movement of lives, entangled, blown by contrary winds. In the days when she had lain warm in Nathaniel's arms she'd never thought she'd need a different cove in which to anchor the hope of her passion.

"Maria?" called Nathaniel, softly.
She turned but did not answer him.

Nathaniel heard her but he could not see her. When she didn't answer, he closed his eyes. The sweetness of the marijuana smoke lingered. He drowsed and wondered, *If you could sing, Tomas, what would you sing of?*

"Would you sing," he murmured aloud, "*Arma Virumque Cano?*" He stopped and half-smiled to himself. The language was rusty, yet it was still in him, the Latin song of war and victory that Caitlin had disliked so much. Nathaniel closed his eyes, to see a man—not the man of arms, but a man armed with obsolescence, who had taught him a language of conquest in a time when such victory was impossible, when war had nothing to do with men-at-arms, or loving honor more than life.

Even when he was a child, the poetry had seemed to him bitterly false, a mocking lie. It hadn't mattered. Only the intricate puzzle of the language and the cadences of verse had mattered. Just as he had learned Latin, so, too, had he learned Japanese, Greek, Arabic, Spanish, Russian, Navajo, English, all these to play with the puzzle of alphabets and please his reloc teacher's autumn days. He was more than just good at it; but when he left the makeshift classroom, he talked only the argot of the reloc. Sometimes, before his mother died, he'd spoken French or Inuit with her. Sometimes, after her death, he would make an Inuit song to solace the spirit of her that lived on in him. And then, in Monkar, he'd found a new language to puzzle about—the strange random code in the papers they'd found in the ruin above town center. He'd tried cracking the code by various means and always failed. This failure always came back to two puzzling questions: UBAS must've been some kind of a name—but what did it name? And if the capital letters did form words, the language was repetitious and tediously limited. What language could be so barren?

But even this had stopped when he finally came to understand that all the languages he could ever learn would not help his child.

Tomas heard no tongue, he had no tongue. He never would.

Caitlin had raged. "Of all the sign-systems you know, why," she'd asked him, "why not the sign language of the deaf?" One had existed, she'd been told about it at an enclave trade by two Monkarians who'd settled on the other side of the lighthouse. After that, whenever someone made a rare foray to the Area, or even gone on simple Monkar trades, he'd searched or asked people to search for him—as he had asked of Ed this time. But he'd never been able to find it. He'd tried to teach Tomas to write—at least that—but the boy resisted, and slowly, after Caitlin's accident, father and son made their own language; they spoke in gestures, with looks, and, as Tomas had gotten older, they had moved toward a strange intensity, a knowing that Nathaniel had chalked up to the familiar and comfortable dance of everyday living. He yawned and sighed. He didn't know of what his child would sing if he could. Whatever it was, though, he knew it would be sweet and fierce.

While the stew simmered, and Maria lingered upstairs with Nathaniel, Emily slipped out the front door. She didn't want to think about what Maria and Nathaniel might say to one another. And she didn't want to remember—

Stillbirth.

She shook her head. Her own never-born sons. And poor little dead Carlo! Death had brought them, she and Maria, together, at quilting, or at the harrowing of the fields, over community meals and celebrations, then, later, over tea on cold winter mornings, or dancing to the racing drums Matty played—over far more things than Emily could find to share with Sean, or Maria could find to share with Nathaniel. Whenever Sean left to forage, Maria stayed with her in the empty house to keep away its ghosts. It had been so easy to sit together in a hug that was as light and as comforting to wear as a shawl on a cool night. When Maria finally kissed her, it was a relief—almost like having Linda back, though not, of course, not. Never that kind of absolute intimacy, a being together she could never bring into words. But when they had lain together on those first summer nights of their passion, Emily had trembled in Maria's hands, sometimes thinking too much of how she'd loved Linda and Sean, sometimes forgetting them altogether.

Summer delirious. She'd craved Maria, shuddered at the littlest touch.

Still, she did not leave Sean. She did not ask him to leave, either—her house or her bed. Maria had wept, at first.

And sometimes, Sean would come to her, come bounding up to her and his heat would rival the stove's. Urgency would seize her and she'd burn the potatoes, leave the supper cold. But her second stillbirth took this and it was to Maria she turned, not Sean.

"Did you notice?" she said softly to the evening air as she stood on the front porch.

"Notice what?"

Emily started and turned to see Maria framed by the screen door, the oil lamp light gentle behind her. "I was thinking of Linda," she said. "And Sean."

Maria stepped out. "Em, about the book—"

Emily shook her head and turned to watch the sun slink slowly toward its ocean bed. The shadows grew long over the beach, and the dilapidated dock and the black pebbles and rocks, the dune grass and the tracks of many feet marking the sand as if giant sandpipers had gone there in search of food. The heart of the day retreated.

"Em—"

"Here," said Emily. "Let's just sit for a minute." She gestured at the steps and then sat down at the top.

Maria followed, glancing across the wide, weedy lawn toward the road. "Where has Alice gotten to, I wonder?"

"Me too. I hope Serena's okay."

"Maybe she had her baby. It's possible—just barely."

"Could be," said Emily. Then she asked, "Maria, how do you talk to Tomas?" She cleared her throat. "I mean, if he's going to be here for a while—"

Maria chuckled. "I can't answer that."

"Why not?"

"Because I don't know how. We don't talk. I—I simply understand." She shrugged. "Watch Nate and Tomas together. You'll see. Stop trying."

Emily shook her head.

"I'm not being facetious."

"Stop trying? That's what my father used to say about love. Stop trying and you'll find it."

"So I've heard."

"Well," said Emily tightly. "I need to be able to talk to Tomas. Somehow."

Maria nodded, thinking. Finally, she said, "Earlier today I heard a cry. At first I thought—"

"—that it was Nathan," said Emily absently. "When he fell."

"I wonder if it was Tomas."

"*What?* I thought you just said—"

"I know what I said, but Tomas can make noises. As a baby, he used to have nightmares. He would thrash about, his eyes wide open. Nathan would shake him. But sometimes, he wouldn't wake up. Once, out of desperation, Nathan just doused him with a glass of water. I remember he cried out—"

"What did that sound like?"

"A bit like—" she hesitated, "—like what I heard today. A wail; a long, whistling wail." She tried to imitate it, but her voice shook and the sound died. "Higher."

"Higher? Like this?" Emily cleared her throat and stood. She was suddenly gripped by a tension of hope, of a perhaps, as she conjured up the music, her dream music, her night voices, and the sound she finally forced herself to make was so high and sharp and somehow grieving, it frightened her as it bounced off the hillside to echo back at them.

Maria caught her breath. "Yes," she said, "yes—almost *just* like that. Almost, almost exactly like that. It was *you*?"

"No. But . . . I've heard it. Often."

"So have I," said Maria angrily. "In my head, in my dreams. Carlo. He cried out to me—"

"Carlo?" said Emily, distressed. She sat back down and slid her arm around Maria, who leaned into the embrace. After a moment or two, Maria said, "Where have you heard that sound?"

Emily shifted. "I had thought lately that I was dreaming it. I mean, I've been hearing sounds like that—sometimes softer, more like music or even speech. I've thought—" She let go of Maria and rested back on her elbows. She said, "It reminds me of Aretina."

"Aretina? That's odd. Why?"

"Not her, exactly. More like some of her old, old stories."

Maria tilted her head. "Tell me."

Emily half-laughed. "You sure?"

"Go on. Please. It'll take my mind off Carlo."

Once there was a fishman who hadn't very much luck. All his fathers, all his brothers and his grandfather and his great-great grandfather, all of them, had been fishmen and had fed their families well. Why, fishmen's nets can lull the fish with their music! But he was unlucky.

Now, one day this unlucky fishman rowed to a tiny, tiny island he'd chanced to see. He had a strange feeling he would have good fortune there.

On the island, nothing much grew except a small, hardy grass, an herb that breathed a sharp sweetness as he walked over it. It covered the land thick and luxuriant, like land sea-weed.

He threw out his nets from this weedy shore, whispering his hope that his fortune could change—and so it did, because, hauling in, he found his net heavy with silver-scaled beauties of a succulent size. Overjoyed, he laid his catch in the grass and cast his net again. But, casting, he saw his catch wriggling back into the water—and plop! the fish were gone.

Now this was terrible. When he hauled in his full nets again, he laid the fishes even higher up in the grass, away from the water. But no sooner had he cast out, than he heard a tell-tale plop! plop!—and his catch was gone again.

On the third try, when the poor fishman laid his fishes in the grass to dry, instead of casting his net, he laid himself down nearby to watch over his silver beauties. They flopped about, wriggling and gasping just like any caught fish might, when suddenly their death throes stopped and, like small sea cows, they nibbled on the grass. In the next moment, they wriggled off toward the sea, almost as if they had legs, or as if the air had become water to them. And then they were gone.

Surprised and curious, he gathered up a bit of the herb and tasted it. The minute he swallowed the sharp sticky juice, he knew that he just had to go for a swim, that he'd just die, in fact, die of a longing so tremblingly intense that he felt it as lust, lust for the sea, and so he threw off his fishman's clothes, abandoned his net, and dove after the smart little fishes—plop!

Once he was deep in the sea's sweet embrace, his new-found passion worked a magic on him. His hair turned green, long and green, his skin turned a gray-blue, sleek and oily; he traded in his thighs for a forked tail with blue-green scales. He became, forever more, a true fishman: Glaucus, newborn child of a new domain, who—

The front door slammed behind them. Tomas dashed down the stairs and over the slope to the embankment, then the beach. He dove into the water, swam straight out, sur-faced, then back and forth, up the cove and down.

Emily stood; her whole body had gone cold.

"Strange," said Maria. "Your Glaucus has appeared."

"Yeah. I was thinking the same thing." She sat back down. "Should he really be out there? It'll be dark soon."

"Nathan has never worried. Besides, he stays in the cove."

Emily sighed. "I guess." She stared after him. "You'd almost think he'd heard me."

Maria inched close to whisper slow and soft in Emily's ear. "Maybe you've bewitched him."

"Oh, hush."

Tentative, Maria leaned closer.

Emily linked her arms around Maria's waist and rested her head against her shoulder. They watched the boy swim until the sun dropped its heavy gold into the sea; then, abandoning the porch, skipping more talk, they went inside. The cloudless night's cold came on slowly. Spring was giving way to summer.

On such cloudless nights, when the sea is nearly as still as lake water may be, the boy always goes down to the cove. The town of Monkar sleeps. This is when he goes.

Tonight there is a full moon. It makes his way easy to see, so he runs boldly across the damp sand into the surf. Circles of watery moonlight waver about his naked hips. He rises and stands there, swaying slightly with the undertow, gritting his teeth against the cold, his thin arms folded to his chest. The sea laps the pebbles off the shore and licks the rotted pilings of the old dock with tiny waves that are all foam and no force.

The boy looks around warily. He glances back at the low-roofed house above the cove. The house is unlit. He lifts his gaze, moving his sight farther up the coast. On a more distant hill, silhouetted by the moonlight, a tower of a building juts. It, too, is dark.

A cool wind blows. Across the bay, a night fog creeps along the peaks of the range beyond the cove. The boy shivers. He wades out farther, letting the sea hold him closer. A quick look back at the darkened house again and then, breathing deeply, he begins to sing—a quiet, piercing boy's soprano. It is a wandering sort of not-melody, shapeless as a cat's raucous love, yet mellifluous and, because gentle, jarring.

He makes an odd sight there, should anyone chance to see him standing in the water, with his head tilted back so that the moonlight finds the tendons in his throat and traces the shadows of their tension as he sings.

But it would be odder still to hear the music that answers the boy's. Pitched to his octave, echoing his not-melody, a low trilling comes back over the waters to him. The sound is neither an echo nor his own voice bouncing off the rugged bluffs. The boy leans forward.

The fragile answering chorus holds to his song. The boy wades out into the black glass of the sea until his shoulders dip and he cannot touch bottom. Drifting, he swims, his head bobbing with each stroke until he ducks below the surface. The moonlight rings spread away from where he'd been, until the ripples of his dive melt into the belt of a new wave and lace into bubbles on the sand.

The sky is cloudless, the sea quite still. As the sun dives down and brings on evening, he drifts in the water. He scans the empty beach, the unlighted house, the cove. He tilts his head as if to listen. Revolving slowly, he faces the dock and, high above it against the full moon, the lonely ruin. A brief, sharp, mournful tone of melancholy sounds, so full of longing that "melancholy" seems a pale word to use to capture it. He strikes out for the dock.

And then, suddenly, Tomas makes an oblique turn. Without breaking rhythm, he swims past the seaweed beds, beyond the safety of the cove, and out into the open sea.

winter's end

1

To Market, to Market, to Buy a
Fat Pig

(4:30 A.M.)

SEAN WOKE, KNOWING that he was missing something, know-ing it was almost too late—but for what? He woke to pitch-dark suffocation, the horror into which he'd fallen night after day, day after night. . . .

Or was it the same?

No.

A dream?

No.

There was a fragile grayish light filtering into the room. Suddenly, he knew this room, it was the same room he'd—they'd—left (and thinking of them, he knew now what, or rather who, he was missing) with so much idiotic unknowing (or so he thought of those days), a little less than a year ago. The familiarity of it, the safety of it, the clean smell of it forced relieved tears from him. He forced them back. He was with Sheila, safe. He'd been there for days. But it was a hard joy to trust.

He was not a deecee pincushion anymore. He would not

hear a distant moaning or a frothy thick cough, he would not smell . . .

He gagged, then sat up.

He glanced over at Christine. She'd been ill since they'd left the Area; she was huddled, with the curve of her back to him, asleep. He straightened his cramped shoulders, reached out to touch her, then stopped. His hand trembled. The tattooed letters on his palm seemed to waver in the half-light, their blue-black precision marred by his weakness. He clenched his hand and watched the shadows lying across Christine's back, to make sure she was still breathing.

Yes.

He reached for her.

A distinct, sharp clang pushed him to his feet in one sudden, terrified movement. Bile filled his mouth.

Now he could see that the gray light came in from the next room. The metallic sound stopped. He rose, pulled on trousers and a sweater, and edged cautiously to the door. Rubbing his face with both hands to clear his head, he stepped into the light.

The sharp clang that had frightened him sounded again. It came from the back hallway. The rear door to Sheila's hole-in-the-ground home was wide open, letting in the morning air. He could just see a metal-shaded lamp hanging from the jamb. In the gentle, predawn wind, it swung. The fanned shade struck the wooden door frame.

He blinked and slipped the pocket watch hung around his neck out from under his sweater. He'd slept only three hours. He rubbed his face again and half turned back; behind him, the miracle of clean blankets, and pillows and comfort, sleep . . .

Nightmares.

That's why he'd wakened. Pieces of nightmare erupted at him, now, again, as he stood at the door, a rough and ugly quilt of splintered, disconnected fears: falling from what seemed to be an endless cliff; a line of baggy, headless male corpses, all naked and flaccid with death. Needles. An arm decorated with lacy tight scars, holding an electric prod; a stinking metal room plastered with feces ceiling to floor . . . a child there, eating shit. Needles. And, later, Ed's eyes, darkening with incredulity as he . . . Sean gagged again and hurried down the hall, to the fresh air.

Just outside the open door, in a circlet of light, Sheila sat bundled in dark clothes on a long, broad rock—the same place where he and Chris had lingered the night before they'd left for the Area. They'd talked then, he remembered, of betrayal and abandonments. If he'd had even the smallest idea of what they'd been about to find—he shook his head and watched Sheila pour tea from a fire-red kettle. The cold air had a bite to it, a welcome, bitter salt tang. He shivered and stepped out.

Sheila glanced up sharply, her lined face catching the full lamp light. She was crying.

He stopped.

She cleared her throat. "Tea?"

"It's not day yet," he said slowly.

"No," she said, and shrugged. "But I couldn't sleep."

Sighing, he glanced beyond her to where the dunes began, the gleam of sand barely visible under a still bright and bare winter moon. The sand was a mere line, like a skinny, flat ghost or a ribbon-shroud of ancient linen, woven in and out and around the black trees, which hung a dark trellis of drooping conifer branches. The sea's distant, half-moaning sibilance made the dark seem denser, thicker. The only vividness was the red teapot.

"Smell it?" she said, making an audible sniff.

"The tea?" He frowned. "No."

"Not tea. The ocean. The salt. Seaweed drying on the shore. That deep, constant, wonderful rich. I need it," she said. "I was born by this sea. Can't imagine living far from it."

He leaned up against the rock, feeling weak. He half smiled and then sat down next to her. "I took Monkar for home. I should never have left."

"Is that an accusation?" she said mildly.

He eyed her. "Only against myself."

She looked away. Then she said, "I left Monkar because I had to. Just as you did. And Chris. Just as Jay and Ed did." The names dropped between them, as heavy as solid objects.

He shook his head and folded his arms across his chest.

"I didn't intend," she said quietly, "to stay away." She coughed and stared down at her hands. "But when Andros died? He—he was the last of those I really knew. And then, I found Ona."

"Ona?" he said, feeling cold. He glanced aside, then looked down at his feet. "But she wasn't—"

"—much company? Well, I was never much company myself."

He frowned. "What happened to her?"

"Nothing. Why?"

He froze. Then, carefully, he made himself calm and able to ask, "You mean she's still here? Where?"

"Around." Sheila shrugged. "Why?"

He forced himself to stand. "Where?"

Sheila shrugged again. "Sit down. Don't worry about Ona."

"How can you say that?"

"First, because I know where Ona is; second, because I know you will not be hurt."

Slowly, he sat down. His legs were trembling. "How can you be so sure?"

"Trust me." She nodded to him and he narrowed his eyes, wondering. But for the moment he held his tongue.

She yawned. "Monkar had become a haunted place for me. And I wanted to forget." She offered Sean her little teacup. He held it with both hands, afraid he would break it or spill the tea, his heart still racing with the knowledge that Ona was somewhere near, that she was not, as he'd imagined, gone.

Sheila took a deep breath. "Taste the new day! It makes up for not sleeping."

"New days," he said quietly, "have terrified me." When

she didn't reply, he added, "But this, right now, this is fine." He sat down again, handing back the teacup. "And the prospect of going home."

"My first memories of Monkar," she said, "aren't pleasant ones. The cove, especially up near what Andros took as his house, was littered in the morning with stuff that smelled neither sweet nor clean. Death. Dead stuff."

"Dead stuff," he echoed.

"The sea," she continued, "brought it. Such death that came up on that cove . . ." She swallowed. "Death without a story. I slept badly as a kid, if at all. Barbara didn't know what to do with me."

"Em . . . Emily never said it was like that—"

"She wouldn't remember." Sheila settled her back against the grassy wall of her home. "It only happened during those early years, long before Aretina brought Emily to us, long before Andros moved away from the square and on up the hill. I was just a baby."

"You knew Barbara well?"

Sheila made a small, slightly confused laugh. "That a real question? Sean? My older sister?"

"Your *sister*?"

"You didn't *know*?" Sheila focused on him, recalled from her memories by his ignorance. "Now that," she said, "truly surprises me. You aren't joking?"

"No," he said and rubbed his forehead. "It's hard for me to believe, but no, I had no idea. So that means you're Maria's—"

"—aunt. Great-aunt. After Barbara's son, and his twins, died during that year that took all the boys, she set great store by little Maria. I didn't like the child; Barbara used to say that I was just jealous. Maybe I was."

"Vibrant," he said absently. "I mean Barbara. That's how Andros described her to me. I wondered if one person could contain such energy."

"She couldn't. I sometimes think Monkar itself exists as

proof of that. She made us live. She—and Eldon, Mejgan, Jan-ice, Serena . . . Andros . . ." She broke off. "The dead."

"Have you heard from home, since . . . since we left you?"

"No." She sighed. "I wish I had."

"Nothing?"

She sipped at the cooled tea. "What are you asking me?"

"For news."

"About Emily?"

"She was fine," he said flatly. "When I left her. But that was a long, long time ago."

Sheila said gently, "Not so long."

"Maybe not to you."

She stood up and threw out the cold dregs. "I'm sorry," she said. "I should have gone with you."

"What for? To die?" He closed his eyes.

"The best route—"

He laughed. "We took it."

"But I know how to maneuver, to wheedle and bribe the introduct, to bargain and trade, to lie—"

"So did Ed." Sean opened his eyes and stared at her. "You taught him, didn't you? You told him everything he needed to know—he said you had. It made no difference."

She didn't speak.

"It made no difference," he repeated, staring at her with a gentle intensity. "We were lost the minute we found Linda. She gave us up."

"Did she? Well. I'm going with you today."

He started. "What?"

"It's time," she said. "Ed was right about it being risky here. Besides, it's time for me to face up to what I ran from. Time to go home."

"You're coming with us?" He smiled widely. "I'm glad. Really."

"Good. I've been thinking on it. I wasn't sure. Now I am. It's been hard."

He nodded. "Because it's too late for Ona, isn't it?"

"Too late?" she said. "Maybe it's too early. But Ona will go where I go."

He stared at her, speechless with horror.

Sheila didn't seem to notice. She said merely, "I need some sleep before the sun's up. If I can get it."

"You can't—" he managed.

"Can't?" Sheila turned towards him. "Can't what? Sleep?"

"You can't think of bringing it to Monkar."

"What?"

"You heard me."

"I see." Sheila sighed. "We have to talk."

"Nothing to discuss."

"You're wrong." She stood up. "But I can't talk about this half asleep." She offered him the teacup and pot. "You want to finish it?"

"I want to know," he said, "where Ona is."

"Safe. From you, it would appear."

"Sheila!"

"I asked you to trust me. And I warn you, Sean. Please. Leave Ona be." With that she left him in the semidark with the tea.

He stared after her, stricken with cold fear. Sheila clearly didn't understand. He shivered and drank the tea. Here he'd been thinking for the past few days that Ona had died; he should have asked! Now, it was up to him to get himself and Chris—and Sheila if he could get through to her—out of there.

Unless—

Maybe he'd been wrong?

Troubled, Sean watched the fog drift, swirling inland from the beach, between the trees. The stars were all but hidden, and the moon had become a mere brightened patch in the distance. Despite his anxiety, he began to drowse. When he'd caught himself nodding for the third time, he leaned back, placing the teacup down with a sleepy gentleness. He stretched his legs out. Something nearby scrambled for cover.

A rat?

Or Ona?

He bolted to his feet, then stopped. Shaking convulsively, he forced himself to breathe deeply and slowly.

A rat, he told himself. *And only one. Rats are not likely to be swarming here.*

"Just one," he muttered aloud, sitting.

"**R**odents survive," JP had said. "They can get by on scarce food and ruined water." Sean could almost hear his voice, the memory was so forceful; they'd been talking just after sunrise on the last morning that their world had been still in one piece.

He remembered how—

Fog had again drifted into their camp, muffling them in a pale wrap as it had every morning, quieting the glow of the breakfast fire. Sean had taken the last watch, while the other three slept. He'd tended the fire, drinking tea—as he was doing now—and had watched the fog shapes drift and dive and swirl. The sun was all but hidden, not more than a brightened patch.

He'd been jumpy, irritable. They were within two miles of the Area's perimeter—within a mile of the spot where Ed had seen Linda. They could see the remains of the magnificent but structurally unusable bridge, the ragged teeth of the cityscape beyond it. Flat, black zip barges dotted the waters below them. The bay. He'd remembered it, the place he'd been born, so very dimly he could hardly believe it was real.

For some reason, JP had waked. He'd turned over and rolled onto his feet all in one swift and sure move, a practiced and instant waking after days and days of short sleep and a constant care. They were all worn thin, but not to frailty, just wiry thin, although Sean could not remember back to that morning before the world ended without an overlay of JP as the living skeleton he had become shortly before he'd died.

Horribly, then, the two of them had talked of rats. The closer they'd gotten to the Area, the fewer trolls and the more rats they'd seen. JP had said, "Rats are sturdier than children."

"Like mine?" Sean had snapped. "Or Linda's?"

JP shook his head, slow and weary. "No. If you stopped to think about it, we've all lost children. Not just Linda. Or you." He'd glanced over to Christine and Ed for emphasis, then asked, "And if your kids had survived?"

"Maybe," he said stonily, "Linda wouldn't have left."

"Left?" said JP. "How do you know—why do you say she *left*?"

He shrugged. "I don't know."

"Left," said JP nervously. He shook his head. "Sean, what if—what if her kids had been as bad off as Carlo—or even Tomas? Jiro? Lindi? What then?"

Sean stirred, to fend off the remembered conversation. He stared at the red kettle, trying to hold on to its shiny blare as an anchor to the present. Trying and failing.

Linda had talked a lot about having a child. It had been brave talk and he'd made promises as pretty as the butterflies his mother had said she'd chased as a child.

Sean finished the tea. He'd never seen a butterfly.

And his mother had said angrily to his father, "There's no place to hide from pestilence. Pestilence is deaf and dumb and very, very patient."

The day before the trolls had come, she'd said this. It was one of the few things he remembered of those last days at home. And now, after being himself so harrowed as scarcely to know what the word *self* might mean, he heard her voice in the back of his head, constant, angry, and provokingly monotonous. And now, after losing her, and his father, and Terence, after losing Linda thrice, after spending night after night with only the stinking, eaten remains of a man he'd learned to love, and there seemed to be nothing left in the world but JF's death, and darkness, her words had come back to him and her voice had stayed on, always with him, a haunting, unshared litany of despair—"pestilence is deaf and dumb and very, very patient."

He must have fallen asleep. He was splayed out on the ground on his stomach. The red teapot was knocked over and the tea leaves had soaked, cold, into the dirt at his side.

He was about to heave himself up when, to his shock, he found Ona staring at him. She ran off at a clip that carried her far across the matted grass and out toward the dunes before he'd the time to breathe.

He sprang to his feet and ran after her.

She was easy to follow. Even in the faint light her trail was unmistakable, her curved footprints with their long toes the only marks in the expanse of wind-smoothed sand. The prints tracked solitary up over the dunes. He followed them out to the exposed flat of the low-tide shore, where they dotted the sand almost to the water, then away, a string that looped toward a tangle of rocks planted in the middle of the otherwise empty beach. The prints disappeared around the rocks. There was no Ona attached to them.

Jogging slowly, attentive with fear and aware of every jolt to his underfed body, Sean followed Ona's track. The lively salt wind slapped him. He bent his head and folded his arms tightly across his sweatered chest, until he reached the lee shelter of the rocks.

No Ona. Her footprints dashed from where he stood, to the back of the hill before him. Doggedly he went on in their wake, around and down into a rock arch. It was almost as deep as a true cave, with a weedy roof of barnacles, anenomes, and seaweeds as fine as wire. Beneath that roof enough night chill had been captured and held to make his breath steam, as if the verge of winter had visited. He eased through the narrow way. He was afraid to stumble suddenly upon Ona in the cramped cold—afraid but determined. Having come this far, he had to know if she was how he thought she was. Knowing absolutely, he could help Sheila understand—if she didn't. Well, she couldn't really, or she'd never suggest bringing it to Monkar! He nodded to himself. He would have to help Sheila understand, so that she could leave Ona to the death that had already begun to take her.

At the arch's end, he cautiously poked his head out. A roil of whitecaps broke against the tip of the rock, and he eased back. Glancing up, he found Ona, perched at the edge of the arch above him.

She had her back to him, and the rush of the sea was so loud there, he knew she would not hear him if he tried to call. She sat motionless, the cabling of her sweater stretched tight over her knees. Her dense mass of curly hair was blown nearly flat by the wind's force until she gathered it back, twisting it into an incomplete knot at the nape of her neck.

He waited, watching.

She leaned forward. Straining over the bare rocks, tensed, she reached out as if to hold the water or lift a wave, as if to embrace the sea.

Sean eased himself to the other side of the arch to get a clear view. Maddeningly, his angle of vision was no better.

She lifted her head a little; the knot in her hair broke loose and she seemed to break away with it, collapsing forward, vanishing from his sight.

Damn! he thought and retreated to the archway. Breathing hard, he hastened back the way he'd come, hoping to find a path around the arch and down to the shore from there. But before he reached the dunes, he heard a hobbling series of moaning, high-pitched, almost musical cries. Instantly, he branched off the doubled trail of footprints to walk the beach at the water's edge, with the wind at his back and his eyes trained on the water. He strode for a while as the sun rose, hoping to catch sight of them, one of those he'd come to know, and to hate.

Finally, disappointed in his search, he moved up the beach toward the house. Those cries had given him the knowledge that he had needed.

Grimly, he thought, *It **is** too late for Ona.*

He put his shoulder to the wind. He bent his head low. As he passed the outcropping again, Ona was standing there, sweatered and small. She darted out of sight.

Shivering, he shrugged and headed back to the house in the ground. There was no need for him to risk himself anymore.

When he reached the door, the fire-red teapot and the teacup were gone and only a wet patch of tea leaves left. The door was open. He stepped inside, shutting the door after himself carefully. He took a few steps.

Ona sat cross-legged in the dim light on the floor of the hall.

Wholly startled, he froze.

She stood up. Her dark, downy face was wet, her hair dripping lank over her eyes. Yet she stared at him.

He started inching away.

She did not move.

He fumbled for the door handle behind him.

She gasped, taking rough hold of his wrist. She made a small noise, a short, whistling moan, and he reared away, banging his shoulder on the wall, astonished that he could not break her grip. She held him and leaned close, so close he could taste her, the salt and sea and sweat of her and when she shook back her hair and blinked, he saw that her eyes seemed to be only shine, shining blankness, no color, no iris, nothing but shine.

He tried to scream but couldn't. He tried to move but was held by more than her grip; he was held in a kind of dazed trance by something like an emotion—it wasn't his own, and it wasn't fear. It was—fascination?

She let go.

By the time he came back to himself and could breathe again, she'd disappeared up the hall. He checked his wrist for scratches and, finding none, he slid down to the floor, his thighs shaking. "Jesus," he muttered. The shaking took over his whole body and he sat for a few moments unable to stop, the blood pounding in his temples. He was tingling all over.

When he moved at last, he moved as if crippled. He felt assaulted by what he kept trying to forget, to dodge and slice up, mentally zigzagging for escape routes.

Zig. "Linda! Linda!" He had called to her loud and urgent through the Plexiglas as she walked away. He'd screamed her name over and over until he'd been tranked to make him stop.

Zag. Roused violently, he was handed a shovel, he found himself on a shore, couldn't tell where. The burst of pure cold salty air pummeled him into something like consciousness.

Zig. Headlights.

Zag. Faceless protective gear. Gloves. Flashlights flickering light up and down bedraggled ranks. He stood there with the shovel they'd handed him. Far down the line, JP.

Zig. The hole they dug in the firm sand seemed to go on forever; he was sure they were digging their own grave. It was only when the sun came up that he saw what they'd been sent to bury.

At the water's edge, in one ragged large cluster and a smaller pile, lay the slaughtered. They had to have been slaughtered, there on the sand holding onto one another, and the black slides of dark blood pooled under the bodies, and the guards standing nearby, their weapons at the ready as if the dead might escape, or as if the threat of death might be held at bay. But as he watched, he saw the reason for which the guards were really there.

From the largest pile, a figure detached itself. At first, it might simply have rolled aside with the unseen mobility of sheer gravity, the unmotivated ambulation of an object. It lay aside from the pile long moments still. No one and nothing else moved out there, except for the calm rise of the tide.

Sean dug.

One of the guards walked down the beach a little.

The sea touched the object, rolling it to one side.

Ever so slightly, it resisted the roll.

The guard hurried closer.

When the tide came back in, the object rose with it, making an awkward lunge after the tide's retreat, staggering. The guard took aim as the figure rose again and lurched toward the vanishing whitecaps, this time running at a burst, a full forward grace. A high, shrieking cry and a sharp-smelling, frying retort stopped the dig for a moment.

Propelled forward, the figure dove free into the waves.

Soon, they were ordered out of the sandy pit, to retrieve the dead. Marching, Sean managed to angle his way over to JP, who gave him a glassy stare as they approached the pile.

It was then that the object washed back in with the tide. Forced to retrieve it, Sean found a burned, bloody, and mangled death; what was left of muscled limbs and a long torso, thickly covered with fine hair so slick with blood it was bluish; a flat, oval face contorted into a grimace; greenish-brown eyes wide open but dulled by a fast-clouding, once-clear secondary lid.

In Sheila's kitchen, Chris sat near Sean, her lowered eyes lidded with tears. He put his arm around her. Sheila stood in front of the fire pit with her back to both of them.

"I say Ona is a child." Sheila spoke calmly, quietly. "Not dangerous—just growing up. That's all."

Ona walked in and Sheila said, "They won't hurt you."

Angry, Sean said, "I'd think you'd be more concerned about protecting us from her."

Ona glanced from Sheila to Sean, then sharply at Chris, who seemed to curl back into herself.

"It's all right," said Sheila.

Sean watched Ona as she walked over to the storage cellar. She carried an empty sack. She knelt and began filling the sack with edible roots—carrots, turnips, beets, onions. Sean stared.

As if sensing his attention, Ona half-turned from her now bulging sack and in an annoyingly high, unadept singsong, said, "To market, to market, to buy a fat pig—"

Chris make a brief, strangled sound.

Ona hefted the sack. She whined, "To market, to market, to buy a fat pig—"

"What the hell," muttered Sean.

Ona parted her tangled hair. "Home again, home again, jiggity, jig!" she finished, and darted out of the kitchen.

"Jesus," muttered Sean.

"Nursery rhymes," said Sheila. "I told you. Ona is a child."

"She's no child now," said Sean. "She's—" He made a gesture of confusion. "She's becoming an animal. And then she'll die."

"We're all animals."

He shook his head. "Not like that. Not . . . bestial," he said awkwardly. "Not deadly."

Sheila laughed so hard that Christine jumped. "You aren't?" said the older woman, still laughing.

He held onto himself, to keep from screaming. He had to be patient. Clearly, Sheila didn't understand. He said in an even, wretched tone, "Listen to me. I watched JP die slowly after he'd been attacked by one of them—and he died like . . . like one of them. I don't know how it happens, but JP died frothing and foaming and looking like one of them. It's ubes— or they are." He glanced toward the room into which Ona had vanished. "She is. On the beach, I heard them. And she was out there, with them. She'll kill you, Sheila. Eventually."

Sheila's manner shifted to somber. "Urban lies," she said flatly. "Scare tactics. Besides—"

"Truth," said Sean, interrupting her. "And I saw enough to be scared for the rest of my life."

Sheila glanced over to Chris. "And you? What do you see?"

Chris shook her lowered head and closed her eyes.

"How long?" asked Sheila. "How long has she been like that?"

Sean took one of Chris's hands in his. "She hasn't said a word since I got away from the deecees and told her what happened to JP." He shook his head. "She knew he was dead. The deecees had told her that much. When she and Ed got me out, she knew he was gone. But she wanted to know how." He chafed her hand. "I shouldn't have told her, I guess." He glanced at Sheila. "I was just lucky. JP wasn't."

"And Linda. And Ed. They weren't lucky either?"

"No."

"What happened to them?"

"I can't," he said, slowly. "I can't talk about that yet."

"You can talk about JP," said Sheila harshly.

"I—" He let go of Chris's hand suddenly, and stood up. "You are . . . you are . . . you have it," he said, trembling. "Don't you? Ubes! You're infected. You're dying."

Sheila looked steadily back at him. "Yes, I'm dying, Sean."

He took a deep breath. "All right. That explains everything. And I'm very sorry for you, Sheila, but don't come near us. Or Monkar. Chris and I will be leaving now."

Sheila sat down and folded her hands on the table. "We're all dying."

"Oh, yeah," he said. "But not like dogs."

"No," she said evenly. "I'm not a dog and neither is Ona. And we can't give you—or Monkar—something it already has. Something it already is."

"Monkar?" Linda had said calmly. "Don't you see that's where ubes might have begun?"

Sean remembered how she had sat there, so composed, smaller than he remembered, and her lovely long hair uncropped, sleek, lovely. She was so like Chris and yet, to him, so absolutely different. She was breaking his heart sitting there. She said, "I eat. I sleep. I have work. Soon, I'll have a safer place to live, a protected place." Her voice came small through the Plexiglas, and its thick distortion made her seem no more real than the dreams he'd had of her. Was still having of her.

But she was no dream. After getting past the deecees, they had found her in the sprawl of the Area-run reloc at the edge of the bay. She was on road repair detail until her i.d. was okayed and she was cleared to move across the bay. And finding her, he had glimpsed his redemption—a chance to end his old nightmare's awful outcome, a chance to have Linda back. He'd embraced her, he'd embraced this new dream—even after she had betrayed them all.

Suddenly she leaned toward him and whispered, "Chris and Ed got away."

"No thanks to you."

"I know. I may have—I may have made a mistake." She swallowed. "Just don't worry about them."

"You expect me to believe you?"

"No," she said. "But—I think they're safe."

"As safe as I am? As safe as JP?" he said, touching the Plexiglas. "All right. How do we get out of here?"

"I'm working on that," she said, leaning back in her chair again. "Your blood tests aren't done."

"And then?"

"That depends," she said. "If you don't have it, you can stay with me. If you do—"

"I don't want to stay, Linda. I want to go home. Don't you?"

"Yes," she said. "I've wanted a home."

"Monkar is better than this," he said with disgust, glancing around. "You know it is. And you should see how it's grown."

"Monkar is a dead-town."

He closed his eyes in frustration. "You knew that, Linda. We all did. That isn't why you left."

"No. It isn't. But I've made a home here," she said.

"And Monkar?"

She looked at him for a few long minutes, then whispered, "I . . . I traded."

"Traded?" He made a fist. "Are you telling me you *were* traded? Sheila said something about people trading children—"

"It doesn't matter." She glanced behind her and nodded. "I can't explain—"

"Linda," he said, "get me out of here. They're bleeding me dry, and they've taken enough—" he stopped and then raised his eyes, feeling his face redden with anger. "They want sperm—"

"They're just making sure," she said smoothly, soothingly.

"Of what? What in the hell did you tell them?"

"If you're not ubes—they'll let you go."

"Whatever that is. And if they decide I am? Then what?"

"Monkar is a dead-town," she said, raising her voice slightly. "I hope you don't have it." She pushed back her chair. "I have to leave now."

"Don't—"

"I'll come back."

"Linda—" He pounded on the Plexiglas. "Linda! Linda!" He had called to her, loud and urgent. He'd screamed her name over and over until he'd been tranked to make him stop.

"I am not ubes," he said to Sheila. "Or I'd be dead. All of Monkar would be dead. So just keep away from us." He put his hand out to Chris, but she'd ducked into the next room.

"I'm coming home," said Sheila. "With you, this morning, or without. It doesn't matter."

"Without," he said. "And I'm telling you to keep away."

"You're being foolish."

"I don't think so."

"Ed knew."

He watched her. She didn't seem ill. Yet she'd said she

was—and there was the proof of Ona. "Of course," he said. "Ed knew."

"We're all 'dying,' Sean. Monkar as it is now will die. Just as it had died once before, when it had the name UBAS."

"Ubes?" He made a quick laugh to humor her craziness. He could hear Chris packing—they would be out of there soon. He said, "Sure. Sure it will. Look, Sheila, maybe you don't have it. In that case, why not come to Monkar with us?" He lowered his voice. "Just leave Ona here. As you've said, she can take care of herself."

"What good would that do? Ona would follow. Besides, it's no different here than in Monkar."

"You brought Ona up from the Area, didn't you? How do you know she didn't have it from there—"

Sheila sighed. "Ed didn't believe my story about trading for Ona. Why did you?"

"I didn't." Sean paused. "I respected Ed's silence."

"I see."

"Well?"

"Trade."

"What?"

"Trade. You tell me about Ed. I'll tell you about Ona."

Chris appeared, her pack in place, his in hand. He took it from her, and slung it on one shoulder. "I already know what Ona is," he said. "Just keep it away from Monkar."

"You're a fool," she said, dead quiet. "You ask but you don't want to understand, do you?" She glanced over to Chris. "*You* know what I'm talking about."

"Leave us alone, Sheila," said Sean. "I ask, and you answer in riddles. I know what I need to know. Stay away from Monkar. I'm warning you."

Chris stood still, as if Sheila had pinned her to the wall.

Sean glanced from one woman to the other. "Chris?"

Sheila nodded slowly. "When you found Linda, she said she had a child. As I do, now."

"You do," said Sean, then stopped himself to listen to her.

Yet, even before she spoke, he thought he knew what she was going to say, yes, he thought, *I know what she is going to say,* and then she was saying it—Ona was Linda's child. And . . . his?

"I'm the one," said Sheila, "who brought Linda south in the first place. She'd come to me, from Monkar, when she was sure she was pregnant. She told me that JP knew."

"JP?" cried Sean. "All these years? That fucking little *bastard*! And you—"

"He's dead," said Sheila. "Isn't he? And she'd *made* him promise his silence. So don't slander Jay's memory. Linda came to me. She ran from Monkar and asked me to take her back to the Area. She'd said, 'Take me home. I want my child to live.' She was afraid. In the Area, she thought, there must be a way to insure that her baby wouldn't be born like Tomas or Carlo. I didn't blame her. We'd lost so many, hadn't we?" She raised her brows. "I didn't know you, Sean. I knew Linda. I did—and I've done—what she wanted me to do. Ed found her by sheer accident. I wish he hadn't. I tried talking him out of telling you."

Sean's heart contracted to a hard knot. "Are you the one who traded her?"

"Traded?" Sheila shook her head. "Traded *her*? I know she'd cut a deal with the deecees. That's how I got in and out. Who told you that I traded *her*?"

"She did."

"What?" Sheila glanced at Chris. "You told him I traded *you*? What in the world for? Why?"

Sean swung around. Chris was still standing stock-still against the wall. He looked at her carefully, slowly, then turned back to Sheila, thinking that the older woman must be far more ill than she seemed. He said, "Go on. Tell me the rest."

She shrugged. "The rest of the story was almost true. Ona did come out here with me—when the child was old enough to start becoming too much what you call 'ubes' to hide it.

Linda stayed. She was still trying, you see, to find a cure for Ona. But I've finally decided—I finally believe—that there is no cure because there is no cure for being what you are. Ona isn't curable because Ona is the future. Ours. Our future. Profoundly different, but ours nonetheless. All the children will be like Ona. That's why I'm going back to Monkar—to see for myself if I'm right. I haven't wanted to believe, but you'll soon see for yourself, as I expect to." Sheila nodded at Chris. "You know I'm telling the truth, don't you? Something happened in the Area to make you stop looking for a cure. Isn't that why you've come home? Was it something Ed spoke of—or was it Chris?"

Sean stepped back, his head spinning. "Chris can't speak."

Sheila didn't move. "I don't think," she said slowly, "that I've been talking to Christine—or that I'm talking to her now. And although it may very well be that Christine can't speak to me, I think that Linda can. Can't you?"

One of the twins—*it's Chris,* thought Sean, *of course it's Chris*—looked steadily at Sheila. Although she hadn't spoken for what had seemed to Sean forever, she did now. She said, "Yes."

"What the hell happened, Linda? Where's Chris—where's Ed? Chris?" said Sean, his voice uneven.

The woman he thought was Christine glanced at him. "I'm Linda," she said. "Don't you know me? Can't you see me, now?"

2

Storm Front

(6:00 A.M.)

A QUIET TIDE shoots to land, goes out, comes in. It is a cloudless dawn, heavy with moisture. The low-roofed house is dark. A half-moon hangs overhead, flat and white against a dim sky just hardening into blue brilliance. Stealthy, the tide goes out and comes in again. Phosphorous trails, like miniature comet tracks, coruscate the unquiet face of the still dark waters. A faint, musical trilling hovers, too steady and too loud to be the sea. Abruptly, it stops. The tide goes out, comes in. Folded within its froth and flourish, thriving, they are borne.

Inside the low-roofed house above the beach, Tomas sat on the master bedroom floor beside the closed double doors to the nursery. He held onto a steaming mug of tea and wore a green blanket as if wrapped in a cocoon, with only his head peeking out. He, and the blanket, were soaked.

From Emily's bed, Nathaniel watched his son. After a moment or two of watching, he sat up and pushed aside the blue down quilt. Emily slept. He made a gesture to Tomas, then another, to ask, as he had been asking over the past several mornings, "Where do you go, where have you been all night?"

Tomas took a long sip from the mug.

Nathaniel sighed, watching his son—whose lowered gaze seemed fixed on the rim of the cup. He'd been awake for some time, according to the rusty alarm clock by the bed. He'd been waiting, staring at the dark ceiling and waiting for Tomas to return. He'd been waiting to ask yet again, "Where, where have you gone, where do you go?"

Tomas stood up, hauling with him the damp green cocoon and mug. He trailed across the room, and looked down at Emily, sleeping. Nathaniel held out his hand, but Tomas dodged the touch. He turned and left.

Nathaniel watched him, thinking that he should resent this, being given no answers, but he found that he didn't, no, not really, not that morning. He was too worn out from all the work of the past several weeks, harvesting seaweeds, wrangling with council, spackling for Alice, rebuilding the boat. He didn't want to move just yet, he didn't want to care about anything just yet, didn't want to ask Tomas again where the hell he'd been last night, and the night before, and the night before that, slipping out from the house each night, Nathan had come to believe, ever since he'd decided to stay on with Emily.

But, he told himself, *it's good to know Tomas can do for himself, even if it took a broken ankle for me to let myself see just how much—*

"He's grown," said Emily, yawning.

"You're awake," he said, laughing. "Mind reader."

She turned over onto her back and gazed up at him. He took a deep breath, surprised that she could still catch at him like that, catch him with a rough, almost raw pleasure. "Emily," he said, touching her lightly.

"What?"

He laughed. "Oh, nothing."

She propped herself up on her elbows a little and frowned. "Are you being kicked?" he asked.

"Not yet." She laid a hand flat on the pregnant swell of her waist. "Tomas—he's not a boy anymore." Her voice dropped. "He's not been a boy for some time."

"No," he said. "I just hadn't—wasn't paying attention. I was too busy chasing after all the day-to-day things."

"But attention *is* chasing after day-to-day things," she said, yawning again. "I feel like a big, old rock already."

"Patience," Nathaniel replied softly, chafing the back of her hand, running his fingers over the old gem in the ring he'd given her—Caitlin's ring, although he wasn't ready to tell her that yet, not just yet.

"Easy for you to say. What time is it?"

"Early. Before seven."

"And what time do you leave?"

"I'm to meet Ki at the boat in twenty minutes."

She sat up, shivering, and reached for her tunic. "I wish you wouldn't do this."

"I know. But I've learned my lesson." He lifted his foot under the sheet. "I'm the soul of caution. No more broken bones."

"Will Tomas and Jiro go out with you?"

"No. As you said, they're not boys anymore."

"Nate?" She sat back down on the bed.

He made a small laugh. "I miss him."

"He's not gone. Wasn't he just here?"

"Yes."

"So? He's still—" she looked away, "—young."

"As am I," said Nathaniel. "Sometimes, so am I."

"Don't I know it!"

"And you?" He murmured, holding her hand tightly. "You were so young and lost, Em, when I first moved in here."

"Was I?" She shook her head. "Was I?"

He leaned back and raised his brows. "Emily."

"What?"

"I wish you wouldn't mind so much. It's a good thing, if we can land a seal, prove they're here."

"Is it?"

"Oh, come on. You know it is."

She shook her head. "I'm afraid I don't. If there are seals out there, Nate—*if*—why hunt them?"

"Christ, I'm not talking about slaughter, Em. I'm talking about knowing, that's all. It might make next winter a little less hard for us."

"It wasn't that horrible this winter," she said. "And it's nearly over."

He let go of her hand. "It is." He hesitated. "I know."

She sighed. "And you know what I'm thinking, now, don't you? They're not coming back, are they? They're not coming back."

He held his breath for a moment, then let it out. "Sandra and George have given up."

She grimaced. "I haven't had the courage to talk to Sandra. We've talked about Jett. Not about—"

"Maybe you should."

"Maybe. Have you—have you been to Maria's lately? Spoken to her?"

He shook his head. "No."

"No?" She folded her hands and looked down at them, as if, folded, they were unusually engaging to her.

He stirred and smoothed out the blue blanket again. "She's still angry. She's still hurt that you and I—"

"Is she?" Emily pulled up the fraying collar on her tunic. "Not with me."

He shrugged. "She suddenly started to argue about the boat. Nobody thought twice about it until she started—"

"Nate, I didn't think it such a good idea, either. Not so soon after being as sick as you were. I thought you should wait to start working—"

"Yes, but you didn't say at council that I'm unbalanced."

"That's not fair. That's not what she's said." She paused. "I asked her to visit with me today. Here."

He didn't reply.

"She doesn't believe you," Emily said gently. "She never has. About the seals. Most people can't—"

"And you?"

She stepped up to the window above her sea chest and lifted the curtains, glancing out. "I'm not sure what I believe."

"Why? Because you've seen something?"

"I told you. A while ago, I used to hear . . . cries. At night." She dropped the curtain and turned to face him. She'd gotten herself to believe that the voices of her dreams had been only dreams, built on the fragile, sometimes frightening, sounds that Tomas could make. She'd come to accept the fact that it had been Tomas weaving cries into her dreams where the sound had become something less prosaic than the voice of a deaf-mute—it was she, only she, who had made his voice into a choir of murmuring promise, a solace of magic, the speech of the fabulous fishman, Glaucus.

What could she have said to Nathaniel? How could she have told him—and how, how could she possibly tell him now—that his son was the stuff of her dreams? Especially now that! She closed her eyes tightly—

"—not barking, though," Nathaniel was saying. "Not like seals are supposed to sound."

"No."

"And? Have you heard it again?"

She decided to change the subject. "You know Ki just wanted a fishing boat."

He frowned and got up from the bed. "Then this morning shouldn't matter." He reached for his shirt. "We're not going to hunt seals, we're just fishing." He finished dressing and lifted an already packed knapsack from the bedside. "I'll be home before dark," he said. "Maria won't be here, will she?"

"No, but I've asked Alice up for supper tonight."

"Good."

"Be careful."

"Promise."

After Nathaniel had gone, Emily stood at her bedroom window, holding in her anxiety. She pulled the curtains aside, and watched Nathaniel climb down to the cove. He still had a limp from his fall. She sat on her sea chest, staring out the window at the blustery, dark morning, and at the expanse of land that he had crossed, left empty.

Then, swiftly decisive, she stood, opened the sea chest, and lifted a blanket. Underneath lay her heart-shaped pouch, where she'd left it so many months ago. She took it out, closed the sea chest. Settling herself in a rocking chair, she pulled at the pouch strings and the flap that held it shut.

The inlaid gold Greek cross her great-grandmother had given her sat in its nest of blue fabric, the same blue cotton of which she had sewn her comforter, a cool, fierce color that always made her think of Aretina. Aretina had given the most tenacious love to Emily, a love both unspoken and as loud as a roar, a love of such ancient-seeming dimension and such unshakable, if critical, permanence that Emily thought she'd never really known true, complete love since.

That thought stung her—for on the right side of the pouch, where Sean's watch should have been—his father's, then his brother's, silver pocket watch—there was nothing. The right side of her heart-shaped pouch was empty, the ventricle chamber drained. All this time and she had not looked, had not known.

A slight sound, close and intimate, startled her back to her feet. She put the pouch down on the rocking chair. Tomas had returned, dressed now in trousers and huge, baggy top, his thick, spongy hair tied back from his face. He stood in the doorway.

Emily took a deep, trembling breath, as Tomas's gaze seemed to eat her up, take her, hold her....

He continued to stand in the doorway.

She was held by his gaze, as he seemed to gather stillness,

to become as motionless as furniture, watching.

Painfully, she turned to the window and peered out. "Why didn't you go fishing?" she murmured aloud in a weary voice, though of course he would neither hear, nor respond. "Are you too old for such foolishness? God. I wish Nathan was." She turned back around.

Tomas came in the room and seated himself on the rucked sheets, one leg dangling. He was not watching her anymore, but staring at his own swinging foot, his gold-brown hair loosened and fallen forward. He looked as if made only of light, perched upon the tangled sheets, one leg folded beneath him.

She walked over to the bed and stood in front of him.

He stopped swinging his leg.

She leaned forward and put her hand on his shoulder.

He stood. He was not so much taller than she, but broader and when he touched her with one spatulate-fingered, flat hand, she flinched and closed her eyes, shuddering as his fingertips traveled down to the small of her arching back and his lips brushed her neck, finding their soft way up to her ear. Her legs shook as she leaned to him, her breath lost and the tears welling past her eyelids. He unbuttoned her tunic as she stood there shuddering, her eyes closed, crying. He slipped his arms around her and the tunic dropped off her shoulders. He leaned back and lifted her just-swollen breasts very, very gently, kissing them, his tongue flicking briefly across the darkened aureoles. He pressed his mouth to them, gentle at first, but he soon began to pull at the hardened nipples, as if he would suckle.

Startled, she took his face in both hands, pushing him away. She would give milk, if he kept at her.

He looked up, shaking his hair back from his too-green eyes.

She frowned. Something was amiss—it was not just this strange neediness, something more . . . what was wrong? His face seemed swollen, his eyes—

He ducked from her scrutiny and she let him go, stepping quickly over to look at his face, to see that his too-green eyes were too green because hooded with a moist, sparkling membrane, and, like spring water glistening over stones, this second lid had made the green of his eyes shine wetly, green jewels. He ducked away again. She caught her breath and let it out; a small whistle escaped her, sharp and high.

He turned back around.

"Oh my God," she said aloud. "You heard that. You heard me?"

He ran. He was out the door and gone before she was sure of what she'd seen, before she could try to follow, or even figure out if she wanted to follow, knowing, too, that she was far too clumsy to catch him unless he wished to be caught. She sat down on the sea chest. Then, mechanically, she got up again, opened the chest, put away her tunic, and dressed. She worked methodically, feeling grim.

What *had* she seen? She'd not noticed his eyes before, but then she and he were so seldom alone now, so seldom that close—she shook her head, wiping away the tears. And had he actually *heard* her whistle? How? To calm herself, she smoothed the bedclothes, settled the blue comforter flat, shook out the pillows, and wiped away the spiderwebs on the headboard.

Maria would know.

She folded her arms on top of the rounded shelf her stomach had become, and went to stand by the window again. The rocking chair creaked as she moved by it, rocking its burden of the heart-shaped pouch. She picked up the pouch, feeling sweaty and miserable but sure.

Maria would have to know.

"**A**nyone home?" said Maria tentatively. She poked her head in the back kitchen door of Emily's house.

No one answered her, so she went in.

It had been a long time since she'd been in this house—a

long time since she'd stood in this kitchen. She took a deep breath, to taste it, to take it in.

"Emily?" she called.

Upstairs she heard a cry and then footsteps. She hastened only to collide with—

"Tomas!" she said, catching hold of him.

He hung his head and wouldn't look at her.

She made a very soft, cautious piping trill.

He whistled a short return and pulled away from her. She heard him go out the way she'd come in.

"What the hell," she muttered to herself, taking the stairs two at a time. When she got to the bedroom, she found Emily sitting on the bed, with something in her lap—a pouch of some kind. She was staring into it, but Maria could see that she was also staring through it and whatever she was seeing disturbed her, caused that slight crease around her lips to deepen, brought that glaze to her eye, made her shoulders slack.

"Emily?"

The younger woman blinked and blinked again before she looked up to answer, "Thank God."

Maria sat gingerly on the bed. Emily took out the cross and handed it to her. It was a wafer of gold, filigreed at the edges and inlaid with blue enamel, heavy in the palm of the hand for so small a thing.

"Aretina's," said Emily. "She'd gotten it from her own grandmother, who had been given it, I was told, on the day her first child was born."

"I see," Maria said, handing back the cross, wondering what had happened.

Emily put the cross on. "I might as well wear it."

"Sure," said Maria. "Why not? Why haven't you?"

Emily let out a deep breath. "When Sean put his watch in here, I put in my necklace. The watch had been in his family a long time. A long time. When he left, he must've taken it. All this while and I didn't know."

"Emily," said Maria gently, "I don't understand."

She shut the pouch. "We put the things in here as a gift to our children. If he took his watch," she touched the flap, "he must have given up on the idea. Of children. With me."

"But, Em, hadn't *you* given up?"

Emily cradled herself, sensing the child she hoped, this time, to bear alive.

Maria didn't speak, didn't move. She'd been assuming—didn't Nathan assume?—that the child was his. But what if Sean—? She'd thought she had seen how far Emily's heart had gone away from Sean long before he'd left, how very dim the once full sun of her love for him had become, but, then, she could not say it had gone entirely, she'd had far too many of her own heartstrings wrapped up in that hope; anything she could have said might have turned into a weapon that would be used against her.

And now?

Maria smiled bitterly. Now? So much—just everything really—had changed. One thing did seem clear—she could not ask Emily if she'd lied to Nathan. She said, "You were lucky to have had Aretina for so many years."

"Yes," said Emily dully, without opening her eyes, "yes, I was. Very." She smiled a little, touching the Greek cross. "But she lived in the past-past, I mean, toward the end, she'd call me Anna—one of her sisters. Anna died young—MHD. The other three died of various recon-bac cleanings; pneumonia VI was pretty bad then. Out of seven, only Aretina survived. Luck, she said. Dumb luck—or maybe not luck at all. Maybe it was a misfortune." Emily opened her eyes. "She would sometimes tell me about her parents, as if we two were in league against them. The things she used to say! It's almost impossible for me to imagine a world like the one she'd been born into." Emily closed her eyes again, letting tears go. "God, I miss her," she said and made a gesture of dismissal. "But you'd think I'd've gotten used to it."

"No," said Maria. "You loved her."

Emily stood and put the now empty pouch back in the sea

chest, under the blanket. "Sometimes she'd talk about simple things, say, 'Mama has baked baklava, let's steal a piece.' Or sometimes she'd tell me that the boy 'down-street' was sweet on me—silly things, little things so familiar to her, yet to me they'd add up to a crazy, marvelous, deadly, confusing, crowded world—a place of incessant talk and music and pain. Gone for her too swiftly—gone altogether now."

Maria sat still on the wrinkled bed, watching Emily at the window. "Em," she asked, "what happened with Tomas?"

Emily turned slowly, slowly and stiffly around. Maria was a little taken aback by the drained and frightened look on her face. "What—how did you know?" she said.

"He nearly knocked me over, coming down the stairs."

"Oh?" She took a deep breath. "You saw him?"

"Well, of course I saw him! I told you—"

"I mean, closely. Did you look at him closely?"

"Emily," said Maria. She gestured at the unmade bed. "Come sit here. Come sit."

"Don't humor me."

"Come on."

Like an admonished child, she did what she was told. "All right," she said. "Humor me. Did you look at Tomas closely?"

"Em," said Maria, "What was I supposed to see?"

She hesitated, then said, "His eyes."

Maria laughed. "Uh-huh. They're green."

Emily pursed her lips. "Did you *look* at him?"

"Of course I did!" Maria frowned. "Why?"

Emily levered herself up off the bed and went back over to the window. Glancing out, deliberately not turning toward Maria, she said softly, "I've missed you."

"Don't," said Maria. "My house has been too, too empty."

Emily fiddled with the edge of one curtain. "How are your mighty ratters?"

"Lazy, but keeping down the rat population." She paused. "What's wrong with his eyes?"

Emily sighed. "After Nathan left this morning, Tomas came back." She stopped.

"Uh-huh," said Maria. "And you saw his eyes?" She laughed, to hide her unease. "They are gorgeous. They always have been."

Emily flushed. "Don't laugh at me."

"I'm not!" Maria stood. "Why so touchy?"

"Are you—" Emily gazed at the floor. "Are you hiding something from me? About Tomas?"

"Don't *you* be absurd. What could I hide about Tomas? He lives here, now, doesn't he?" She was saying what she thought was best, but her panic began to singe through her words.

"Then something strange has happened to him." Emily turned to face Maria, her own expression calm, hard, certain. "And no, he scarcely lives here anymore."

"Emily—"

"Stop lying, Maria. I want to know how much I should worry about my baby. I want to know whatever it is you know about Tomas."

Nathaniel stood at the edge of the dock, looking over the dory he and Ki had built—or rebuilt, since they'd started with one of the wrecks left in the cove. The little craft was plain, and the sails patchwork, but the boat was seaworthy.

He folded his arms, trying to warm his hands under them. Ki was late and it was chilly. The sun, barely creeping over the hills behind him, shed a weak, pale light through a gathering cloud cover. He turned, shaded his eyes, and gazed at the ruin on the hill, wondering if George would ever agree to venture up there again to work on it, now that Sean was gone. Sean— and Ed, and Jay, and Chris—and Linda, he reminded himself, but recently he'd only been thinking of Sean, and, shamefully, he knew why. He was selfishly relieved. He didn't want to face the man, didn't want to find out if what Emily insisted upon was actually true—that Sean and she had fallen away from one another long before Sean had left for the Area, long before Nathaniel had hurt himself and come to her. It was better simply to believe her. Better to have Sean gone. For good.

But, of course, no one knew whether the group was lost. George and Sandra had given up—but many others had not. Ki, for one. She had been—still was—adamant that Ed would come home. At winter's end.

Nathan stamped his feet, wincing a little. His ankle had healed but the healing had left him weak there, a little numb, so that his gait was off—and would always be. Alice had said no, he should give it more time, but he knew he'd never run as he once had, race Tomas across the sand, if not swift, at least surefooted. He stamped his feet again, impatient.

"Where are you?" he mumbled aloud, glancing back toward town. But the white ribbon of road was empty. Ki was late.

He swung back around and looked out over the choppy sea, to Gideon's Point, from which he had fallen. If they could sail out there, beyond the cove into the open sea, and so get a look at Gideon's involuted caves from that vantage, maybe then he could spot the seals he knew *had* to be there.

He sighed. Emily was right, no one believed him. Not even Ki, although she was excited about the boat. The seals had remained a solitary obsession, nurtured, he had to admit, by dreams. These dreams had taken a strong hold on him when he'd been laid up. Lying fevered and delirious in Emily's nursery, he'd seen seals in his dreams, he'd heard them.

Later, when he was no longer feverish, day after day he'd gone back over his fall, examining it from every angle, trying over and over to figure out what had happened, how he'd gotten off that cliff. He became absolutely certain that he had, in fact, seen seals that day. Right before he'd lost consciousness, and in the confusion of nearly drowning, he'd seen seals swimming around him.

Footsteps. Nathaniel turned, expecting Ki at last. But to his surprise, Tomas stood before him. Surprised, pleased, he gestured at the boat. "You will come with me?"

Tomas shook his head and, in emphatic silence, told Nathaniel not to go. And, in silence, they argued.

Nathan laughed at first, assuring Tomas, as he had assured Emily, that he meant to be careful, that he had learned a lesson from his broken ankle, but soon he realized that assurance was not what his son wanted, especially when Tomas started to pull him away from the boat and the dock. He was shocked to feel his son's full strength, a physical strength that caught him off-guard. He found himself dragged bodily to the end of the dock. There he finally realized that Tomas was adamant, and understood what was happening—or believed it—that Tomas meant to keep him from sailing that morning.

"Hey!" called Ki. "What the hell—"

Nathaniel caught his son's lifted arm, but the boy twisted away and ran, ran flat out, but with an oddly unbalanced gait, as if carrying an unusual, unaccountable weight; he ran down to the end of the dock, shed his clothes, and dove off.

"We were always together," said Maria, lying back against the pillows on Emily's generous bed. "When Tomas was a toddler and Carlo just born. It was a good time, a good time for me."

"Do you still—" asked Emily.

"I miss them both," said Maria. She pulled at a few stray tufts of hair near her ear, relieved that Emily had at last relaxed a little, and did not sit as stiff as if she had been positioned on the edge of the bed for sacrifice or some other such ritual; she said, "Nate's a gentle person."

Emily made a low, knowing chuckle.

"And stubborn and maddening but gentle. And I miss him, yes. But not all the time. And not," she smiled, "if you will believe me, not the way I miss you. But I'm also not jealous, if that's what you're asking."

Emily half smiled. "I was."

"I know." She cupped her hands behind her head, stretched.

"But, Maria, there's more, isn't there? About Tomas?"

The older woman sat up. "You asked me to tell you what I know, and I did—yes, Tomas does have those extra lids. They've come in, like eyeteeth, just lately. I noticed, but then they don't seem to be bothering him, do they?"

"No, but—"

"—they're peculiar."

"That's polite," said Emily. "Does Alice know?"

"She must," said Maria. She shrugged. "What does Nathan say about it?"

"I don't think he's noticed," said Emily. "And—Tomas *can* hear?"

"A little. Not everything," Maria said. "Only very high-pitched sounds. I found that out accidentally. He could hear my teakettle. But he couldn't hear us talking."

"I wonder how long? How long he's be able to—"

"Don't know." Maria sighed. "But I'd be surprised if Nathaniel *hasn't* noticed, they are so close. Are you sure?"

"He hasn't said anything."

"Did you think that he might be afraid to?"

Emily stared. "Of me?"

"I didn't mean of you. I meant *for* you. And the baby."

"Then he should have told me."

"Yes," said Maria. "Still." She plumped the pillow, sitting back against the bedpost.

Emily got up off the bed. She unbraided her dark hair, letting it hang down her back in three long waves. She picked up a brush from the table. "Did you know," she said uneasily, "that Jett is deaf?"

"What?" said Maria, startled.

"Sandra's known for some time." Emily started to brush

her hair. "She's calm about it. She says she expects now that every child born in Monkar will have some kind of deafness."

"Here," said Maria, "let me brush it for you."

Sighing, Emily held the brush out.

"Don't sound so resigned. I don't have to do it."

"Please," said Emily. She sat back on the bed, folded up her legs under the comforter. "Please do."

Maria ran her fingers through the coarse, black waves, to loosen them from the shape of the braiding. She rested her chin on Emily's shoulder and whispered, "Rapunzel, Rapunzel let down your long hair."

Emily laughed. "I'm not a blonde."

Maria leaned back. "Thank God for small favors," she said and began brushing. Static snapped.

"Don't you like blondes?"

"Of course. I *was* one, before this gray. But dark ladies are always more intriguing. Didn't you know?"

Emily whistled and eyed her companion over her shoulder. "You should watch what you say. I might take you seriously."

"Ai, mama!"

"I'm not a mama yet."

"Ah, *perdika* . . ."

"Yeah, yeah, yeah."

Maria chuckled and gave Emily a light rap with the back of the hairbrush.

"Maria?"

"Mm?"

"I've been . . . I've been hearing the music again. I thought perhaps I was mistaken—"

Maria put her hand on Emily's shoulder. "Wait. Didn't we decide it was Tomas? Your Glaucus, remember?"

"I know," she said, looking down and feeling the heat of a blush rise. "I know, but it can't be," she said. "It can't—because it's not just one voice. I'm sure now. Not just one voice—not just his."

* * *

"Hurry," said Nathaniel.

"All right, here," said Ki as she lifted the sail to the wind and the small craft eased away from the dock.

Nathan searched the choppy, foam-tipped waters.

"He's a good swimmer," said Ki over the rhythmic flap of the sail as she jockeyed it to catch the steady breeze. "He's always been. I don't know why you're so worried."

Nathaniel nodded, but he kept his gaze on the sea.

"There!" called Ki, pointing out toward the cliffs. She jibbed the sails. In a moment, they began to scoot toward the breaching figure.

Nathan held onto the mast, stepped over the harvesting scythes, and leaned forward. Tomas was headed for the other side of the sheltering cliffs—out beyond the cove, out where Nathan had nearly drowned in the ocean's full fury, out where he'd told the boy never, never to go.

And the waters were darkening to a dull cold gray as the sky's increasing cloud cover came down, lowering with the heavy-bellied thunderheads of an impending storm.

3

Home Again, Home Again, Jiggity, Jig

(9:00 A.M.)

THE BEACH SPREAD out before them for what seemed a long and impossible distance; the fine white sand was swept in low, stinging trails. Sean let Chris—

Chris, she's Chris, he told himself. (He knew the difference between the two. He knew. He'd always known. Didn't he? Didn't he?)

Sean let her keep several paces ahead of him, cresting the sandstorm and showing a flat-out determination. He watched the beach behind them. They were alone. He didn't think Sheila could have followed them—not yet.

He glanced overhead. The sun struggled but it was losing a battle against rainclouds.

He looked backward over his shoulder again. If they could just get down to Monkar! Then they'd have time to get the story out clear before Sheila showed up to confuse things.

Unless Nate had found his "seals"! What if—

Sean blanched. He hadn't thought about that—he nodded to himself, rapidly thinking through the jumble of the past, to sort out what he might say, what he might have to do . . . about how Ed had died . . . no, he couldn't try to remember that just yet—he'd have to be careful about that. JP was easier.

And then there was Linda.

He stared at Christine's back, thinking of Linda. What to say about her, the absent cause of so much loss? She seemed to him, now, a fantasy, the missing aim in a journey to nowhere. He wanted to say it was all her fault, all her fault, everything bad in his life had really just been her, the mere slim, compelling fact of her. And only Emily understood. She understood the power of the woman. But that would sound crazy. He knew it sounded crazy.

Linda was dead. She had to be dead. That was the only way to begin to explain how they'd gone away four and come back two, when they'd been hoping to come back five. He nodded again, as if he were talking aloud already, as if the faces of Monkar were peering at him with disbelief and he had to convince them.

Spurred by this imagined disbelief, Sean felt he had to get it all arranged in his head at that moment: how Sheila was sick, yes, she'd lost her mind. Monkar would have to guard itself against her—and Ona. Sheila'd gone crazy living alone with the ubes. Both she and Ona would die soon—they were lost already. Sheila had said herself that she was dying.

Sean shook his head, closing his eyes momentarily, and walked into Chris, who'd halted. He steadied himself. She was staring off across the beach, out toward a small hunch of sea stacks and scattered rocks. "What?" he said.

"You don't know me," she said gruffly. "You don't know who I am, do you? Do you?"

He frowned. "It's good to hear your voice again," he said.

"Sean?"

"I know you."

"I'm—"

"Chris." He put his hand on her shoulder and held onto her gently. He made his voice as quiet as he could over the rising wind and sea. "Listen. You confused Sheila with this lie about Linda—about being Linda. But don't go on with it. Not here, not now. And not with me."

She stared at him, an unwavering stare that was hard, very hard. He stared back. For moments he saw, in her face, in the lostness of her eyes and in the way in which she was, after all, Linda, the conviction that fed her lie; then, the Linda that was made up and made out of her twin was gone and he saw Chris. He said so. He said, "Chris."

Her eyes glittered. "She killed herself," she said, glancing away from him, trembling in a sharp, feverish shudder. "My fault." She shook her head. "Did you ever kill?"

For a moment, he couldn't answer her, afraid that somehow she knew what he'd done. It was as if in finding her voice for this question, she'd forced him to lose his. He managed at last to squeeze out. "She *is* dead, then."

"My fault. Even though she'd slipped the deecees when they took you and Jay, she still believed me. That quarantine was temporary. That it would end." She shook her head. "But the Area is all one big QC now. Not like when we were kids, when there were still a few places—remember? In Monkar, I kept remembering our childhood until Monkar became unreal to me whenever I thought about the Area. And all these years since I left Monkar and have lived in the Area again, I thought if I could just get back across the bay, to those narrow, safe-seeming streets where we grew up! I kept forgetting about the deecees; I let myself forget the trolls. I lost knowing how and why we left. I blocked out the deaths—Mom and Dad." She closed her eyes, then opened them. "You know what's over there, across the bay? Nothing like what we remember. They give you a little teeny space, a box really, where you sleep during the time between laboring, food lining, deecee needles, fucking, forced births and forced abortions if you're not lucky—and then you die—"

"Hey," he said, and held her to try to stop her shaking.

"What do you know?" Her voice was still gravelly from

lack of use. "I killed myself," she said, "and I'm still alive!"

"Stop," he said. "Stop it."

She glared at him. "Sheila's story is true—about Ona. She's right."

"Is she?" he asked tightly. "Then why didn't you stay?"

She stared over his shoulder into the distance from which they had come. "It was easy," she said. "To kill. I never knew."

"Let's go," he said, thinking, *I know.*

She looked at him. "I never knew how easy—"

"Let's go—"

She focused on him. "What?"

"Let's go," he repeated.

"Sean? Do you understand? I killed her."

"Yes. I understand."

She hesitated. "And—"

"What?"

"Do you care?"

He let a few moments pass, a few moments to look at her without speaking, a few moments to look as soft as he could manage, to keep his anger and grief and terror far away from his eyes when he said, "Yes. Of course I care."

She shrugged off his light, restraining embrace.

"Okay?" he asked, thinking, *Poor Chris, she's worn out. If we can just get home, get some decent sleep . . . maybe then I can tell her. . . .*

"Sheila—" she said.

"Sheila is not well."

"Sheila knows," she went on as if he hadn't spoken, "that the old-townies cut Monkar off. No contact. They knew what was happening—it's not an illness anymore. But the deecees keep up a fantasy of a cure, they keep saying some people can get well. And I believed it—"

"Come on," he said, interrupting. "Let's get home first. We can talk later—"

She grabbed him. "It's happening—it's going to happen—

everywhere. All the deecee controls, all the precautions, it's all fucking nonsense. There's no place to go. Sean? Didn't you hear Sheila? I tried to escape. I thought that there was a cure. And I'm still scared. Do you hear what I'm saying? I didn't want it—I was afraid of ubes! And now—now I'm afraid of myself."

"What," said Sean, "are you *talking* about? Stop it. Monkar will be safe. Wait and see."

She looked at him with grave solemnity. "It's not a disease, Sean. Ona's not ill. I'm not ill."

"I hear you," he cut in, back on familiar ground. "Of course you're not ill. Neither am I. But Ona is a different story."

She made a hiccup of a small laugh.

Sean's frown deepened. "We need to get home."

She began to cry. "It's an old, old story, isn't it? To decide that some people aren't people?"

He gritted his teeth. "It's not a decision. It's real."

"Real?" She laughed. "Are you an animal, Sean? No. But you were one, to the deecees, in that place they'd put you." She sighed. "It doesn't matter. Sheila will bring Ona to Monkar, eventually."

He shook his head. He couldn't go on with this crazy talk. If Chris kept at it, or if she said any more, he might have to talk to her about Ed, and he couldn't. "Come on then. We've got to move. We've got to get home before they do."

She didn't answer, but when he started walking toward the sea stacks, she followed him across the long cold expanse of the beach. The sky became darker as they went. Sean kept pushing their pace, much as he'd done when they'd first come this way.

The wind picked up so sharply, and sent such a stinging blizzard of sand at them, they had to huddle together in the face of it, holding one another against the onslaught until Sean could think of nothing except getting off the wretched beach. Absorbed by pain and his desire to escape the wind's lashing sandstorm, Sean did not see the dark swimmer, just a figure on the sea's foamy skirt, who followed them. The moment they ducked into the shelter of a small cave, the swimmer darted in from the deep water, to cling to one of the sea stacks, just out of reach of the sea's roil. As the travelers rested, the swimmer watched them stealthily, as if a spy marking an enemy's progress.

"Are you asleep?" whispered Maria. "Em?"

Emily's answer was a murmur, an unconscious sigh. She pulled the pillow that she held with both arms into a tighter hug, her eyes closed, her lids trembling a little and her breathing even.

Maria smiled. Lightly, she played with the ends of Emily's hair. She wanted to run her fingers through it again as she had done when she'd brushed it. But Emily probably needed to rest—

She glanced around the warm, worn room. Her glance took in the tea she'd made for them both, a chipped white pot and two mismatched cups, the frayed curtains, and the old filigreed cross Emily had taken off. Maria took a deep breath and then another as if to speak aloud. But she didn't want to wake Emily.

I belong here, she told herself silently. *I belong here.*

She closed her eyes and gritted her teeth to keep her vehemence inside. Where it was that she thought she belonged, and where it was that she was wanted, these had been, for a long time now, two very different things.

She had waited. She had been patient. She had left Emily and Nathan alone. She could see that the two had closed a circle together, so she had stayed, without argument, at its periphery. They'd not been cruel. And she'd tried not to feel exclusion, she tried not to feel the pain of being both left behind and left out—by two people she had loved and still loved. She had given herself over to working, to being closer to Lindi and to the other children, trying to help them live with their disabilities. She'd learned from Tomas how to speak to him and how to understand him with the most zeal. For after all, although neither Emily nor Nathan could see what their circle had done, she could—she could see Tomas standing lost at the periphery. Just as she was.

I've been patient, she thought. "But I'm not getting any younger, now, am I?" she whispered in a very low voice. She glanced back down at Emily.

No, she thought, *I'm not getting any younger and I'm not getting any wiser, either.* She stared at a sudden patch of weak sunlight on the wooden floor. A powdering of bright dust swirled idly in its trail. Then it went out.

What did she know, really? She could "talk" with Tomas, it was true, but what exactly had he said? He was lonely. He loved his friends. He missed being with his father. Hardly unusual things. Hadn't spoken about his eyes, though. Hadn't said a word about those strange lids. And the other children. Everyone knew they were suffering. But was there more?

Maria shrugged to herself and rubbed her forehead. She hadn't known about Jett's deafness. And Serena's baby? Had they checked its hearing? Pat had been as premature and as underweight as Jett—in fact, the newborn looked a bit like Jett—ill-formed ears, a flattened nose, and more hair than seemed likely. The resemblance had set up some good-natured ribbing for George and Serena, though Serena had insisted . . .

Slowly, cautiously, Maria edged herself off the bed. Standing, she stared down at the woman whose fragile beauty had always made her shiver and whose now generous curves and full-flushed face made her want to sit and weep and scream all at once. She wanted to kiss her lightly, everywhere, hold her. Hold her. And be held.

But Maria did not move. She stood beside the bed, watching.

What if Emily was right? What if there was something more to know about the children than they'd all let themselves understand?

She bent down and kissed Emily's cheek and turned to leave. She was tired of patience. If there was something to find out, she would find it. For Emily's sake.

A tiny, guarded fire lit the scoop of the just-barely-a-cave. After Sean had made a scanty meal—of bread (Sheila's), seaweed (Chris had insisted), and a few tough mussels that he'd pried from a nearby bed to boil in the fresh water they carried with them—he'd proposed that they both nap. Then they would push on. If they kept pushing and quick-napping, they might make it home before the day was gone.

The campfire snapped as he fed it driftwood twigs. It was getting dark again, as if the night were coming right back in after just departing. But it wasn't night, it was the closeness of long, rolling rainclouds, scudding across the sea, making what had looked, at dawn, to be a bright day damp and dark. It would rain soon.

Sean glanced down at Chris, who seemed to be sleeping fitfully, shifting now and then. Watching her, he felt a terrible wakefulness. He thought, *When she's ready, we'll push for home,* and whispered, "Home," and then nearly laughed at himself for the superstition that had made him speak the word. He hadn't been sure he could actually say it. Speaking it, hearing his own voice, reminded him of what Chris had given him before she'd fallen asleep—his journal, battered and shorn of pages. Somehow, she'd gotten hold of it, saved it. He had no idea how.

Shifting himself closer to the fire, he leaned over the scantily etched page. He knew he'd written the words there—he felt the recognition of his hand, the familiarity of the printing—

LEFT EMELE

it said, and the peculiarity of the e's and the l's knew him.

He rifled forward through the thin, brown sheets, seeking

clues to himself in the smudged lead. And he found traces of someone and clues to something, someone brief and sparing faced with something capacious. Neither made for himself.

LEFT EMELE

Ed had thought him cruel—truly, deliberately cruel. He remembered that, the shock of it, of hearing Ed call him mad, of hearing Ed curse him for Jay's death—Sean remembered . . . Ed in the dark, just sobbing. He never thought he'd sit and simply listen to Ed sob, it never seemed a likely scene, but there he was listening to the dry and quiet sobbing. It finally ended in a declarative cry that had an object but could muster no response—"Jay," he'd cried. Just that, a name that was just the sound of a letter.

"Jay was my strength," Ed's voice cracked. "Did you know that? I made him come along with me. I couldn't tell you that I just couldn't leave him—not like you left Emily."

LEFT EMELE

Sean stared at his handwriting.

He hadn't simply left! They'd talked it over. They'd decided together. Hadn't they?

He tried to remember across the scorched horror of the past months. What had he said to Emily, or she to him?

LEFT EMELE

The journal had a flat, accusatory sound to him, almost as if his handwriting had acquired Ed's voice.

Chris moaned and rolled over, waking slowly. He watched her sit up and gather herself compactly, for warmth, rubbing her face with her hands, brushing away sand, not looking at him until she'd come into herself—so like Linda, he thought, so like, but not.

Not. Not Linda.

"Your turn," she said to him.

"No. I think we should go on."

"Oh." She frowned. "All right." She stretched her legs out and reached for her feet. "Give me a minute."

"Do you remember," he said hesitantly, "how Emily seemed to you, before we left?"

"How she seemed? Why? What do you mean?"

"Was she well?"

She stared at him. "Sean, you said she was. You told me she was. What are you saying? Wasn't she all right?"

"Yes. Never mind."

"Sean?"

"Yes." He stared at his own hands, wondering. The tattoo on his palm had no l's and no e's, just a plus sign, an x, two y's, then a plus sign. "Yes," he said.

She crawled to the end of the cave and stood up, brushing more sand from her trousers. He stood also.

"It's getting dark," she said. "How long have I slept?"

"Not long. It's going to rain."

"Maybe we should wait."

"No."

She nodded and collected her pack, as he stamped out the feeble blaze.

"I wondered," said Sean, "if, as you'd said, she might have been pregnant."

"Oh, God," she said, turning to him. "Oh, God. And you *left*?"

He winced and stared at the dead fire, the last puff of smoke drifting away from its ruin and—

He was standing beside Emily at dawn, near Alice's, where they'd rushed when the contractions had started. Her second pregnancy—seven and a half months and they had allowed themselves to hope. Under fading stars, on the beach, she'd squatted while he'd frantically hauled Alice out of her house half-asleep. Somehow Maria had appeared—and Sandra and Chris—he remembered their faces; then, blood soaking into the sand and Emily's hoarse voice, her slick, sweaty shoulders—

"That's it," murmured Alice, encouraging, coaxing, unruffled. Sean remembered her voice viscerally, as if it had become a smooth fabric muffling his heart. It kept him from running. Each time Emily moaned, his calves tingled to take him away from the pain, and her panting, the heat of her clasping hands. He tried to focus on her face, he tried to ignore the stiff power of her body as it labored.

She clutched him; the muscles of his forearms jumped. He leaned forward, his legs straining, and said to her—"Hold on, Em, hold on . . ."

When the baby's head had crowned bloody, and Emily's fingers had dragged furrows in his flesh, he wanted to leap, to grab his child, to pull his son to safety. . . . He remembered closing his eyes at that moment as if laboring with her, his own hands locked around her wrists. And her hands, gripping his forearms for support as she pushed their stillborn boy into the world. He'd waited for a sound he was never, ever to hear, for the sound of his son's untried cry . . . stillborn.

Rain. Maria glanced up and then out across the bluffs above the sea caves. She stood at the end of the thready path that led down, the overgrown path whose packed soil held all the memories of Carlo she'd placed there, whose very air held the echo of his dying cry, the imprint of his loss.

She squinted into the rain, glad that she'd stopped in at Alice's and sent her up to Emily's early—Em hated being alone in the house, especially in a storm; she'd be worried about Nathan, too. Maria nodded to herself and quickly started down the path, down toward the sea caves, as the rain dashed, light and furious, to earth. She felt herself matching that seeming fury of the rain with her own determined, angry stride. She'd been waiting on Tomas, waiting on Emily, not asking, not listening perhaps. Waiting, waiting, waiting.

She'd come to the end of it.

She shook the wet from her face and hurried. She could feel strain in her thighs, she slipped and regained her balance with some trouble, but she pushed on. Tomas and Lindi had taken the sea caves as a kind of hiding place, a secret place, theirs only when the tide left, precious because so rarely open. She'd known about it for a long time—she'd been trying to keep Nathan away from it, increasingly sure that the seals he'd seen before his fall had simply been the children—but she'd not gone there. The memory of Carlo had kept her at bay.

Not anymore. She would talk to Tomas. Now.

At the bottom of the bluff, she could see the caves clearly. She ran out across the exposed spit to reach them. The low-tide surf was up, growing wild under the dull, rainy sky as the storm winds blew in from the north.

Sheltered against the rain, she dried her face on her shirt-tails, and smoothed her wet hair. The cave was damp and redolent with ocean, the thick, salty air chilled. In the dark she stood, waiting for her eyes to adjust.

The caves did not cut deeply into the bluff, or at least she remembered them as convoluted, shallow and self-involved. She'd nearly gotten caught once by the tide there, and in her panic at the rising water, she'd blundered into two dead ends.

Blowing warmth on her pained hands, she peered into the caves and then, quietly but with force, made a low whistle that piped up, then died, a questioning sound. The cave carried and amplified it. She called again. This time, at no great distance, she was answered in kind. Tomas. Tucking her hands under her arms, she made the piping sound he'd taught her to use as his name. For an answer, she heard someone approaching from the cave's retreat.

"Maria?"

"Lindi!" Maria moved forward, bending low to the lowering roof of the cave. "Where's Tomas?"

Lindi tilted her head questioningly. "Not with you?"

"No." Maria reached for the girl, but Lindi held herself back. "Where's Tomas?"

"You shouldn't be here," she said decisively, "without Tomas."

"Perhaps. I must speak to him."

"I just told you. He's not here."

"I'll wait then." She sat down on a rock, knowing the damp would soon push her back to her feet. She said, looking up at the girl in the dim light, "He is here, isn't he?"

Lindi glanced behind her and folded her arms across her chest.

"I know this is your special place, Lindi," said Maria gently. "I know. But—"

Her explanation was cut short by the light, soft music, a chorus so crystalline and startling that for a split second Maria felt caught in the snatch of a suddenly erupting dream.

"What is it?" she asked.

"No!" muttered Lindi.

Before the older woman could speak again, the girl had taken her by the arm roughly and was pulling her out of the cave, away from the lovely, enthralling sound and into the rain.

"Stop, stop it, Lindi, what—" she protested, twisting away from the girl's grip. "What's wrong?"

"Come on," she said. "Come away—please!" She was sobbing now. "I'm afraid for you—"

Maria stood firm in the rain outside the cave and held Lindi's shoulders to hold her still. The girl stared at her, her eyes shining in the dull light, shining with tears and—

Something else.

A clear, second lid.

"Why did you think she was pregnant?" Sean asked Christine.

She looked over at him, her face drawn and sweaty. They were resting under the cover of the pines. The rain had let up a little, and the pine-needle carpet where they sat was nearly dry. He could almost see them all as they had been once—JP and Christine and Ed, with his map. He didn't want to see them. He closed his eyes again and took a drink of water from the canteen.

She said, "You stopped here." Her voice was weary.

"Come on, Chris. You must remember the troll—"

She closed her eyes. "I don't. I'm not Chris. And, just now, I don't want to remember anything."

"Chris—"

She blinked. "Look at me, Sean."

"I'm looking."

She handed him back the canteen. "Then see."

He said nothing.

She shook her head. "What if I told you that I want to forget. Everything."

"You will," he said. "If you want to, you can."

She smiled, slow and knowing. "Wishful thinking."

"I suppose."

"And why do *you* think Emily was pregnant?"

He frowned. "Because you did, I guess."

"Sean—"

"Hell, I don't know." He screwed the lid on the canteen. "She never said anything to me. But I began to wonder. And maybe now I wish, for her sake, that she might have been."

"Only wishful thinking for her sake?"

"How do you mean?"

She eyed him with mild surprise. "She wanted you to love her, didn't she? I know she wanted that. It hurt me. And you? You wanted a son, didn't you? More than anything. It's pretty simple. It's always been pretty simple."

He stood. "Nothing's all that simple."

"Better sometimes to make things simple." She stared up at him. "You want to keep moving?"

He nodded toward the muddy road. "We could be home soon. We could be home before nightfall."

" 'Home again, home again, jiggity, jig'?"

He threw her a sharp look of annoyance. She stood. "Come," she said and they began making for the road. When he turned to glance back at her, to see that she was following, he stopped dead. He thought he saw—

She spun around, crouching. "What?" she whispered.

4

Seal Hunt

(Noon)

A SLASHING, BITTER, stinging rain lashed down on Nathaniel and Ki. The sea bucked the boat.

"We've got to go back!" Nathan heard her shout over the fierce wind.

"No!" she cried.

"We won't find him. Not in this!"

Nathaniel shook his head. Huddled in the stern, half turned so that he wouldn't have to see Ki's fear, he did not answer. He was soaked through—so was Ki. Watching, hoping, he'd believed that the bitter, biting rain would stop. It had to stop. But it hadn't, didn't. He glanced upward, his dark face pummeled by the fine, light, burning shower. It wasn't going to stop. He leveled his gaze on the choppy, grayish sea, wiping his eyes and staring across the waters.

"Nate!" The boat tipped as Ki shifted her weight and jibbed the sails. "Nate?"

"A minute," he said. "One more minute."

"Goddamn," said Ki, barely audible.

Nathan ignored her. He wiped at his face again as if this might bring Tomas into view.

"What?" said Ki. "I don't see anything!"

Nathan squinted and folded his arms.

"Nate?" said Ki. Her tone had become flat and her words carried a determined finality. "I'm taking us in."

Nathan turned around. He could feel his face settling into a frozen acquiescence. He nodded.

"I'm sorry," said Ki. She eased the boat windward. Shudderingly, they sailed past the rocky bluffs. Ki was heading for the shore down near Maria's beachside cottage. They'd come far, searching for Tomas—too far along the coast to turn around in the storm. Better simply to land.

Nathan stared bleakly at the waters stippled with steady rain. Ki was right; they'd lost sight of Tomas. He'd been swimming hard and swift, just out past the cove and then he was gone. To find him on the open sea in the rain was folly. And the boat was shipping too much water.

"He's a swimmer," said Ki as they picked up speed. "He's young. He's strong."

"Just take us in," he managed to say. "Just get us back."

"Nate."

"What?"

"He was swimming away from us."

"Was he?"

"You saw."

Nathaniel shook his head "I don't," he said. "I don't know what he was doing."

Ki put her hand on Nathan's shoulder, a brief touch, and then gestured out to the bluffs. "There," she said. "You can see them now. Your caves."

He looked out at the rocky land, and the black sockets where the water rushed white. No one he knew had seen these bluffs from this angle—and how many sea caves riddled the hillside! More than he'd expected. He stared, transfixed. He'd been working so hard for such a view. Yet as they passed by the craggy, pocked sheer of the hillside, wet and dark and sea-battered even at low tide, it told him nothing. Forbidding, the hill and its myriad caves gave him nothing.

He kept staring at the nothing and felt blank. He had believed for so long that this moment would bring the discovery for which he had dreamed. For so long he had believed he would find the seals out here, as a talisman for the future of Monkar, a token of renewal, a sign that the name of dead-town was a misnomer. For how long had he believed that seeing the bluff from this angle would reveal the secret haunt of the seals? Almost his whole life's time—or so it seemed to him as he stared with a dumbfounded awe at the eerie emptiness he faced. And the rain fell with such steadiness he thought even the sky was mocking his foolishness.

He glanced up to the top of the bluff, tracing downward the way he had fallen months ago—he fancied he could even make out the marks of his fall, that he could see the torn foliage of his passage, and the rocks that had followed in his wake—as if he could, indeed, see himself, a black shadow of a figure pinned to the sheer cliff. Andromeda struggling to get free before the waters rose, a black shadow of a figure betrayed by her people, saved by a hero. But his own savior, his son, his Perseus, had been lost.

The boat dipped and leaned, shipping more water, soaking their already soaked and numbed feet. Ki mimed bailing at him and so Nathan bailed what he could with cupped hands. The boat angled them steadily away from the open sea. The wind was contrary, fickle, dangerous; the brackish, lightly burning rain fell harder. Nathan kept bailing.

Ki managed to carry them around a small point where the land angled inward. Nathan could see the beach flats, long and empty, shrouded here and there with rainy fog, especially where the caves met the sand.

"Look!" said Ki suddenly. "There, look! Is it Tomas?"

Nathan leaned forward. Someone—a slight, bedraggled

figure, half hidden by fog and rain—was on the beach. "Is it? Tomas!" he said aloud to the crying wind, echoing Ki. "Who is it?" He scrambled to the prow, trying to stand up.

"No!" shouted Ki.

In the distance, on the long, flat beach where the caves met the sand, someone stood briefly.

"Tomas!" shouted Nate, aware of the ludicrous hopelessness of shouting. He stared. Whoever had been on the edge of sea and land, it wasn't Tomas. No. Not Tomas. And not someone he knew, either. He stared across the gray waters, until Ki's warnings forced him back to the labor of saving the boat. Straining against the surf's strength, the two of them urged the craft up from the water, away from its grip.

Ages later, it seemed, Nathaniel finally leapt from the stern to help Ki pull the boat roughly in to land. They staggered, half blinded by the still driving, still bitterly acid rain.

Nate tried to see down the length of the foggy beach to where he thought he'd seen—who? Strangers just didn't suddenly appear in Monkar—rarely, anyhow—and there had been something odd about the dark figure, something that, even at so great a distance, hadn't seemed—right. Not Tomas. But . . . someone.

"Jesus," said Ki. She leaned against the beached boat, her dark hair plastered to her face. She'd gone sallow in the dingy light, she was soaked and panting. "That was close."

But Nathaniel, intent, barely heard her. He strapped on his pack and slowly hefted one of the slick harvesting scythes from the boat. Without another word, he jogged down the flat through the gradually lessening rain, jogging away from Ki's cry, jogging with a strong though unsure purpose toward the caves.

Away Point.

Poised as if for flight at the precipice, Sean gazed across the jumbled buildings of Monkar and up to the black silhouette of the lighthouse, blinking tears that the steady rain masked. It all looked so quiet. So utterly calm, so much the same as it had the day they had left.

He lifted his gaze, sweeping back down across the whole of the straggling community—Maria's crazily patched cottage, perched at the edge of the beach, content with its own dubiousness; George and Sandra's large nest of a house, smack in the middle of town, where the clock tower he'd tried to mend stood pointing to the sky. Here and there, from the Row houses at one end to where his home (not his anymore?) stood, widely scattered lights glimmered in the rainy dark. Monkar wore a calm, waiting look, expectant, welcoming. It seemed so wonderfully the same, as he stood on the edge of Away Point, that he felt suspended for a moment in the illusion that he had never left. He folded his arms against his chest so that neither his deecee tattoo nor the QC needle-track scars would show.

"Home," she breathed. She stood beside and slightly below him, her face half turned away so he could see only her profile, this whip-thin, dark woman with bronze hair shorn to the scalp who was Chris, she was Chris, and not Linda. Her lined face, her arms, her hands, and trousered legs were muddy; he could see her shoulders tremble with the fatigue he shared as she shifted the weight of her pack and began the rocky climb downward.

Following her, concentrating on every step, he wondered if he looked as worn as she did; following her, he wondered how it would be for them both, this coming home with only grief and loss to show for their journey. Robbed and beaten. Following her down the slope, he had a sudden, fierce urge to hold onto her for the rest of his life.

As they reached the sandy silt and flat, scrubby land at the bottom of the Point, he touched her shoulder. He wanted to talk now, now that they were home, yet before they went in, he wanted to tell her what had really happened to Ed. The story he'd told her was a lie. He felt suddenly that he had to know that they both knew the same things. He let his hand drop the length of her arm to find her hand.

At his touch, she halted and turned around. But as she turned to him, her questioning expression shifted radically, rapidly into a quiet smile and then, to his surprise, she leaned against him. He put awkward arms around her as her head fell softly against his shoulder. She lifted her face, began a gentle kiss. He took it gratefully and gave back more, opening his mouth, tonguing urgency to her, to—

Linda?

Blindly, violently, he tore away, bruising his own mouth, tasting salt blood. She cried out to him, she reached for him but, with a sharp burst of shocked strength, he backhanded her; she fell to her knees and rolled hard into the scrub.

"Linda!" he cried at her, accusing, disbelieving, angry—ashamed. It was then that he saw Ona.

Emily lost her brief, panting release to a flood of sheer pain. She spoke to herself, talking herself through it; she knew, distantly, that she probably sounded bizarre, but it didn't matter. Alice wouldn't care and she needed to speak, to talk about anything, even about the singing of her dreams. . . .

"—they always sounded so cool, so utterly calm. . . ."

"Here, cold water," said Alice, giving her a tiny sip.

Pain came, held her fiercely, went; she strained and tried to hear the dream music to soothe the pain. The contractions had come on so fast. Too fast . . .

Alice dried her forehead. "Don't fight so," she said.

Several days later, it seemed, Emily heard the house creaking in the steady wind. She heard a heavy rain shushing on the roof. She heard the murmur of her own voice. More days seemed to pass. On one of these long, wearisome days, she called for Maria.

"I'm here," said a woman's soft voice.

"Maria?"

"She'll be back soon."

"Alice." Emily leaned against the pillows, her face to the white-painted ceiling, as Alice fussed and wiped her forehead. She felt drugged and dimmed, she felt at once too large and too small. She cried—with pain, with vexation, with a wanting that felt endless, imperious, and childish. She wanted the voices that she had heard pattering the midnight silences to sing to her, *now*. She wanted to be alone, she'd had enough of this; she wanted the pain to go away, she wanted Alice to go away, she wanted the baby to go away and leave her alone, she wanted to be alone to hear the murmur of the high-pitched not-music. . . .

"Alice—" she managed to ask (yet more days of pain and release later), "Alice, it's too early, I am too early again—isn't this—too early—again?"

Alice probably answered, but the pain was so swift and enveloping, Emily couldn't catch hold of the answer. Laboring there in the semidusk of the rainy afternoon, alone with only the pain and yet, she knew (irritated) not alone, she caught a glimpse of a glimmer, a dull glint off her great-grandmother's filigreed cross. It occurred to her, in this stray moment of lucidity, that Aretina would have called her—

"Shameless!"

Aretina Zafieras gathered shape now out of the rainy, gray dim of the room and the hallucinatory sweat and gravidity of this strangely swift and terrible labor. She sat down in the rocking chair and gave her great-granddaughter "the" look, as Andros had called it, "the" look of admonishment that had always preceded something harsh, something pointed.

Emily whispered to her, "Tell me it'll be all right."

"It's all right," said Alice.

"What—a grown woman like you needs lies?" The ghost was sad and forbidding. "Shall I tell you how you've become a shame to the family, child?"

There's no family left, Emily thought and thinking it, even to a ghost of her own conjuring, made her weep. *There's no family left. Just me.*

"Em, I'm here. It's all right," said Alice.

But the ghost looked even sadder and nodded as she rocked. Emily closed her eyes against the gray vision of her great-grandmother, against the slow illumination of pale gold sunlight peering in the window, breaking through the cessation of the rain. Yet still Aretina seemed to speak, murmuring about the long-gone past time—

—when such things still happened, and the world was still the world, there lived a fishman and his daughter. They had become very poor, you know, because so many fish had died out. He had refused to become a company man and so he fished for the few that still swam free. Whenever the toxic quotient was small enough, he sold the catch to the highest deecee bidders, who took great pride in serving up to their guests a piece of the diminishing wild. She mended the nets and, most of the time, took care of their household deecee quota and so, together, they kept hunger from camping too near the door of their home and kept the chill of too little from taking all the joy of their days away from them.

One evening the fishman did not come home. The girl finally went looking for him at the docks—only to hear that the boat was lost; some said it had been sunk by greens, others said it had been boarded by big blue and the fishmen made into bait. Already some had begun mourning. For a long time she stood there and said nothing, did nothing. Then she screamed once, a sound of disbelief and rage. They wanted her to come away but she would neither move nor sit when they brought her a stool. She stood as if planted, she stood as if she would never move again, she stood to wait for him until long, long after the moon rose and all the rest had gone away.

At last she turned and walked the highway to her empty house where hunger had now moved closer to the door. She left the light on at the window—a last hope. And then she went to sleep.

A knocking on the door woke her. She leapt from her bed

to lift the latch and lo! there stood her father, bedraggled but alive and she gave herself to his arms, sobbing out his name.

When she could see beyond her own joy, she saw that he was not alone. A woman stood at the threshold by his side. Not a woman from the city, nor a woman from across the hills, not this small, very dark creature with soft, dark eyes. She was a stranger. Something about her made the girl grow cold.

He brought the woman into the house and told his daughter that she had saved him from drowning but as he told the story he had a quiet look about him, as if there were more to this tale than his words. What it was the girl did not know and could not guess and so, puzzled, she thanked the stranger and fed them both and it was during the meal that her father said he would marry the small, dark stranger on the morrow.

The girl didn't argue. It wasn't her place to argue. She was his daughter. He was her father. She did not like this woman. She did not like to have to feed another, or wash for another, and mend for another. But she said nothing.

And as the days passed, it became clear to the girl that this woman, her stepmother, was terribly, amazingly ignorant; she knew not a whit—neither how to microwave nor vacuum; she couldn't run the washer, she couldn't mouse, she didn't even drive. It amazed the girl and, ashamed, she strove to teach her stepmother, and to hide the bad bargain her father had made in a so-called wife. But he never seemed to notice and her stepmother never seemed to care and so the girl soon gave up teaching her about the proper ways of being a woman. Indeed, she began instead to watch her stepmother's ways because despite her terrible ignorance, she was a happy woman, probably the happiest woman the girl had ever known. She sang all the time; while washing down the deck, or out on the docks, over by the abandoned oil tanks where they went to gather weeds, or down in the monthly food line—it didn't matter who heard her or where they were, she sang. In the summer she would swim and swim, sliding through the green waters.

Soon the girl grew lazier and lazier—at least according to the local deecees, though they merely grumbled when her quota was late, and did nothing more. The truth is that she began to forget the propriety of being the woman her mother had taught her to be and became instead the companion of the stranger who had saved her father's life. She became, in short measure, a small, happy, singing woman.

And so things went on like this until the sad day that the fishman did die. On the night after the cremation, the girl and the woman went home hand in hand, to grieve.

But they say that, after the moon rose, the girl found her stepmother lying wide awake in her marriage bed, her green eyes looking at the sea. And the girl sat beside her stepmother, to find her cold, as if she had caught death from her lost husband. And the woman took the girl's warm hand in her cold one and then, they say, something was passed between them— something powerful and changing passed from the woman to the girl.

And they say the two vanished that night the father died; when they came to look, the woman and the girl were gone, and the poor house was empty, but out on the sea's broad back two sleekly dark and singing sirens leapt and dove in the foam. . . .

Sean cursed, breathing roughly. Maria's cottage was empty. He leaned against the sagging door frame. He calculated swiftly, or tried to. He tried to, but he felt so worn with shock and so suddenly, breathlessly hot, it was hard to think.

What to do now? Which path to take? The rain was letting up. Should he head home? To town? Out to the fields? Up to council? Someone would be up there without question. But where was Maria? Should he head over to Sandra and George's?

No. How could he possibly explain—

"Linda," he muttered, staring at his tattooed hand. It trembled. He couldn't stop it, remembering how fragile she'd become and that he'd hit her, hit her because—

Why?

For shock? Disbelief? Confusion?

And, tucked inside that violence, he strove not to remember how he had once, long ago, hit her before, in much the same way. He closed his eyes. She'd promised. He'd hit her because she'd promised never, ever to touch Emily again and because she had; he'd found them in *his* bed together, and then she stood there and lied about it to him.

He explored his torn lip with light, unsteady fingertips. He was still bleeding, though he had washed the wound. He sucked at the bloody edge, wincing. He glanced back inside the dark cottage. He'd left his pack on the floor by the hammock. Next to it four shining reflective eyes watched him. The surprise sent a bolt to his stomach and amplified a sweat he had started some moments ago, even as he knew what eyes, whose eyes . . .

"Cats," he said to reassure himself. "Maria's ratters." But the sweat remained. He had to find somebody, talk to somebody, he had to find somebody.

Go back now and find Linda?

No. No. He'd managed to lure Ona away from her, managed to drag the ubes down to the beach, into the sea. It fought, it had spat at him like a cat, but he'd checked himself, he hadn't been bitten, and he'd seen it swim off a little.

He wiped his forehead on his sleeve, felt the weight of his pocket watch slide beneath the notebook he'd slipped in his shirt pocket. The notebook Maria had given him. He took it out and held it for a moment. It was damp and bent. He flipped through the pages. The pencil marks were fuzzy, some smeared to illegibility. A bead of sweat fell from his face to dot the open page. He let go, letting the book flutter shut, and went back inside the house. The four eyes scattered, two by two, at his approach. He set the journal on top of his pack, then turned on his heel and left, running up the thready path that led to the cliffs and then down to the beach—he would have to find the ubes. Find it. Kill it.

"Em?" said Alice, gently. "They always arrive hungry."

Emily nodded, huddled to herself, exhausted on the fresh-made bed. She smiled at Alice, who had worked so hard, had washed and fussed and washed and fussed and now stood near the rocking chair quietly holding the baby. But she didn't move yet. It was over—somehow she'd made it past the impassable and the pain was over. Her whole body throbbed with relief, release. The house was quiet, except for the baby's high-pitched snuffling. The rain had stopped altogether. In a heartbeat, she heard the baby take up crying again. But she had not looked yet. Not just yet. She listened to the child make the small hungry cry.

"Em?"

She laughed weakly and shifted herself, lifting up into the afternoon light that barely warmed the worn wooden floor and the bed's edge. She balanced herself carefully as Alice handed her the tiny, tiny child wrapped close in flannel, warm and limp but alive and hungry. Mottled brown-and-red skin, thick-lidded eyes swollen shut, nut-shaped head with a mass of fine, thick, dark hair, and dark hands clenched against the rawness of air, the baby wailed until tiny flush-red lips found her nipple and the slow nourishment came. Alice sat down wearily in the rocking chair and watched the baby suck.

"You look about as racked as I feel," said Emily.

Alice nodded and then spoke with a slow deliberation, as if choosing her words with extraordinary precision. "This labor comes on so quickly, and goes so violently, so terribly fast. How do you feel?"

"Racked," said Emily.

"I was worried."

"I'm okay."

Alice nodded. A few moments drifted by in silence. Emily

felt them drift but she let them go, absorbed by the gentle pull-pull-pull of the baby's greed, warmed over by a growing drowsiness. But—there was trouble in the drift; she knew Alice. "What?" she said at last. "Tell me. The baby—?"

"—seems fine."

"Seems." Emily took the cue of worry. She glanced down at the child, pulling aside the blanket a little, exposing flat nipples. "Alice?"

The older woman responded by gently unwrapping the flannel down past the bloodied remains of the umbilical knot, unwrapping until the tiny baby was wholly naked and, having lost its grip on the milk, started to cry.

"I see," said Emily. She stroked the short legs, touched the curved toes and the fine layer of light downy hair. "A boy?" she said. "Or a girl?"

"I can't tell," said Alice, her voice cracking as she smoothed some of the child's down away from its groin. "Can you? It's—" she said, her uncertainty palpable. She shook her head. "I've been thinking all these years, with so few children born alive, all right, we've a problem with birth rate and birth defects. Birth defects. Hardly a surprise, with so small a population. Tomas's deafness. Before that, Jorge's clubfoot. Sometimes an extra finger. Poor Carlo. We've all known—and it's hardly surprising, given all the other sickness out there. It's partly what made Barbara and the rest come to settle Monkar in the first place, wasn't it? All the deaths, multiple incurable sicknesses, rampant deecee incompetance. I couldn't have been a doctor to all that—neither could my mother. That's why she joined Barbara here. And this—" she gestured at the baby. "It happens sometimes. But—"

"But what?"

"Well, birth defects shouldn't be so regular. They should be much more random. I mean, ever since a few of our children survived and ever since those few made it past two years old, I've helped people to see what they wanted to see, to decide—you know? Sandra and George saw Lindi as a girl. Even my own grandchild—" Alice frowned. "Ki just 'knew' Jiro was a boy and so I knew it, too. Sandra was less sure with Jett. And little Pat? Serena's been half crazy with wondering." Alice hesitated. "And . . ."

"And? And Carlo?"

Alice shook her head. "No. I meant the first time I helped someone here decide. I meant Tomas. Cait and I made a deliberate decision when he was born. Nathaniel wasn't home and she got so terrified, I was afraid she'd do something to the baby. So I just told her. It's a boy, I said. And she hid Tomas— she even hid him from Nathaniel—at least until he was four or five months and then . . . it . . . it started to grow. At least enough to be able to say confidently, 'boy.' After that, it seemed the least of his troubles, what with his deafness, and then your father started all the talking and worry about the sheer number of birth defects in Monkar, sounding as if he'd like to become a deecee, to start that urban craziness here. You remember—" She broke off, gazing at the child. "And then Carlo was born. At the time, I thought, it's Nathan, poor Nate, he's especially cursed. But now—"

Another sound, scathingly familiar, thrillingly close, ended talk. Emily lost the thread of Alice's worry and was caught up by the aching, whispery music, so terribly, so gorgeously near.

"Do you hear it?" she breathed, afraid to speak too loudly and so break the newborn's lilting music.

Turning, the tide crept back into emptied, rain-swept tide pools. The shallow ones filled to disappearance, while the deep ones came slowly back to the life that shut or hid or slept out the short dry spells. The rain lingered in a few halfhearted drops, but the heaviest gray had fled across the sea's face. From out behind the sheltering mountains that hugged Monkar to the sea, sunlight tore brightly through the few remaining clouds.

Maria sat at the edge of one wide-mouthed and fast-disappearing well. The sun, though weak, seemed to lay a light blanket against her back. It brought no comfort. She pulled her legs against her chest, clasping her arms about them. She rocked herself a little. The panicky tears she'd shed had dried to tiny, hard, sharp, little kernels. Her throat was sore from the scrabbling cry she'd made. Lindi's double-lidded eyes, so like Tomas's, had jolted her to a profound dread; she'd lost her voice, her calm, her tears.

She remembered the scream she'd made. It had filled the cave—

"God," she muttered inconsequentially, and she glanced across the spit to the fast-closing sea caves, where the tide did not enter gently. The sea spoke roughly to itself in those dark chambers. Was Lindi still in there? She caught her breath—she couldn't believe she'd run; she couldn't believe that she had seen in this child who trusted her nothing but a sign of something so frightening that her whole self seemed to collapse into it. And although each moment she sat on the boulder above the tide well dragged at her, although she felt hooked with the remains of her dread, she couldn't move.

She glanced down into the calmness of the slowly filling tide well. Plump, heart's-blood ribbons of marooned sea-weeds floated, rippling out as the sea exhaled, dropping soft like an ancient woman's skirt with the sea's inhale. Startlingly bright green and red, the soft mouths of the once shut anemones bloomed all along the cragged face of one wall. Crammed together and open flush, the fat tendrils of the anemones mingled, as if vying to grab the edge of a sparkle, or a quick flicker of the sun's dance across the crystal surface.

She let the shivering light and the warmth on her back lull her away from fear, away from the memory of doubly lidded eyes—

"Maria!"

Her name sounded low, shaped by a familiar but long-unheard voice, flew at her from out of the rumbling silence of the beach. The voice making her name pulled her out of the terror and to her feet as he half ran, half stumbled across the sand. Emaciated, bloodied, his pocket-watch hanging like a lead weight around his neck, Sean collapsed at her feet as she tried to hold onto him, what was left of him anyway, her strength no match for his weakness. She held onto him as best she could, feeling the starkness of his ribs under the worn clothing, feeling him strain for breath. He was muttering at her. She could catch very little of it. She spoke back to him, held him until he quieted, half lifted him away from the encroaching tide. By the time she laid him down there, she was shorn of resilience. He looked at her, but his bloodshot eyes didn't focus well. His shaggy face was damp and swollen, his lip torn.

"Kill it!" he cried.

"It's you," she said helplessly. "My God Sean! It's Maria, you're all right, you're home—"

He shook his head. "It's there—" he said and pointed.

Maria turned. The slender, slight one who looked at them from the other side of the tide well's increasing fullness had long, thick, curled hair, was very dark and nakedly sleek, glistening wet. Maria squinted, cursing her imperfect sight. Who?

Not Lindi, nor any of the town's children. Not familiar and, Maria saw, badly hurt?

Yes. She was bleeding, her bare shoulder and arm slashed open, the dark flesh split with bright red, like bloody rent fabric. The apparition stood there, swaying, but only for a moment because as Maria moved, it shuddered and knelt, and slipped into the deepening tide well.

5

Alchemies

(2:00 P.M.)

"THIS FEVER," SAID Alice, as she stripped a limp and unresisting Sean. She checked for broken bones, swift, expert, and sure. "We've got to bring it down. Soon."

"I'll get more water," said Ki.

Maria sat back on her heels and watched Alice, watched her, she hoped, dispassionately. The walls of Emily's living room were closing in on her, however—a crushing, airless vacuum of the past.

They'd carried him—she and Ki, who'd appeared at Maria's side on the beach, seemingly out of nowhere—had carried this fleshly phantom home, home to Emily—or rather home to Alice, who, with her usual calm, set about doing what needed to be done without questions.

All the slow way up to the low-roofed house on the hill, Maria had wished fiercely, selfishly, guiltily that maybe he'd die before they got him up there. He was bones, a sweat-slicked, bloodied nothing. He'd raved—about Linda, about Ed, then he'd stopped. He'd either passed out or had fainted—

or perhaps he'd died. Maria hadn't known which until they'd laid him on the living room floor.

Ki came back from the kitchen with a metal bucket. "I went to the well," she said. "It's cold. Will it do?"

"Is there any colder?" asked Alice. "Alcohol?"

"Not here," said Ki. She set the bucket down and knelt next to Maria. "I checked. I'll have to go back to council. Mom—do you need your kit?"

"Luckily, most of it's already upstairs—"

"Mother? Can you handle him?"

"For now," she said. "But hurry. This fever's spiking fast."

Ki nodded. "Nate!" she said, lurching to her feet. "What the hell happened to you?"

Maria glanced up.

Nathaniel stood at the threshold between kitchen and living room, soaking with sand and mud, one hand stained brown. He was staring at the nothing of Sean on the floor.

"Nate?" said Ki.

"You all right?" he asked, then glanced down again. "Is that—is it Sean?" He seemed dazed. "How? I—It can't be. It can't be—"

"Hey," said Ki softly, stepping toward the kitchen. "Nate, listen to me. Did you find Tomas?"

Alice said suddenly, in a quick, matter-of-fact tone, "Nathaniel? You have a child."

"What?" said Maria, in surprise. "But I was here this morning and she didn't seem—"

"I did," Nathaniel said blankly. "I did have a child."

"What's happened?" said Maria, catching Nathaniel's blankness, even as she knew her question had too many answers. "Nate? Where's Tomas?"

He shook his head. "Drowned."

"You don't know that," said Ki violently. She turned to Maria. "Tomas was caught in the storm—out past the cove. Swimming. We went out after him, lost him—"

"Later," said Alice peremptorily.

Ki cut her a quick, irritated look. "Mother," she began.

"Later," Alice repeated. "I need that alcohol."

"He's dead?" said Emily. "He's *dead*?"

Maria's heart jumped as she saw Emily coming down the staircase to stand at the foot of the stairs unsteadily. "He's dead?"

"Jesus," swore Alice. "He's not dead yet, but he will be if I don't get some help! Maria, Nate—get Emily back upstairs. Ki, the water. Come on, come on, move, move—"

When Maria went to do as Alice bid her, Emily didn't resist. Still, she found herself nearly carrying the younger woman up the stairs.

"How?" murmured Emily, glancing halfheartedly over her shoulder toward the living room. "Nathaniel?" she called out weakly. "Where's Tomas?

"Upstairs, Emily," said Maria, trying for a stern tone. "You shouldn't be on your feet."

"Was that . . . was it . . . was that Sean?"

"Yes," said Maria. "And he's not dead. Em, help me out. I can't lift you." The two women clung to one another and straggled up the steps, back into the bedroom. Emily wandered about aimlessly there and then began to cry, long silent tears streaking her face.

Maria felt her heart crack. She spoke Emily's name twice, three times, but wasn't heard. Finally, Emily sat down at the head of her bed and leaned against the ornamental bedposts, staring at the flannel-wrapped child, who was in the very middle of the blue comforter.

Maria sat in the rocking chair.

"No," said Emily, in a whisper. "He can't be dead. Not now."

Maria murmured, "He's not, Em. Alice will take care of him. Just you rest." She stood up and gazed at the sleeping newborn, remembering how Carlo had lain so assuredly in her lap, as if the world had been safe, as if the world had been his. She said, "Did you choose a name?"

"We did. Nate and I . . . but it can't be, not now, not now, if Tomas is dead. . . ."

Puzzled, worried, Maria sat gingerly on the bed and lifted the sleeping baby to her knees.

Emily seemed to flinch. She leaned back against the pillows and Maria could see her arms trembling a little. Her dark hair was restrained, pulled away from her face, but errant tendrils, made curlier and darker by the moistness of sweat, had escaped. The frame of tiny wet curls made Emily look both haggard and somehow very young. Maria held out one hand.

"Em?"

Emily stared at her for a few moments. "Sean's downstairs?"

"Yes."

"And Nathaniel?"

"Yes," said Maria, still offering her hand.

"Don't let him see it yet," she whispered earnestly.

"See?" Maria let her hand rest on the bed.

"Don't let him—"

"Emily?" said Nathan. He stood at the threshold, breathing hard as if he'd just come in from a run. "Alice told me—I didn't understand when she told me—Em, how do you feel? Are you all right?"

"She's fine," said Maria, turning half around.

"And the baby?"

Emily lifted the newborn. "It's fine," she said almost shyly to Nathaniel. "You left."

"Emily." He started across the room to her. "I wouldn't have gone this morning if I'd known—"

"But you needn't hunt for seals anymore." She held the baby out to him. "Here's one for you." She laughed a short bitter cut. "You've wanted a seal."

Nathaniel stared, his dark face going gray. "And I found

them. I . . . it . . . I think I might have killed one." He held out his stained hand, which trembled, and then he glanced at Maria. "I was down at the caves," he said.

"So was I," she said, watching him. Gently, she took the child from Emily's outstretched hands. "So was Lindi. And—" She kept her voice as even as she could. "And another child. A stranger. Did you—" she paused. "Nate. What happened?"

He passed his clean hand over his face. "You saw a stranger? No." He shook his head and sat on the end of the bed near Maria. "Not a stranger. But—something. Something attacked me. In the dark, in the cave. Maria, it was no child. It was—it was wild. Vicious, growling." He turned his stained hand over. "I had one of the harvest scythes and I—"

"Oh my God," she said, standing up with the baby tight in her arms. "You hurt a child—" She went to the window and looked out. "I saw her, down where we found Sean, near Gideon's Point. When Ki and I tried to find her, she was gone, vanished—and we had Sean to take care of, so we left."

"You're wrong," he said emphatically. "I don't know what you saw, but it wasn't a child." He stood up. "Let me hold my baby?"

Emily made a small, startled sob. "Tomas?" she whispered, but neither Nathaniel nor Maria heard her.

"Hungry, I bet," said Maria, still rocking the child. She didn't want to let it go, just yet.

"I should have told you," said Emily into the silence.

"Told me?" said Nathaniel, irritated at Maria's unspoken refusal to let him hold his child. "What? Emily, look at me."

Emily whispered, "Tomas . . . Tomas . . ."

"Emily?" said Nathaniel, his voice breaking. "Didn't you hear me downstairs? Tomas is—I lost him. . . . I—"

"You don't know that," said Maria. "Ki said that you don't, you can't know for sure."

Emily made a small noise, halfway between a word and a sob.

He turned and touched his chest lightly. "I know it here."

"Nate!" came Alice's voice from downstairs. "Nate, I need you. Now."

"All right!" He sat on the bed and touched Emily's arm. She shook her averted head and pulled away from him.

He looked to Maria. "Will you—can you manage?"

She nodded. "Go on."

He stood, glancing back at Emily. "We'd decided to name a girl May, didn't we?"

Emily finally turned around. "We don't have a girl. We don't have a boy. I'm not even sure it's—" she grimaced. "It's not yours."

Nathan frowned. "Of course it's mine."

"A seal," said Emily, her voice brittle and flat. "Isn't it what you've dreamt? I have. I've dreamt it. Now, it's true."

Nathaniel asked uncertainly, "Are you trying to tell me this . . . is this Sean's baby?"

She laughed again. "Oh no. Not Sean's," she said.

"Emily—"

"Nate," said Maria, interrupting. "Please. I don't know what's wrong, but Alice needs you and Emily's not—"

"I'm fine," said Emily. "I know what I'm saying." She glanced from Nathaniel to Maria and then rested her gaze miserably on the unnamed baby. "When you hear it, you'll know," she said, touching the edge of the baby's flannel blanket, closing her eyes so that she wouldn't have to see Nathaniel's face. She dropped her voice to a whisper. "You'll hear his voice. You'll hear Tomas."

"Ed? Ed? Where are we?"

Alice wiped Sean's face and smoothed back his wet hair. "It's Alice," she said and then shouted over her shoulder again. "Nate! Nate, goddamn, you get the fuck down—"

"I'm here," he said.

She turned. "Jesus—"

"Whose baby, Alice?"

Alice shut her eyes and rubbed them wearily. "Help me carry Sean upstairs."

"Alice, whose baby?"

"Emily's!" she said angrily, her voice lancing fury. "Now help me—"

"Mine . . . or my"—he took a deep breath—"or my son's?"

Alice stood up. "I need your help right this minute. Do you hear me?"

Without another word, Nathaniel lifted Sean from the floor and carried him upstairs to the nursery. The nursery room, and the sickbed—it was all too familiar, a now cloying familiarity of his once too-constant occupation here. The room, from faded wallpaper to musty odor, seemed to speak to him loudly, too loudly—of Tomas, of Emily. Tomas? Emily? He stepped back as Alice worked to save the man whose presence Nathaniel had so often—so foolishly?—dreaded.

"Ed?" Sean stared upward unseeingly, calling. "Ed?"

"Did you try to talk to him?" whispered Nathaniel.

Alice nodded. "He think's I'm Linda. Or he did, a moment back." She leaned closer to her patient. "Sean? It's Alice. Can you hear me?"

Sean grabbed weakly at Alice's hand. His breathing was heavy, ragged, thick. "Watch," he said, "Watch out."

"Sean, it's Alice."

He closed his eyes. "Alice?"

Nathaniel stood with his shoulders against the closed double doors that separated him from Emily.

"Ki should be back soon," said Alice. "I'm going out to the well. It's not cold enough, but it will do. Make sure he doesn't try to get up."

"He looks too weak for that," said Nathaniel. He touched her arm. "Should I go to your place for your things?"

"No. Most of what I need is here already." She nodded toward the master bedroom.

"And if he wakes?"

"He's semidelirious now. He might do anything. That's why I want you to stay here. I don't have your strength. Stay and see that he doesn't move. If Ki gets back in before I do, start dousing him. We've got to get his fever down out of the roof." She stepped over the stool and back from the narrow bed. Sean sighed and tossed a little, but he did not open his eyes.

"See?" said Alice, nodding at her patient. "I don't think he'll come 'round until we break the fever. But I can't be sure." Then she gave Nathaniel a hard look, a look he had grown familiar with as his foot had slowly healed. "You?"

He made a brief, hard laugh. "Me what?"

"Are you going to remain in one piece?"

"How should I know?" He shook his head. "Don't worry. I'll watch him."

After she'd gone, he pulled the stool she'd been using back from the bed and sat down. Sean had not opened his eyes, or moved, and his breathing was shallow. Sitting in the rough-breathing quiet, trying not to listen to his own thoughts, Nathan rubbed at the dried blood that coated his hand, remembering the weight and shudder of the scythe as he'd struck. And he'd struck something—solid but yielding—he'd hit it. The shriek had made him drop the scythe. Dropping the scythe, he'd rushed out of the cave—he hadn't checked, he hadn't tried to—he'd just headed down the beach for home until he'd seen, impossibly but apparently, Sean, Sean Rider, a living nightmare, rushing clumsily across the wet sand where Maria—

Maria did not see a child, he told himself. *She could not have seen a child.*

And she hadn't seen him, no. Neither she nor Ki had seen him; they'd been focused on Sean and then, thinking of how Maria hadn't seen him, a piece of his long-ago escape from the cliff side slipped in on him, a piece that he had not remembered before—

—a brush of warmth in the cold. A pressure against his ankle. A shudder ran through him as his body remembered the leap he tried to make, a leap of panic. Even in that long-ago, semiconscious state he'd feared sharks, and now he remembered that he had tried to leap away, had nearly snapped his leg in two, frightened of the light he'd seen just below the surface. He was sure he'd seen something, movement, dashes of movement and—

Eyes. Lovely, huge eyes.

Music. A strange but audible, underwater music.

Something worried at his foot. That was the end of the memory; if there was more he couldn't find it.

Maybe he'd seen Tomas; or maybe it had all simply been part of his delirium—or . . . what? He knew that he had never wrenched himself free of that rock. He knew there was no way he had, by himself, crawled free. He had thought, all this time, it must have been Tomas—

Tomas.

The shock of loss brought emptiness. He sat with this emptiness and stared over at the wasted, scarred, sweating man whose return he had hoped would never happen. None of it made sense to him. A murmur came from beyond the double doors. Unintelligible words but familiar voices. They were calm. He rubbed his face.

Sean opened his eyes. "Ed." His voice rasped.

"It's Nathaniel."

"Ed . . ." Sean reached out weakly. "Jay's dead."

"Sean," said Nathaniel patiently. "It's Nathaniel. You're home."

He made a weak and sputtering laugh. "Home again, home again . . . jiggity, jig."

"Sean," said Nathaniel softly.

"We'll never get home." He looked straight at Nathaniel, his eyes unfocused and strangely fogged, as if full of gummy tears. "Jay's dead—you see him there?" He pointed, his hand shaking. "I'm going to die like that."

"Sean—"

"Hot, so hot. Can't see. That's how it starts. That's how it starts . . . that's why I had to . . . had to. I did it. She doesn't know. I never had the chance to tell her. I killed him. Ed . . . he had the fever, and then his eyes—his eyes! Like Jay. Just like Jay." Sean fell silent for a moment. "I'm going to die."

Nathan stood and took both of Sean's sweat-slicked hands in his own, trying to calm their dancing agitation. "Ed was strong," he said, feeling the foolishness of the words, but not knowing what else to say. "Alice is here."

Sean lay back. He did not let go of Nathaniel. "Alice?"

"She's here. She'll take care of you."

Sean frowned. He rubbed Nathaniel's hands in his own, closed his eyes, and opened them. "Oh my God," he wailed suddenly, pulling his hands away and covering his face. "I'm home."

"Sean, it's okay," said Nathaniel.

But before Sean could speak again there was a cry, liltingly musical, piercingly high. Nathaniel dashed from the nursery into the narrow hall. Maria was there before him.

"Alice?"

"She left," said Nathaniel.

Maria frowned, listening. "It sounds like . . ." She glanced over at Nathaniel. Without another word, they hurried down the stairs together, Nathaniel first.

"Tomas?" Maria asked.

No one answered. The kitchen was empty. The back door was open. Nathan took hold of Maria's hand. They ventured into the living room.

Small, dark, bloody, and wet, the stranger sat in the middle of the room—or rather, crouched there, huddled within its tangled hair, in a low, somehow gracefully sleek pose, a pose of readiness, as if about to run or dance, glidingly. It stared at them with an unblinking and glittering force. It sang in a sharp, low, crooning purr that soon ended in a lilting, painful shriek, an anguish, terror.

Maria knew this wounded child. It had been there, on the beach when she and Ki had found Sean—or Sean had found them—and it had disappeared into the tide well. It rocked back and forth. A small puddle of bright red was gathering on the rug.

"What—" said Nathaniel, touching Maria's arm. His voice was uncertain.

"She was on the beach," said Maria. "Earlier. I told you—"

"Not possible," he said. "Not this—"

But before she could answer, the child sprang, leaping from the floor in an impossible arc toward Nathaniel. She hit him, full body, and he fell. Maria grabbed at the stranger, only to be knocked aside. The blow sent her tumbling across the rug, sliding to her knees on the wooden floor, and into the fireplace. She stood, grasping the mantel awkwardly. Her hand sent one of the clocks off its perch. As it hit the ground it cracked musically, scattering pieces of itself across the floor, in a shower of glass shards.

The child growled savagely. To Maria's horror, Nathaniel's hands were bloody. In another moment, he'd managed to get clear of the child, who fell to her knees, panting. He scrambled on all fours, kicking something round and silver and sending it zipping across the room. The child was uncontrollable, wild, back on her feet and making that high, despairing, and horribly familiar cry. Maria lunged at her, catching as she moved a glimpse of another running in from the kitchen. She snagged her foot on the rug, lost her balance, and the room exploded in light.

Emily got out of bed. Her legs held her, though her whole body resisted and she was nauseated. She stood listening. The cries from downstairs—lilting, musical, speakingly familiar—told her that Tomas was at least alive. She shut her eyes, trembling. He was alive and home. There had been a horrible scream, a muffled thumping. Then, the music of his voice. Now there was nothing. Quiet.

She carried herself with care, as if she might break, across the room to the basket that Maria had set on the sea chest near the windows. Incredibly, the baby had fallen asleep through all the noise. Already the trauma of birth was fading from its delicate downy skin. Its sloe eyes were closed by heavy, swollen lids and it sucked its spatulate thumb.

"May," Emily whispered, shaking her head and touching one tiny, involuted, nearly invisible ear. "What foolishness. You won't need a name. You won't need one, will you? It—it probably won't really matter. Whatever it is that you hear, it won't be a name. And you won't need me." She mused to herself for a moment, then murmured, "Tomas." She straightened and glanced out the window. The waning day had become bright, clear, windy. Small clouds scudded across the horizon and the ocean sparkled under the new-washed sunshine, a dazzling dance of fluidity and foam.

And there in front of the dance of the sea, she saw.

Linda.

Linda had, at last and terribly, come home.

She turned away from the window, shaking. First Sean, now, impossibly, impossibly, Linda . . . she leaned against the wall. The whole miserable past had come back to collide with the now, with what she and Tomas had done. The past that she no longer wanted to remember. The past that should have stayed gone. The past had come back from the away-place to which she had consigned it; it rose in the flesh, out of the deep burial of forgetfulness, and it would find out, it would find out that she'd, that she and Tomas, that she'd lain with him and that they'd . . . had a baby.

This was worse than Nathaniel knowing—or even Maria. Worse because Linda and Sean had been protected, they had been dead and so kept away from the horror of her shame and the yearning imperative hunger that had driven her to Tomas.

Emily glanced at the baby, then yanked open the window. Maybe she'd been mistaken. The woman there on the bright, wet grass was Chris. Yes, that was it, Chris, not . . .

"Linda?" she called. The too remembered, too loved, and suddenly too loathed face flashed a look up at her, and Emily felt again the shudder of sudden and absolute hunger, the irresistible need that she'd once felt for Linda, long ago, long ago . . . and that, incredibly, crazily, despite Sean, despite Nathan, despite Maria, she had come to feel for Tomas. Emily shut her eyes. "No," she muttered. "No . . ."

The woman lifted her arms and made a high, light, wordless cry of joy, beckoning.

"No," said Emily, and then, "NO! Go away, go back! I don't want this—I can't bear it. I don't want you here!" She ducked inside, her face hot, her head swimming. She paced up and down the room, shaking. A small, deep groan from the nursery arrested her attention.

Sean?

First, she checked the nameless baby, who slept peacefully on. Lifting the whole basket away from the window, she set it down at the head of the double bed, soft on the pillows at the very edge of the blue comforter, far away from the window, away from the past lurking outside. Then she picked up the gold filigreed cross and, opening the sea chest, found the pouch Sean had made. Her arms shook as she set the cross back inside the pouch and then put the pouch at the baby's feet for safekeeping.

Finished, she walked to the double doors and cautiously pulled them open. Sean lay in the narrow bed there, sweating, semiconscious.

"Sean," she whispered.

He opened his eyes—or he tried to, but struggled against a filmy whitish membrane. The membrane wouldn't lift or break, though he blinked and blinked. Emily choked. Mercifully, he closed his clogged eyes.

"Linda," he muttered, his voice graveled with phlegm.

"Kill me . . . kill me. Please. I'm going to die."

Emily gagged, shaking her head. "Sean, it's Em."

"I'm dead," he mumbled. "I'm dead already."

"Sean," she said. "Sean, it's Emily."

"Left," he said. "Left Emily." He blinked whiteness again. He held out his hands. "Hold me?"

"Sean," she whispered. "You're home."

"I didn't mean," he said, his voice dropping, broken. "I didn't mean . . . don't. Don't hurt me. I'm sorry."

She flinched and bent down to him, as if to lift him and cradle him in her arms, and although she shuddered at another piercing scream from downstairs, she ignored it.

"Hold me," he whispered. "Hold me until I die."

She eased herself into the small bed next to him, the furnace heat and heavy sweat of him, the thin loss of him. She folded his shaking arms around her. Feebly, he clasped her and she held onto him.

A long time later, or so it seemed, Emily heard the high, moaning, musical cry of her dreams—

No, she realized, it was her own little seal, crying in that lovely and familiar song. This was not a chorus and not a dream, not just the wind, or the sea. Not Tomas now, no, not her seducing Glaucus, but a thin and haunting cry, the cry of a newborn who sang to her this song, familiar and clear, this song, the one she'd heard the night before Sean left so long ago in the now unburied, horribly still alive past, a song that tore her up with shame.

And then, all at once, Emily smiled with an absolute wonder that lifted her heart. She could hear a clarity in this voice, she could, finally, know what the song meant. She knew it was made for her and just for her, and that it was speaking of what she could do that would make everything all right again, to put the past back into the past and leave the singing future untainted by her confusing shame. She heard a solution to her unrest; it was distinct and very clear. It told her what to do. She raised herself from the bed and went to find Alice's kit.

*   *   *

Maria rolled over, waking to uneven splashes of dancing darkness; she was on the floor, on the braided rug, she could see her hands supporting her as she tried to get up, but she couldn't focus, couldn't clear her sight of dark splotches, couldn't get the floor to stop moving. The explosion of light was gone, the room was darker, her head was pounding. She sat back on her heels and closed her eyes.

Gradually she realized someone was crying in a high, keening whine—Tomas? Sounded like Tomas. And underneath that, there was moaning, a muttering *nonononono.*

She opened her eyes again. Beyond the black splotches and jiggling floor—"Chris?"

"She's dead, Maria. Chris is dead."

"Linda?"

"Goddamnit," muttered Alice, on her knees by the kitchen door. "Maria, can you move?"

"I think so."

"Then get the hell over here—"

Maria pushed herself to her feet, still trying to clear her head. She glanced back at Linda (!) who seemed to be holding someone—Tomas? Or—

"Nathan," said Maria, swinging around, looking for him, finding him beyond Alice, sitting in the kitchen, haggard; it was he who was moaning *nonononono.*

"Leave Nathaniel," said Alice sharply. "He's not hurt badly and he's no use right now."

"Nathan?"

"Goddamnit, Maria," said Alice, her tone strained. "You want Tomas to die?"

"Tomas," said Nathaniel. "Is he . . ."

"No," snapped Alice. "But I'm afraid he will be if either you or Maria don't help me. Maria?"

Maria picked her way around the pieces of broken clock, across the glass-littered room, past Linda-not-Chris, who was holding—who? what?—

"I've slowed the bleeding," said Alice, looking down at Tomas, lying naked on his back across the kitchen threshold. Maria was confused. Undressed, the boy looked strangely bloated to her. Alice was pressing hard on his thickly haired groin, where the skin was slicked dark with blood. "The glass must've cut deep, maybe nicked an artery, though I can't—it doesn't look that bad—" She narrowed her eyes. "I've got anesthetic upstairs, my scalpels, scissors . . ." She looked to Maria, who'd knelt beside her. "Can you keep the pressure on here—that's it, here—"

Maria reached down. "What is this?" She touched a series of small symmetrical growths buried in his belly hair. It seemed a trail of tiny tumors. "Alice—"

"Ona is hurt—" said Linda-who-was-not-Chris.

Alice glanced up, startled.

"Alice, please," said Linda as she carried the girl across the room. The huddled, frightening thing that had attached Nathaniel was quiet now, her large eyes hidden beneath her spongy abundance of hair.

"Hello?" said Ki from the back door. "Mother?"

"In here," said Alice. "Thank God! I can't cope with all this myself. Did you bring the alcohol?"

"Got it, and I've brought Sandra along with me—hey—what the hell—"

"Oh my God, oh my God," said Sandra. "Linda!"

Linda smiled briefly, slightly, mournfully. "I'm home."

Sandra sank to her knees at her sister's side, as Ki took over for her mother, who got up to check on the stranger, the one whom Linda had called Ona.

Maria knelt there, dazed, afraid. "Alice," she asked. "What has Tomas got—"

Suddenly Tomas came to, his startling moss-green eyes snapping open—or half open, since the clear, nictating lid still sheathed the green. He made a strange lurching, gasping breath and tried to sit.

"Hey," muttered Ki, restraining him. "Lie still."

But Tomas struggled, his whole body shuddering, straining.

Maria took hold of the youth's shoulders and made the high whistle sound that he'd taught her, to calm him. But even as she began, another lilting, eerie whistling took over from her own hesitant one. She glanced up.

It was the stranger. Sitting deep in Linda's embrace, the child she'd called Ona sang out a series of rapid notes in that same chillingly high tone Maria had come to know as Tomas's, but, too, the sound went through her to the place where Carlo had died and in a haze of remembered loss, she put her arms around Tomas, as if to hold him back from dying.

But Tomas brushed her away. Then he sang. He sang out, as if in answer to Ona, a song gorgeously rich, a trilling tone, a song far more complex and colored with variation than anything she'd ever heard.

Nathaniel got to his feet.

Maria sat back, struggling to understand.

"What the hell—" said Nathaniel. "Maria?" He leaned down, staring at his son, offering a few shaky gestures, and Tomas made a small noise, the old noise he'd made since he'd been a baby, a little clicking tick-tock, the cricket sound. He reached out for his father but Nathan shook his head. He shot a glance of agony to Maria as Tomas reached out again, then he shuddered, and stumbled away, toward the kitchen.

"Lie still!" said Ki to Tomas. "Maria, can you get through to him, tell him to lie still? He's bleeding badly—"

Ona made a quick, sharp whistle. Tomas answered in kind. Then he closed his eyes.

Slowly, glancing from Tomas to Ona, Maria stood up, carrying the beginning of an understanding with her. There had been much to know about the children, more than she'd even guessed. She made the inexpert whistle that Tomas had taught her. His eyelids, all four of them, slid halfway open, showing a quick bright half-moon of green. A shudder of pain took him and he grimaced; a sudden tear slid down the side of his face.

She went into the kitchen after Nathaniel. But he wasn't there. She called to him, stepping up to the screen door and peering out, but he was not there, either. She turned back and her foot hit a silver pocket watch. Sean's. She stopped and picked it up. "Alice," she said, "you need your kit?"

"Yes, yes, yes, and water. Hot. Boil it. But first you've also got to get that alcohol to Sean. My kit's by the bed—I'll need one of the scalpels sterilized, and—"

"Sean?" Linda broke in. "Is he all right?"

"No," said Ki. "He's got a bad fever." She glanced over to Alice. "Mother? Tomas's bleeding isn't right, he's—"

Alice made a wordless sound. "Hold this taut to the wound," she said to Linda and then turned her attention to Tomas.

Linda looked at Maria. "How bad? How bad is Sean?"

"Bad. I'd better take the alcohol."

Linda shook her head. "He'll die."

"Not if I can help it," said Alice grimly. "Maria, get that alcohol upstairs. Go."

"You don't understand," said Linda, her voice certain and heavy with pain. "He can't—he won't live." She caressed the child in her lap, who seemed to be crying. "Ona—"

"Aunt Linda?"

"Lindi!" said Maria, starting up. "I—"

"Aunt Linda?" said Lindi again, staring. "Where's Aunt Chris—Uncle Jay?"

"Gone," said Linda heavily. "Dead."

Before anyone could react, Ona made a quick cry. Lindi seemed to shake herself and then answered the stranger as Tomas had done. Swiftly, she sat down beside him, took his hand, and began crooning.

"Upstairs," said Alice peremptorily to Maria. "Now."

Maria nodded automatically, hauling a bucket of water and the alcohol that Ki had brought. She checked the kitchen, calling to Nathaniel softly, but he'd gone. Careful in her shock, she mounted the stairs, the bucket of water sloshing. She went to Emily first but when she got there, no Emily. The nursery doors were shut. The newborn lay alone in the room, its basket-crib perched on the pillows and guarded by two little spiders that were studiously building their lace between the bed's ornamental posts.

Maria set the bucket down, to make sure the baby slept. She was surprised to find Emily's pouch lying in the basket; the surprise reminded her of the silver watch she'd put in her pocket, but even as she pulled it out, remembering Emily's story of the watch and the cross, a flash of knowing hit her, as if someone had just doused her with the bucket she'd carried. Dropping the watch on the bed, she swept her glance across the room, searching for Alice's missing kit even as she yanked the double doors to the nursery open, and so it was Maria who found them, lying close together on the nursery's bed in a thick red-brown puddle, their throats slashed.

6

Where Luxury Late Reigned

(8:00 P.M.)

WHEN MARIA SAW the lamp up in her house's window, she halted among the rustling dune grasses; then she turned away to stare out over the dark, choppy seawater. After she, Alice, and Ki had seen to it that whatever could be—whatever had to be—done for Emily and Sean was done, she'd become unable to bear that house anymore, unable to think, unable to respond, and Alice had told her to go, sleep if she could (sleep!), come back in the morning. She'd left, but couldn't go home; she'd been walking by herself for hours, just walking, as alone as the sunset, not wishing to see anyone, too stunned to have even one word left to speak.

And so, when she saw the light, she knew two things. She knew who had lit the lamp. And she knew she didn't want to go in there. How could she face him? Nathaniel—

Emily was dead.

And Sean, and Chris, and JP, and Ed . . .

And Tomas—! Tomas—! She shook her head. He hadn't died but what was he? She stuffed her hands deeply in her pockets and stood buffeted by the light wind, shuddering as if in the full blast of a winter storm. She tried not to hear again what Linda had said, tried not to know what she knew, what she'd seen, and heard—

She glanced again at the lighted window.

Did Nathaniel know? What did he, what could he, know? Would she have to be the one to tell him? She didn't want—she couldn't—she closed her eyes.

Doing as Alice had bidden her, going upstairs with Sean's alcohol, she'd found them dead. She hadn't been able to call out; she hadn't even been able to move her lips. But she'd dropped the bucket; and after, she'd still been unable to make even a whisper, even as Ki had held her, even as they both went downstairs—downstairs to—

After seeing what was, impossibly, happening downstairs, after that, she had no tears and doubted she would have any ever again.

The tide would be coming in soon, eating away at the shore; all her favorite tide pools would be gone. She shifted a small wand of driftwood she'd idly picked up from one hand to the other and watched the dark foamy waves jig and break on the retreating sands. Standing there, avoiding Nathaniel, she took refuge in remembering his son, their child—a strange refuge, since Carlo's loss always gave her such pain. But at that moment the old aching loss of her child seemed an oddly comforting way to obscure all the rest.

Carlo had loved the soft secrecy of early evening walks, just after supper, especially those times, like now, when the sun was low and the tide high. And she used to carry him down to the sea on her shoulders. He used to laugh, hiding his odd, lipless mouth behind a small, nearly fingerless hand, even when there was no one else around to see him.

She unclosed her eyes. Tonight, for the very first time, she was glad that he hadn't lived.

She turned from the water and headed across the grasses to the ramshackle house that sagged where the sandy earth had begun to shift years ago. She kept her eye out for her two cats and called to them softly. Then she glanced back over the hill far away and up at the tiny darkened remains of the light-house, barely visible. She'd found the cats up there, years and years ago, when Monkar had decided to clean the place out. Of the five starvelings she'd found that day, only two had lived long enough to be called cats—her twin ratters, one a tom and one a thomasina. She shivered. That distinction, so basic, seemed, after what she'd seen that day, suddenly super-fluous. The twin ratters greeted her as she crept up the uneven stairs onto the porch. Setting down the driftwood, she petted Sister, while Brother held himself aloof. She went over to the moldy chair and sat in it, to put her shoes back on and warm her feet. She peered over her shoulder through the house win-dow. It was a glass window, one of the few left in Monkar. The glass was nubbly, and the dimly lit world inside looked nubbly through it.

Alone in the near dark, the old woman sat across from the nubbly window, her hands folded upon the wooden kitchen table; a gray woman, quiet with her waiting.

Sheila? Maria started. The early rising half-moon struggled out of the little shreddings of the rainclouds, and flooded in through the back windows of the house, cooling a throw rug's bright stripes. Stunned, Maria watched the dim room pale, watched the gray woman grow silvery, softly burnished by the moonlight. She found that she wanted nothing more than to just curl up on that cooling moonlit floor with her ratters to sleep. She didn't want to speak to the silver woman, she didn't want to speak to her aunt. Great-aunt. Sheila. She was weary of thinking and sick to death of surprise—she just wanted to stay forever on the porch, held by the musty old chair, touched by the gentle night wind, her mind a blank. The rat-ters became bored with the silence and left the tilted porch for the more interesting yard. It wasn't until her great-aunt stood up and went over to the stove that Maria got herself out of the chair. She pushed open the screen door. The two ratters dashed from nowhere inside before she did, beelining for the silver woman, who stood with her back to Maria in front of the stove. The woman spoke first. She said, "I'm making tea. Would you like?"

"Sheila," said Maria. She let go of the screen door. "I never thought to see you here again."

"A long while," Sheila said, turning around slowly. "How about a hug?"

Maria found her reluctance gone in an instant; she hung on to the embrace as if after ages of deprivation, folding her tallness down against the smaller woman, her arms shaking with a kind of strained release. "I never thought to see you," she murmured.

"No," said Sheila. "Me neither."

"Did you come with Sean?"

Sheila shook her head, letting Maria go. "Not exactly. Ona and I—" She hesitated. "I've already been up to Andros's," she said, and then trailed off. They both let the silence pool until Maria said, "Alice told you that I'd left."

"Yes. Yes, she did."

"And Nate? Had he come back yet?"

"No. I would've stayed for Ona, but there didn't seem any need. Not with Tomas and Lindi there. Though Tomas is—"

Maria nodded and stepped over to her stove to check on the fire; she added wood; got a teapot from the store shelf. "I thought, when I saw the light, that you were Nathaniel." She started pacing.

"Alice said you'd go home. I decided to wait."

"Maybe I should check his place—"

"Maria, sit."

"I can't." She stared at Sheila. "You know Ona?"

"Linda left Ona—"

"Yes," said Maria, interrupting to make a brief, pained, almost angry smile. "So she said. But *what* is Ona?"

"Older," said Sheila briefly. "Come, sit down. That's what I've been doing. Waiting for you, just sitting."

"I can't," she said again. "I don't want to give my mind too great a chance to find me just now."

Sheila laughed. "Still or moving, one always has a way of finding oneself. Especially and most decidedly when you don't want to."

Maria stopped pacing. She sighed and took a seat at the table. "Yeah," she said wearily. Brother leapt up, waving his sandy-striped, club tail. She scratched between his ears.

"He's got eight toes?" asked Sheila.

"Eight," Maria nodded. "Did you see Sister?"

"The other one? She's here—" Sheila picked the cat up off the floor. "She's got only one eye?"

"Look closely," said Maria. "There isn't even an indentation for the socket. Just a slight hollow. The rest of the litter died. Remember when I found them up at the lighthouse?"

"I don't think it was a lighthouse," said Sheila. She put Sister down on the floor. "Or maybe it was, a long, long time ago. Before—" she stopped.

"Before?"

Sheila gave her great-grandniece a brief, frustrated look. "Before it became something else. Before Monkar became something else. Because I don't think Monkar was just a fishing town—or even just a town. I think it was a community, yes, but what was that community doing here, exactly? What does UBAS mean, do you think? I think Monkar was built for some particular purpose. Of course, I'm not sure. All I've got are fragments and possibilities—like those letters on the scraps of paper Ed and Nathaniel were trying to piece together." She shrugged. "And I was never as interested in piecing together the past as some. Not like Ed. I was more like Andros—more interested in just going on, in doing."

"Doing what?"

"Living," said Sheila and she shrugged again. "Doing all the little daily things—you remember, don't you? It used to drive Barbara crazy. No plans. Just doing. She thought I was pissing away time until I died."

"Weren't you?"

"Was I? And you?" she snapped. "When you were little, you never could keep your mind on anything."

"I was just a kid," Maria said. "I'm sorry."

Sheila took several deep breaths. "Sorry," she whispered and closed her eyes. "I am too. And—" She grimaced. "And I was wrong to leave. I was wrong. You can't just get away from things you don't control. At the end of her life, Barbara used to say that. I thought that I could run—or ignore it. The funny thing is, all I did was find—" She stopped. "Ona."

"And Nathaniel thought he was going to find seals."

"In a way, he might've been right. Maybe it started with seals. Or at least the concept of a seal."

"What?"

Sheila sat down. "I don't pretend to know, Maria. I told Ed as much—and not even as much as I should have told him, I guess. I tried to tell Sean, too, but it was too late for him, he just couldn't hear me. I should have told them both more about Ona. And Barbara. And maybe—maybe about what Aretina used to say."

"Aretina?" Maria frowned. "Why?"

"She liked to come by the house and talk. Before she'd gotten—well, you know. Before she gave up on living in the here and now." Sheila settled back in the rickety chair, shaking her head. "I didn't believe a word of it, until after your brothers died." She shook her head again. "No, not even then I didn't. But that's because, after a while, Barbara absolutely forbade questions. And I didn't want to know."

"Jorge?" said Maria. "Eduardo? I don't—"

"They were boys."

"So?"

"That one year, all the boys died," said Sheila. "All."

"It was flu, Sheila. I had it myself."

"Yes, you did. But I don't think it was just a flu," said Sheila. "All the girls lived. All the boys didn't. We lost them, and we hadn't many to begin with. Jorge, Eduardo, Tino, Drew—should I go on?"

"No," said Maria. "Don't. What did Aretina say?"

"That it was God's doing, that He'd given Monkar the means to change, so that we might survive the Second Flood." Sheila chuckled sadly. "Never mind that, so far as I remember, Aretina's God had promised his creatures never again to destroy the world by water."

"What are you saying?"

Sheila grew serious. "That the flu changed you girls? Left a trace of itself? That's about all I *can* say at the moment, except that it didn't come only here, it isn't just happening here and it won't stay in one place, no matter what the deecees do. Sandra, Chris, Linda—they must have it. You. But the effects aren't the same for everyone, every time—"

"Carlo . . ." said Maria, stumbling over the name, her voice carrying shocked tears. "You mean Carlo was . . . Carlo . . . You moved away from Monkar just after he—"

"I told you. I ran."

"You *knew*—"

"I didn't—and I don't—know fuck all," said Sheila roughly. "At least, not exactly. Maybe Barbara did—maybe all of the first townies here did. Sometimes I think they're the ones who wrecked the roads, who tore out the very idea of electricity, who made of a thriving community a dead-town— that they isolated themselves. I was the youngest back then, remember, younger than Andros even. I was born here, and born long after it had been given Barbara's name."

"And Andros? He must have known, to hate so—"

"I doubt it, Maria. Janice might have. Maybe. Alice thought we were seeing a cluster of birth defects because there were so few of us. And you know Andros came down from Vanseaport. God knows what he saw there. He was afraid. He might have seemed callous or cruel—and council, of course, voted his suggestions down. But he was afraid." She sighed.

"He was only doing what he'd believed was the right thing to do."

"Murder," said Maria dryly.

"Maybe. I think Barbara, and the others, I think they made absolutely sure that we didn't and couldn't know much—made certain by the sheer force of their own understanding that whatever would be passed on to you—and to me—wasn't anything like knowing."

"But why? *Why?*"

Sheila gazed at Maria calmly. "So that we wouldn't kill each other off?" She shrugged. "Linda says they're killing each other off pretty methodically down south, using those they identify as carriers of what they call 'ubes' like buffers—a living, or rather a dying, buffer zone. That's what she found out. She wasn't going to get cured and she wasn't ever going to get back across the bay, except as, well, as something like a slave, so far as I can make out. When I was younger, I thought the killing would surely have to stop. And maybe it will. But not in my lifetime. That's part of the reason I came back home. I'm going to have to watch, to be a witness. I'm too old to do anything else." She regarded Maria quietly. "I'll be a relic. And so, in a way, will you."

Maria stood up. "I don't believe it."

"Neither did I. But raising Ona, and tonight, seeing Caitlin's little Tomas grown to childbearing—I'm convinced."

Maria sat back down and then just lay her head on the table. She whispered, "Tomas—"

"—will mother both children, I think—the one he has fathered with Emily and the one that he gave birth to. As different as they seem to be. But maybe not so different." Sheila sighed. "I just hope Tomas has enough milk, without Emily."

"It's not possible," said Maria, her voice muffled.

"Alice will tell you otherwise."

Maria pushed herself back from the table and stood up. She gazed around the room blankly. "I've got to find Nate."

"He'll turn up."

"I've got to—" She tilted her head, squinted, and then pointed to what looked to be a backpack near the door. "That yours?" she asked.

"No." Sheila went and brought the things to the kitchen table. "It looks like Sean's. This was on top." She handed Maria the journal, which flipped open to—

LEFT EMELE

Maria sat down and wept.

Nathaniel carried the tallow lamp carefully as he crawled through the broken back door to the lighthouse. They'd never bothered to fix it, once they'd gotten the place cleaned out. Standing, he set the lamp down on the floor and rubbed his face roughly with both hands. He could hide here, away from everyone, everyone, and try to get a thought together. No one would look for him up there, not for a while at least. Not even Tomas—

He picked up the lamp and swung it before him, stepping carefully past a heap of crumbled concrete blocks. The uneven light bounced around the smallish space, which was long, windowless, and narrow. It led to an entryway. The air was musty there, the heavy greenish paint chipped from the walls in large, curling flakes. He nearly caught his forehead on one of the protruding metal hooks that lined the wall as he stepped past several more broken concrete blocks.

Gaining the second room, Nathaniel set his lamp down on one of the glassless windowsills; the room was banked with window spaces that commanded a fine, expansive watch over the coast below. In one corner, he found a rumpled pile of moldy blankets, all marked in bold letters UBAS; two cracked ceramic mugs; dust and woodland trash—dead leaves, twigs, some rocks littered the cracked linoleum floor. He folded his arms. This room had been sparsely furnished when they'd first ventured into it and yet crammed full of paper. Anything and everything usable—bits of glass and glassware, beakers, tubes, needles, ceramics, mirrors, cabinets, drawers, pencils (the pens no longer worked), other odds and ends of metallic furniture, instruments (some of which Alice was grateful for)—they'd taken down to town center, leaving the cavernous place stripped. He rocked for a few moments on his heels and then sat down in the semidark with his back to the window-lined wall.

Tomas, he thought. He folded his arms, curling into himself—

—*it, the wild thing that had attacked him in the sea cave, the thing he'd tried to kill, it was there in the living room*—

A noise, a slight scritch-scritch.

Nathaniel looked about, tensing, straining to see in the dark. The noise stopped. He reached for the lamp and held it out before him. The flickering light caught this dusty corner and that, but it couldn't reach across the entirety of the room, nor into the hallway beyond. The noise had ceased. Nathaniel set the lamp down on the floor.

—*and Emily, the baby upstairs, Maria by his side, but what was she saying? She was saying the incomprehensible, that the dangerous thing was a child*—

He stared into the darkness, shivering. Had he hit a child? With a scythe? Had he? Had he been struggling with a *child*? He shut his eyes, feeling sick, conscious that he still wore the blood of that sea-cave struggle, and still, horribly, too, his own son's blood, Tomas's blood—

—*Tomas had knocked him over. Tomas had hit him, hard, and in his shock he'd dragged the boy with him as he fell, fell across the shards of broken glass*—

A noise, a scritch-scritch. It grew to scratching.

Nathaniel shot to his feet. Was it coming from the far end of the room? He had no scythe with him now, nothing but the lamp—which he picked up. Bouncing the light from wall to wall, he checked the room again.

Nothing visible.

He took a careful step forward, then another, holding the lamp out before him. Nothing—and the noise had stopped.

Rats?

As he stepped across the cracked linoleum toward the hallway that led to several other rooms, he found a good-sized stick and hefted it, in case of rats—or, worse, a dog. At the doorway, he gazed down this second dark and windowless hall.

Nothing.

He took a few more steps and gained the entrance to another room. He stood for a moment, musing. He'd always wondered what this space had been used for, it was so oddly designed, with four sunken rectangular vats, larger than a full-grown man, like four concrete gravesites cut into the flooring. The roof was wholly gone here, and the spaces were filled with blackish, bitter-smelling rainwater that reflected his lamplight and the growing moonlight glassily. The place was damp, almost rank.

He left the odd room and retraced the way he'd come. Whatever was crawling around back there, in whichever room, he didn't need to find it. He stepped gingerly across the hall and was heading across the linoleum when he knew, suddenly, certainly—

In the dark behind him, someone.

Gripping the stick he carried—although it felt useless, not like the heft of a scythe—he turned swiftly around.

What he saw looked back at him with large reflecting and quietly intent eyes, shining in the hollow dark; it was no child, no slight thing like the one on the beach although it seemed somewhat like—flat, narrow nose, those huge eyes, but this one was powerful, its short, dark limbs taut, showing thick musculature. Its body glistened, as if wet, and it watched him just as Maria's ratters had often done, silent and unwavering. He saw that it held a lamp of some kind, and that its inner forearm had been heavily tattooed with what looked to Nathaniel like a series of capital letters, similar to those he'd found on the papers in the lighthouse years ago.

Another, smaller pair of eyes appeared over the shoulder of the first, so suddenly that Nathaniel made an involuntary sound of fright, only to be answered immediately by a high-pitched, musical whistle. It was the little one that made the noise, a dreadfully familiar, dreadfully *speaking* whistle, so haunted and tantalizing, and so like the sound the one he had tried to kill with the scythe had made, so like, so like—

Tomas.

That which looked at him from the hollow dark spoke. It spoke without speaking anything Nathaniel could recognize as words, yet he knew what he heard as a language, he felt the meaning, a part of which said to him *this place is a shrine*. Yet the emotional effect of the calm, almost inaudible audibility was far more immediate than word meaning. It was a language so densely complex with both loss and a profound reverence that it made him want to cry. That which looked at him from the hollow dark held out the light it carried, then set it down on the floor. It moved swiftly, faster than a quick breath and was gone through the empty window bank, disappearing silently into the woods beyond before Nathaniel could understand it was gone, that he was alone, that he was unhurt, alone and left with a dawning sickly fear for (and of? and of?) Tomas. He dropped the useless stick and blew his own lamp out. Gingerly, he stepped over to the other light; it was a perfectly round, quivering circle of illumination that broke, like mercury, into a thousand liquid sparks when he tried to pick it up. As he watched, it collected unto itself again and moved across the floor, away into the other room, leaving Nathaniel in the dark. Grimly, he scrambled out of that place through the glassless window frame.

"I loved her. I once—I loved them. Both of them," said Linda brokenly as she stepped onto the porch of the low-roofed house on the hill. She handed a steaming mug out to Alice, who was sitting on the porch steps, with Maria and Ki.

Maria couldn't bring herself to speak.

"You should rest," said Alice, turning to Linda. She cupped her hands around the mug. "God knows I should." She took a sip and closed her eyes. "And you—" she said, opening her eyes again and looking to Maria, "you should have *stayed* with Sheila and gone to sleep. If you want something to help you sleep—"

"No," said Maria. She shrugged and cleared her throat. "Nathaniel will return here, and I want to be here when he does."

Sandra appeared in the screen door, carrying with her the calm strength she always carried, as if it were a palpable object. "I'm heading home," she said. "Linda?"

"I'll stay. For Ona."

"Lindi will be here," said Sandra evenly. "Alice?"

"I'll stay. I could sleep on this porch this very instant and maybe forever. I'm tired beyond tired."

Ki stood up. "Mother, come home. Sandra's right. There isn't anything more to do here. Not now."

Ki's "not now" hung in the evening chill between the women. For a few long moments, no one spoke.

Finally, Maria couldn't stand the silent implication of Ki's words. "Linda," she asked, trying to keep the rancor out of her tone, "why did you say that Sean would die?"

A few minutes more of silence passed before Linda replied. "Because," she said, "Because Jay had. And Ed—" she paused. "Sean told me about it. A fever that comes on like lightning, suddenly, violently. Both Ed and Jay—" she stopped.

"Sean had been hurt," said Alice peremptorily. "He was underfed—so are you. So, too, no doubt, were all of you. Made you susceptible to whatever was out there or came along. So. Sean had a fever and he was weak, but he needn't have died, Linda. I might have—I could have brought that fever down."

"No," said Linda. "He wouldn't have survived. Not after—"

"After what?" said Maria. "Linda, after what?"

"After a man's been bitten."

Ki laughed uneasily but Linda went on. "I mean it. When Ed, Sean, and I had camped on the bluffs above the Area, I thought we were safe. It was the first night I really felt secure since Jay had died. But I was tired. I begged to sleep and when I woke, I just couldn't believe it. Ed had died. Fever, Sean said. Took him like *that*. They'd gone down the coast a ways, while I slept off my exhaustion. They'd gone down to the water. Ed had been attacked, just like Jay—" Linda broke off.

"They left you?" said Sandra with incredulity. "They just left you, unprotected? What about trolls? Or—"

Linda glanced over to her sister, a glance that shut Sandra's worry down. "I think Ona must have bitten Sean," she said to Alice. "Protecting me. Ona must have seen him hit me."

"He *what*?" said Sandra, gone from incredulity to anger.

"He hit me," Linda repeated wearily, this time not looking at her sister. "I'll explain later."

"Explain now," said Sandra.

But Linda shook her head. "If Ona had bitten him, then he was going to die. That's what happened to Jay—and to Ed. Maybe," she said shakily, "maybe to Chris, too, though I think women usually survive." Now Linda gazed up to Sandra. "I lost her, San. I just lost her. It's my fault. My fault."

"Fault?" said Sandra. "I don't know fault, tonight. I just know what has happened is all too much. There's way too much. Let Lindi stay here and come home with me, where you will be safe."

"San—"

"I've lost them too," she said, "my little Jay, and Chris. Ed. Emily—"

"Nathaniel," said Alice suddenly, narrowing her eyes, looking thoughtful, "didn't die. Nathaniel had that fever, but he didn't die. And I'm sure he'd been bitten."

"What do you mean?" said Maria.

"His ankle was all torn up, remember? He'd broken it badly, all right, but I remember asking Emily about it because the flesh had looked, well, eaten. Gnawed at. And then he had that high, that incredibly high fever. Spiked that night."

"I remember."

"Well," said Alice, "Tomas had been at my bandages earlier that day. Maybe—maybe there's something Tomas did to or for his father that helped him survive. Maybe it's not always fatal. Maybe there's some way that the effects can be—"

"Maybe," said Linda bitterly. "But it doesn't matter, does it? Sean thought he was going to die and it's over—"

"It matters—to us," Alice began. "It's important to know—"

"Is it?" Maria broke in. "Is it? They're both dead." She dragged open the screen door and brushed past Sandra, heading for the stairs.

"Maria!" called Ki, then Sandra, Alice—a chorus of worry. She stopped; turned around. "I'm all right."

"Are you?" asked Sandra. Her voice held an edgy beware.

"Yes," said Maria. "Yes. Enough craziness has gone on in this house tonight. I'm not going to add to it! I just want to talk. To Lindi."

Panting, Nathaniel jogged slowly and limpingly along the shoreline, his way lit only by a half-moon's light. He'd followed the broken trail through the forest as far as he could, then gave up and climbed down from the woods and across the dunes to the cove. It was, he judged, long past midnight and he was certainly long past exhaustion. Everything ached and, for a brief moment as he jogged, he thought of simply lying down in the sand and sleeping.

Far ahead of him he could see the dock, and the harvesting baskets lined up like humped sentinels on it; two of the still unrepaired dories bobbed at the end of the flattened pier. Beyond the dock and above the cove, even more distant, the small light of Emily's house—his home—glimmered.

He slowed his pace, thrusting his stained hands into his pockets; it was so late, so nearly the next day. Emily would be asleep, he hoped, and the baby—

He stopped, shaking his head again as if to clear it of the question—*whose baby*—and impossibilities—*Tomas*—crowding him, as if he might also shake out yet another thing, a mocking word, that lingered there. He pulled his hands roughly out of his pockets and looked at them. They shook. He felt suddenly and somehow permanently ancient and, over and over, over and over until he wanted to laugh aloud with it, the mocking word nagged at him, chided him, haunted his ears and chuckled at his blindness, at the foolishness of—

Seals!

He stuffed his shaking hands back into his pockets and strode toward the seaweed beds. As he came within yards of the dock, he heard it again, that sound, the sound he'd heard as he'd blindly swung the scythe in the sea cave, a fluid sound he did not want to believe Tomas had made, those cries that Emily must have been hearing all along coming up from the dark waters, sounds she'd said she'd heard but that he had never heard before this day and night, sounds shriekingly high but so frighteningly, gorgeously musical that it was ravishing.

They all lay quiet, asleep, in Emily's bed, the cool blue comforter spread like still water beneath them—Lindi, with thin, paled lips set in a small, troubled smile; Ona, wearing Alice's neatly done but stark, blank bandages on a startlingly shaved head and wounded shoulder; between them, as if wedged against them for protection, Tomas.

Maria sat in the rocking chair by the window, watching the gentle rise and fall of Tomas's darkly haired chest, and, lower, there against his compact, lightly sweating body, the two newborns grasping at the tits, suckling with their swollen eyes closed, the one of them very, very small, smaller than any human child Maria had ever seen and yet also recognizably human. The infant's soft, nut-colored skin was pelted sleekly with tiny, flat, tawny hairs; it was not fur and yet like it, but also, unmistakably somehow, just hair—

What were they becoming?

What were these children, nestled so tightly together?

Maria stood up, thinking in an exhausted amusement, *Whoever or whatever they are or might be, right now they're asleep.* She picked up the rusty alarm clock on the bedside table, but it had run down. She nearly laughed aloud at the appropriateness of that, and tiptoed quietly to the window, pulling aside the curtains. The window's shutters were open; the long-past-midnight, nearing-dawn sky was swept clear of any rainclouds and brilliant with the stars. The flat half wafer of a waning moon hung high and snow white over the bluish cove.

A piercing soprano note caught the still night air, and then another, a chorus, pitched at the very edge of her hearing so as almost to hurt.

Maria leaned out the open window. *Emily's voices,* she thought and then, *the children,* for, in answer to this chorus, she heard behind her a wandering not-melody, not-song, shapeless as a cat's raucous love and yet mellifluous, gentle, almost musical, almost speech. She turned around.

They all lay awake now in the generous bed, awake and huddled close to one another. Although it was only Tomas who sang with Emily's voices at first, both Ona and Lindi soon added their own trippingly high, unmelodious notes to the song. And yet it was no song. Maria could see that now— she could see in their faces, in the way their eyes danced with sharp intelligence. This not-music, so deliriously rich, this was speech, a language of some kind, but a language so full of a presence that it surpassed what she knew as language. For a few moments, she stood at the window, enraptured, listening, wondering if she might ever come to understand how this crying music was the language it surely was, wondering if her own unskilled and perhaps even physiologically deficient vocal chords could ever speak it, wondering if Lindi or Tomas might ever have enough trust or patience to teach it to her.

"Lindi," she said softly, but got no answer as Lindi lifted the tiny, impossible infant away from the teat. Tomas watched without moving.

"Lindi," said Maria again.

"I'm going home," said Lindi. Her voice now sounded crippled, much too low and rough. She looked at Maria through closed nictating lids and rocked back and forth, jiggling one shoulder to shush the squalling newborn's maddeningly painful pitch. "Come swimming with us—for a little while?" she asked.

Maria forced a smile. "I won't be a nuisance?"

Lindi gazed at her some long minutes. "I've told them that you promised to love us. I swore that you'd keep your promise. And you have—you always will. I believe that."

Maria felt her chin trembling, a trembling that threatened to take over the whole of her. She looked to Tomas, who was cradling the other, sleeping newborn. She tried to speak, then to make a whistle, but found no voice to do either.

Tomas whistled softly for her. The trill had a physical jolt—it brought a feeling of closeness that terrified and yet it held her off at a hungering distance.

"Maria," said Lindi, and then repeated the trill Tomas had just made. "Maria?"

She gazed from one to the other in confusion.

Lindi trilled.

"Is that," said Maria, her words sounding like stones, "how you call me?"

Lindi nodded and stroked the tiny, quieted head of the strange newborn, glancing down. "Tomas says we'll call this one after you." Lindi repeated the trill gently, and Maria followed after her, as if held by that chord, down the stairs, toward the front door. Everyone had gone, it seemed; the kitchen, the living room, the porch, all were empty—or nearly so; Maria tried to put out of her mind the burden of death held by the storeroom near the porch. Sean and Emily. She failed. Hesitating for a moment in the hall between the front door and the storeroom, she made a half-finished, reaching gesture to Emily that even she could not name a meaning for; then she followed the two children, and the song that her own name had become, out the door and across the slope, down to the brightening beach.

A damp wind, tasting of winter's end, blew. Across the bay, a morning fog began to creep along the peaks of the range. Lindi waded into the water and, taking a deep breath, sang out again. The odd chorus answered in kind. Drifting, both children swam into the black glass of the sea until Lindi let the newborn go and it wriggled easily on its own, letting the waters hold it closely until it slipped into the arms of another who waited, bobbing on the foam of the quiet waves.

Maria stood in the water, letting the warm sea lick her bare feet, letting the water lap at her ankles, watching Lindi join the others in their leap and dive and play, trying to keep her eye on the newborn. She lost sight of it among the roiling, almost boisterous waters, yet she trusted its safety. When she finally looked away, the sky was lifting to a steely clear possibility of dawn and in that possibility of light she saw Nathaniel walking doggedly away from the dock, toward her. At that distance she couldn't see his face well, only the grim set of his shoulders and the pace at which he made for her. What she had to say to him, what she would have to tell him—these were things better left unspoken.

He broke into a limping jog. She cringed inwardly. And when he stood before her in the thin brevity of light that touched his haunted face with a fine rime of a pale, pale gold, all she could do was lean against him, and grasp him, all of him, with a tender violence.

Epilogue

... all dwellings else
Flood overwhelmed, and them with all their pomp
Deep under water rolled: sea covered sea
Sea without shore; and in their palaces
Where luxury late reigned, sea-monsters whelped
And stabled.

—John Milton, *Paradise Lost* Book XI, 746–752

On cloudless midnights, when the high, acid-hot sea tumbles rough and whitecapped to the changing shore, the children of the new world come to this part of their Land to remember what had been, and to speak of what was. Monkar sleeps. It does not wake as it once did and it cannot hear its children's remembrance.

On this night there is a full moon, making the way clear and easy for them. And when they've touched the past and sung of other times, they run boldly across the thin strip of damp sand into the surf.

Circles of watery moonlight waver about naked hips. They rise in the slight undertow, their strong arms oft-times folded against their breasts as they let the currents take them. The sea laps the pebbles of the shore and licks the few rotted stumps of the ancient dock with tiny waves that are all foam and no force.

One of them halts the play and, with several uneven strokes, swims to the low, warm waters near to shore. This one stands, swaying gently with the tide, and looks up to the roofless house above the cove. The house is unlit. The windows gape open.

Gray and tattooed and finely wrinkled, this one gazes silently for a moment as the gorgeous language of his own kind echoes behind him, as a wet wind blows, and the little waves coming in from the cove slap and dance. Often this one will stop and gaze that way, more silent than the rest, until a gentle trilling calls for him, a sound neither an echo nor a voice, but rather unmelodious music, and then, diving backward into a leisurely, still powerful swim, Tomas ducks below the surface. The moonlight rings spread away from that dive until the ripples of it melt into the belt of a new wave and lace into bubbles on the abandoned shore.